The Man Who Wouldn't Stand Up

Jacob M. Appel

CARGO
publishing

"The Man Who Wouldn't Stand Up"
Jacob M. Appel
First Published 2012
Published by Cargo Publishing
SC376700
ISBN: 978-190-888-511-1
Bic Code: FA Modern & Contemporary Fiction

www.dundeebookprize.com

Cover design by Chris Hannah
Typeset by Craig Lamont

Printed by Bell & Bain Ltd., Glasgow

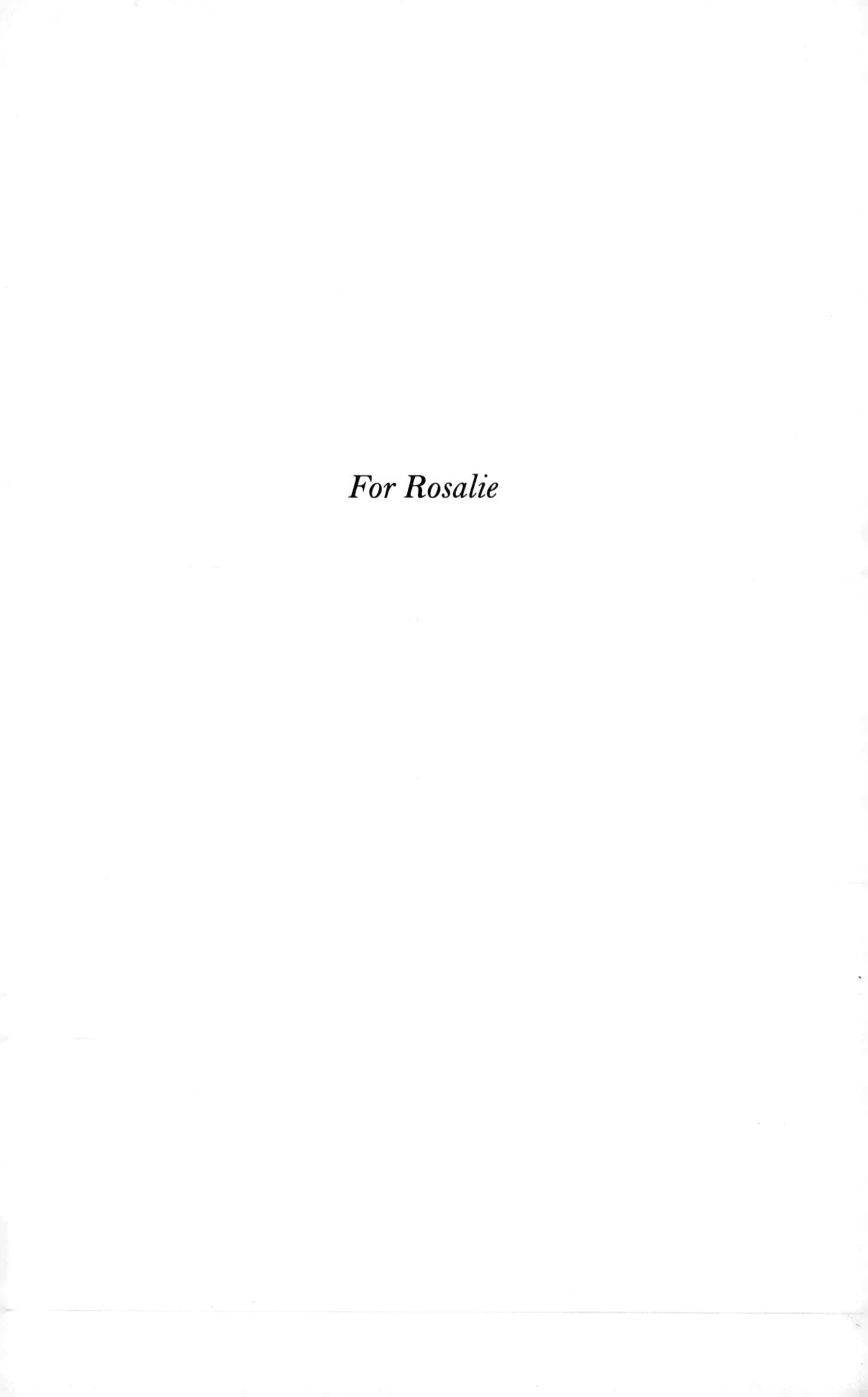

For Rosalie

PART I
Spring 2004

CHAPTER 1

One thing led to another.

That was the only way to explain how Arnold Brinkman, who considered both professional sports and young children unjustifiable, had ended up at Yankee Stadium with a nine-year-old boy. The boy was his nephew, the son of his wife's younger sister. The child's mother, Celeste, was honeymooning in the Aegean. The child's father, now Arnold's *ex-brother-in-law*, had fled to Fiji—as Fiji did not have an extradition treaty with the United States. It seemed unreasonable, even provoking, that a hustler who'd built his fortune trafficking sex slaves from Eastern Europe should live scot-free in the tropics while Arnold, who recycled scrupulously and overpaid his taxes, got stuck chaperoning this trip to the ballpark, but Judith had promised the kid a baseball game. (Why his wife couldn't take the boy to the game herself remained a mystery to Arnold—*she'd* done the promising—but when he suggested as much, she just kissed the inside of his wrist and shook her head.) So here he was. Yankees versus Red Sox. It was hard to imagine a more perfect spring afternoon to waste watching baseball.

They sat in the upper deck, near the foul pole. The boy, Ray, had brought along his baseball glove in the hope of catching a home run. He stood up with every pitch and then sunk back into his seat in disappointment. If the batter made contact with the ball, the child's head followed its trajectory as though drawn by a magnet.

Arnold found the stadium claustrophobic. It was like riding in an airplane, only warmer—and accompanied by a hostile soundtrack. All around him people shouted down the visiting team with the vehemence of right-wing talk radio. Viewed in the proper context, this enthusiasm was indefensible: Millions of Africans died each year of malaria and AIDS, gluttonous ranchers defoliated the Amazon, rebels in Indonesia cut the hands off prisoners—and these people cared whether Mickey Mantle or Willie Mays was a better centrefielder. Okay, maybe not Mantle and Mays. But whichever self-interested, cocaine-addicted troglodytes had replaced them. Arnold conceded he'd enjoyed baseball himself as a kid—but that was in the days before free-agency and multimillion dollar salaries and the designated hitter rule. It was also before he'd recognized the game for what it was: Bread and circus. "*Panem et circenses*," he told the boy. Then he checked himself—he didn't want to put the idea of going to the circus into the kid's brain.

While Arnold counted down the innings, he eavesdropped on his neighbours. To his left, an overweight couple with nine school-age children had corralled both a pretzel vendor and a hotdog vendor simultaneously. Their conveyor belt of offspring, all sporting team paraphernalia, distributed the snacks with the efficiency of third world relief workers. Meanwhile, to Arnold's right, a bald man lectured a girlfriend with a glaring facial rash on the conspiracy to juice up the baseball. "They tie the seams tighter," he explained. "The media can say it's steroids, but it's really all about the ball. My grandmother could launch one of those babies." This was the amazing thing about democracy, thought Arnold—everybody felt entitled to their own pet theory: That Lyndon Johnson had orchestrated the Kennedy assassination, or that Queen Elizabeth I wrote Shakespeare's plays, or that Glenn Miller had survived World War II in a Soviet gulag and formed a marching band for prisoners with Raoul Wallenberg. Judith had a colleague at school, an eighth grade teacher in his forties, who taught his classes that Amelia Earhart had been shot down and tortured by the Japanese. If history judged nations by their pet theories, no one could ever doubt that Americans were creative.

The four black men behind Arnold—all in their twenties, all wearing baseball caps—grew rowdier with each round of beers. One of them told a vulgar anecdote about a woman he'd worked with at a bowling alley. Another tossed an ice cube at a Red Sox fan several rows below who'd been criticizing the mothers of the home team players. "If that nigger don't shut the fuck up," warned the guy directly behind Arnold—but he kept the threat nebulous. The ice cube skimmed the arm of the Red Sox fan's seat. The intended victim didn't notice.

Ray tugged at Arnold's sleeve.

"Can I ask a question?"

The child was always asking permission to ask a question.

"You just did," said Arnold.

"Can I ask another?"

"Sure," said Arnold. "Fire away."

Ray stood up with the pitch, but the batter fouled it off.

"What's a nigger?" he asked.

The boy's question came at a lull in the action. It carried across their little swathe of grandstand like a cloud of plague. Arnold felt his head grow hot. Sweat matted his shirt to his chest. He hadn't brought along tanning lotion and now the nape of his neck burned like a slab of meat in the sun.

"I'll tell you after the game," he said sharply.

Ray rose for another pitch. A called strike. Arnold felt short of breath.

"Can I ask you another question?" the boy asked.

"If you have to."

"Why won't you tell me now?"

"I'll tell you *after the game*," Arnold repeated.

"It's a dirty word, isn't it?" demanded the boy.

Arnold didn't answer. A man of a certain breed—he thought of Gregory Peck playing Atticus Finch in *To Kill*

A Mockingbird—would have been capable of sitting the boy on one knee and instilling tolerance. Arnold didn't have that gift.

"Nigger," said the boy. Very loud. "Nigger. Nigger."

The mother of the nine children shot them a look of disdain.

"You can't say that word like that," warned Arnold. He spoke at top volume so those around him might hear his disapproval.

"Why not?" asked the boy, no longer seeking permission for questions.

Arnold wanted to say, *because it's a racist slur only used by retrograde bigots and shameful morons who don't know their own history*, but he was fully aware that the four black men behind him were listening, and he was in no mood for confrontation. He suffered a sudden urge to urinate.

"It's one of those words that some people can use but others can't," he said. "It means different things when different people say it."

"What does it mean when I say it?" asked Ray.

"I don't know," said Arnold. "*But don't.*"

The loudspeakers punctuated Arnold's answer with a cry of "Charge!" After that, a scuffle broke out in the neighbouring section and police swarmed the walkways. Ray's vocabulary-building episode was soon forgotten.

Arnold passed most of the sixth inning negotiating with himself over exactly how long they had to remain at the ballpark. He didn't want the boy complaining to Judith that they'd left early. It was a tie game, too, so he couldn't plead the "blow-out" defence. On the other hand, he had no desire to share a subway ride with a mob of drunken hooligans. "We'll leave after eight innings," he told the boy. "Eight innings is enough."

"Okay," said Ray. "Then you'll tell me what nigger means."

The seventh inning stretch couldn't come soon enough for Arnold. Not that he gave a damn about stretching—or singing *Take Me Out to the Ball Game*—but it marked the beginning of the end, the start of the mass exodus. For him, only nine outs away from freedom. If they caught the express train, Arnold decided, he'd have time to replant his day lilies before their dinner date with the Cards.

When the break finally arrived, American flags appeared on the video screens. The public address system paid tribute to two Bronx soldiers killed in the line of duty. "Please rise and join us," the announcer said, "in singing *God Bless America*." All around Arnold, Yankees fans and Red Sox fans clambered to their feet. Beer vendors rested their trays on the concrete steps; crackerjack men stopped hawking. The father of the nine children ordered his clan to remove their baseball caps. Ray removed his too.

Arnold remained seated.

"C'mon, Uncle Arnold," said Ray. "Stand up."

"No, I can't do that."

He vaguely recalled hearing about this *God Bless America* nonsense, possibly on public radio, but he'd dismissed it as so much jingoistic, post 9-11 claptrap. *The Star Spangled Banner* was bad enough—how many of these nitwits knew what a rampart was?—but the national anthem might at least be justified as a tradition without meaning, akin to printing "In God We Trust" on coins. In contrast, *God Bless America* was new. Propagandic. Also somewhat farcical—part of a musical program that included hip-hop and *Sweet Caroline* and The Village People's *Y.M.C.A.* That's right. First they sang about gay hook-ups at the YMCA. Then they asked God to bless their country. Nothing like a well thought-out display of patriotism. Arnold wanted no part of it.

"You've *got* to stand up," insisted Ray.

All around them, the spectators had begun to sing. One of the nine children—a chinless little girl with chocolate-smeared cheeks—pointed at Arnold. Her mother stopped singing long enough to say, quite audibly, "Ignore the bad man, honey." Then she sang even louder.

Someone behind him shouted: "Love it or leave it."

"Please," begged Ray. The boy tried to lift Arnold by the thumb.

"This is bullshit," Arnold answered. "It feels like a Nuremberg rally."

It did feel that way, too. He was probably the only person in the stadium not on his feet—certainly the only able-bodied adult. (There wasn't much overlap, he suspected, between baseball enthusiasts and civil libertarians.) Besides, how did these people know he wasn't standing because he was an obstinate jerk? He might just as easily have been a Jehovah's Witness or a paraplegic or a Canadian. His entire body, he realized, was trembling.

Arnold imagined confronting the mother of nine: pointedly informing her that he was a Vietnam veteran and that he had ten sons serving in the military. Not that this was true—*but it could have been.* He had fully immersed himself in this fantasy, exploring its various permutations, when a chorus of jeers and hisses drowned out the final bars of patriotic music.

Arnold looked up. All eyes were glued to the video screen. That's where he saw himself, enlarged for an audience, sitting through their fascistic song. The boy stood at his side, yanking on his fingers.

How dare they?! It was suddenly personal—an aggressive invasion of his privacy. And the man behind the screen kept the camera focused on him.

Arnold might have raised a fist or flicked his middle finger. That was the macho thing to do—one way to put the incident behind him. He could have played the coward and fled. In the long run, that would have been the wisest course. But Arnold couldn't help feeling he was being bullied, taunted, challenged.

He responded instinctively. He stuck out his tongue.

CHAPTER 2

They rode a gypsy cab home from the stadium. The driver, a rumpled looking Irishman with bumblebee glasses, was listening to the ballgame on the radio. While the taxi inched along the West Side Highway, the outraged Yankees broadcasters took turns denouncing Arnold. *You gotta wonder what's going through a guy's head,* said one. Another, an old-time Hall of Famer, explained what his navy buddies would have done to *a loser like that* during World War II. The third broadcaster, a woman with a heavy Bronx accent, offered a slightly different take: *He's clearly a nutcase. I say give him medication or shock-therapy or something.* The cabbie turned to Arnold and said: "Some wiseass wouldn't stand during *God Bless America.* I say we turn guys like that over to Al Qaeda," continued the cabbie. "If they like the terrorists so much, they can go live with them." The driver then offered several thoughts on "camel-jockeys" and people who wiped their asses with their bare hands. Arnold threatened Ray with a stern glare, but the child wasn't going to say anything. He looked frightened, a bit shell-shocked. Arnold patted the boy's bare knee.

The Brinkmans lived in a Greenwich Village brownstone they'd purchased on the same day that President Ford had told New York City to drop dead. The property included a small side yard surrounded by a stockade fence. Raised beds for flowers and a lilac-canopied arbour gave their modest eighth of an acre the feel of an English vicarage. There was also a birdhouse occupied by a pair of downy woodpeckers and, for Judith, an elevated artist's studio built into a linden tree. It was the perfect home for an urban botanist and a painter of cityscapes. "He chose me and he chose this building," Judith often told guests, winking, "so he hasn't had to make any good decisions since." But the truth was that they'd evolved alongside the neighbourhood. Judith now taught art part-time at St. Gregory's. He'd traded in academic botany for a rather lucrative plant nursery. They were just as bourgeois, Judith quipped, as any other civil servants or small businesspeople. She usually qualified this by adding *in the West Village.*

That afternoon—in the coming days they would call it *the* afternoon—Judith was waiting for them in the kitchen. She sat cradling a porcelain tea cup in both hands; blotches of crimson paint stained her fingers. For the kid, she'd set out a mug of chocolate milk and a platter of baked goods: Oreos, chocolate chip cookies, sugar wafers, but also miniature éclairs, napoleons, cream puffs. They had Ray for only two weeks, she'd argued. Weren't they entitled to ruin him?

"How was the roller coaster?" asked Arnold.

Judith had gone to Coney Island to paint. She was quite acclaimed in a "below the radar screen" sort of way for her "reversal of role" canvases: armoured natives greeting loin-clothed European explorers, female sailors catcalling male pedestrians. Her latest project placed senior citizens on amusement park rides.

"How was the roller coaster?" Arnold asked again.

"It had its ups and downs."

Arnold poured himself a glass of pink lemonade.

"You're mighty quiet," he said.

Judith rested her teacup on the table top. She looked from Arnold to Ray, then back to Arnold.

"Did something happen at the game?" she asked.

"Why do you ask?"

"Dammit, Arnold. I *knew* it was you. As soon as I heard on the radio about what happened, I knew you were behind it."

"You were listening to the game?"

"I was listening to *the news*."

The kid looked up from his plate; he wore a moustache of milk. "I tried to get him to stand up, Aunt Judith."

"I know you did, darling," she said.

She crossed into the dining room and began setting the table for the Cards. "I know it's a ridiculous ritual," she said. "I understand that as well as anyone. But why *just once* couldn't you go along with it anyway?"

Arnold helped her lay out the cutlery. "It's about the principle."

"Do you see me going around the city topless on

principle?"

Arnold knew the situations weren't analogous, but he also knew not to suggest that the situations weren't analogous. "What about freedom of conscience?" demanded Arnold. "What if I were a Jehovah's Witness?"

"But you're *not* a Jehovah's Witness."

"That's what they said in Nazi Germany, Judith. You know how that thing damn goes: First they came for the trade unionists…."

"Great. Now you're comparing Yankee Stadium to Nazi Germany."

"It felt like Nuremberg."

"Good God, Arnold. What world do you live in? We were *in* Nuremberg. Remember? Even Nuremberg doesn't feel like Nuremberg anymore."

They faced each other, separated by the marble table. The shadow of the unlit chandelier swayed in the soft afternoon light. "Do you put the fork to the right of the plate or to the left of the plate?" asked Arnold.

"Left. Spoons on the right."

He circled around the table, rearranging flatware. She adjusted the hyacinths and jonquils in the vase.

"Okay, maybe I didn't need to stick out my tongue," he said.

"Maybe not," agreed Judith.

And then they were both laughing. The sort of mutual, tension-relieving laughter one can experience only after twenty-nine years of marriage. It took Arnold half a minute to regain his breath—and then he was laughing again.

"So much for your bourgeois husband," he jibed.

"I can't let you out of my sight," said Judith. "Even for a second."

"I wouldn't want you to."

He wrapped his hands around his wife's delicate waist, drew her face to his. Three decades had gone by since she'd first knocked on the door of his greenhouse at Barnard—she'd wanted to borrow a carnivorous plant for an art project—and she still had the most stunning features he'd ever set eyes upon. Also the most inscrutable. Often, he still couldn't tell whether she was pleased or upset.

Arnold rubbed her nose with the end of his. Laughter rapidly melted into longing.

"Control yourself, lover-boy," she warned. "The kid…."

On cue, Ray entered the room, and asked: "What's so funny?"

Arnold devoted the remainder of the afternoon to his flowers. He'd once feared he'd find an eighth of an acre confining, that maybe they should have chosen a larger plot in Queens or in the suburbs, but over the years he'd come to realize that an eighth of an acre was the maximum amount of soil one man could tend effectively—unless one resorted to artificial herbicides; that was unthinkable. But natural gardening meant daily weeding and pruning. Every morning, before he walked across the square to open the nursery, Arnold spent several hours on his knees with a spade. In most aspects of his life, the botanist was a gentle man—probably too gentle for the world of business. But in his own garden, the kid gloves came off. His neighbours might be content to decapitate their weeds, to let the offending stalks desiccate under the afternoon sun, but not Arnold. He dug up each trespasser by the roots, scooping liberally like a surgeon excising a tumour, and then hacked apart the condemned plant to shake free every last clod of pilfered soil. The scraps of betony and nutsedge and wild radish were carted off, trussed in biodegradable bags, and ultimately composted in a bin behind the tool shed. In the evenings, he did his trimming and separated his perennials. Since it was April, he also set aside at least an hour after work for breeding day lilies.

Everybody asked Arnold the same question: How can you spend all day growing plants for strangers and still want to work in a garden at home? But it was *because* all of the plants that he raised at the nursery were carted off to other people's apartments, presumably to be starved of light or choked on tap water, that he savoured the chance to cultivate for himself. He frequently compared his experience to that of a celebrated chef cooking his own meals, but he actually felt more like an off-duty prostitute taking pleasure in a lover. In his own garden, Arnold might do as he wished. No need to raise hundreds of identical begonias and petunias and geraniums. Besides, he didn't spend that much time at the nursery anymore. Ever since his books had started selling—first *Please Do Eat the Day lilies*, then *The Flower Power Diet*—most of his workday was consumed by lecturing, and writing his weekly horticulture column, and leading foliage-eating walking tours for the Department of Parks & Recreation. He was also finishing a manuscript on the role of plants in classic novels—or plants and fungi, to be precise, because he had given over a full chapter to the pivotal mushroom-picking scene in *Anna Karenina*—so his manager, Guillermo, more or less ran the nursery on his own. Guillermo was a flamboyantly gay Venezuelan in his sixties. He had two dozen employees to assist him.

When Arnold squatted down that afternoon to replant day lilies—carefully labelled stems he'd sorted out the previous summer—the sun had already dipped behind the jagged red wall of the opposite building. That four-story structure had once been an egg candling facility, but now it housed office space and a sex toy museum. A faded advertisement for Goldstein's Packaged Meats still discoloured the brick. While the wall reduced Arnold's daylight growing time by nearly an hour, it also shaded his plants on torrid summer afternoons. That kept the hydrangeas from wilting, the rhododendrons from shedding petals. Arnold worked carefully, but quickly. He was tamping down the earth around the final set of day lilies when Gilbert Card wandered through the kitchen door. The bearded immigration lawyer carried a highball garnished with a cocktail umbrella.

"You're certainly earning your keep," said Gilbert.

"Just thinking," Arnold answered.

He'd actually been doing the opposite: actively not-thinking, working off steam. He kept replaying the afternoon's events—altering his own behaviour every time. He didn't regret remaining seated. Not for a moment. But he wished he'd done something more symbolic, more dignified, than sticking out his tongue. If he had prepared in advance, he would have brought along a political placard. Something like: "The Earth Is Full — Go Home" or "Ignore Our Forests and They Will Go Away." But if grandmother had testicles, as the saying went, she'd be grandfather.

Gilbert settled onto the arm of a wrought-iron bench. "We heard you had quite an adventure this afternoon," he said. The attorney spoke with a syrupy tidewater accent that made him sound folksy, despite his Ivy League credentials, and that had lulled the suspicions of many a credulous juror. Because he was a southerner, the direct descendent of slave-owning planters, people often assumed the litigator shared their own "down home" values. He didn't. "What got into you?" asked Gilbert. "I'm supposed to be the radical one."

Arnold dusted off his overalls. "I figured our lives were growing a bit too comfortable…."

"I hear you. Whenever I feel complacency setting in, I make a point of thumbing my nose at the entire country."

"Get your facts straight, Mr. Big-Shot Attorney. I just stuck out my tongue. No noses involved."

Arnold peeled off his heavy leather gloves. He rinsed his hands under the spigot and stepped behind a wooden divider to change out of his gardening clothes. Storing his overalls and boots in the tool shed had been one of the first concessions that Arnold had offered his bride in the spirit of domestic tranquillity: Judith went through the roof if he tracked up the carpets. "To tell you the truth, Gil," said Arnold, "I was stunned. I thought the days of groupthink were gone with Joe McCarthy."

"That's what I've been telling you for years," answered Gilbert. "You delude yourself that you live in a free country because you never test the boundaries of that freedom."

"Have I earned another lecture on open borders again?"

"I'm just saying…."

Judith completed his sentence from the top of the back stairs. "He's just saying that it's all about borders. That all the ills of the world are derived from immigration restrictions." Judith grinned. "What's that you said last time? 'Patriotism is being convinced your country is better because you were born in it.'"

"I didn't say it," retorted Gilbert. "George Bernard Shaw said it."

"Well I doubt he said it on an empty stomach," said Judith. "You can tell us all about open borders over vichyssoise. And bring Johnny Appleseed with you."

Bonnie and Gilbert Card were their closest friends. Judith and Bonnie had first met when they'd shared a hospital room during the blackout of 77. They later belonged to the same support group for young women who'd undergone hysterectomies. Perpetual childlessness permanently allied the Cards and the Brinkmans. As the other couples they knew were sucked, one-by-one, into that unrelenting world of pre-schools and play-dates—even most of the women from their support group acquired children through adoption and surrogates—they found solidarity in their ongoing independence. Bonnie, an eminent professor of bioethics, wrote extensively on the subject of childbearing. She opposed it. Adamantly. In fact, maybe as a personal coping mechanism, she'd made a name for herself by denouncing motherhood as immoral under present social conditions. Arnold was grateful for Bonnie's views, as radical as they were, because he had no desire to raise offspring himself—and, if Judith harboured any latent regrets, her friend's withering attacks on parenthood took the edge off.

Judith had opened the bay windows in the dining room and the breeze carried with it the sweet green scent of blossoming peonies. For supper, Judith had poached wild salmon on a signature bed of edible flowers: yucca petals, chive blossoms, violets. The wine was a cabernet handpicked by the blind Greek merchant on the corner.

"So where is your little terror?" asked Bonnie. "It isn't bedtime, is it?"

She said the word "bedtime" with unmistakable condescension.

"He went to sleep an hour early," answered Judith. "We bribed him."

"I hope with something good," offered Gilbert. "Like a nine year old girl."

"Or another baseball game," suggested Bonnie.

"I promised him a trip to the aquarium," said Judith.

"I hear they have a flag there," said Bonnie. "Maybe Arnold can set it on fire."

"Okay, have your laughs. But the whole episode was pretty damn terrifying."

"Do you mean you were afraid for your physical safety?" asked Bonnie.

"Yes, that too. But there was much more to it."

Bonnie removed her spectacles and rubbed the bridge of her long nose. "What do you mean?"

"I mean there's something unnerving about armchair patriotism. If I'd been at the Tomb of the Unknown Soldier, it would have been different. And I probably would have stood up too—just to show respect. But what does standing up at a baseball game have to do with loving my country?"

"Here, here," echoed Gilbert. "What's that Chesterton one-liner? 'My country, right or wrong' is like saying 'My mother, drunk or sober.'"

"In Arnold's case," Judith interjected, "it was mostly drunk."

Gilbert and Judith laughed. Arnold smiled too—although his mother, a settlement worker, had never touched even a drop of medicinal brandy. But his mother *had* been a temperamental woman—Judith said irrational—and she was more difficult as a teetotaller than most people are intoxicated.

"Let's keep mothers out of this," said Arnold.

"To keeping mothers out of this," said Gilbert, raising his wine glass.

Bonnie's expression remained hard and intense. She didn't take her eyes off Arnold. "Well, *do you* love America?" she asked.

"What's the supposed to mean?"

"It's a pretty straight-forward question, Arnold. *Do you* love America?"

Quintessentially Bonnie Card. She had a knack for

asking these sorts of questions: What was wrong with child pornography? Why was one-person one-vote a good way to organize society? How could meritocracy and inheritance co-exist simultaneously? Bonnie had nearly lost her university post several years earlier when she'd delivered a commencement speech at N.Y.U. in which she'd proposed mandatory infanticide legislation. She'd advocated a strict utilitarian standard that argued for drowning disabled babies before they experienced pain. She'd even compared parents of cystic fibrosis sufferers to child abusers. There had been protests, boycotts. But Bonnie had stuck to her guns. And she'd picked up supporters as well as detractors: The Hemlock Society had given her its public service medal; Jack Kevorkian had written to her from prison. But then the September 11th attacks occurred and the media had little room for baby-killing philosophers. The episode had done nothing to dampen Bonnie's premise-rattling interrogations.

"I'm not going to answer that," said Arnold.

Gilbert raised his glass. "The defendant pleads the Fifth."

"It's beside the point," Arnold added.

"I don't think so," said Bonnie. "I think it *is* the point."

"You're badgering the witness, honey," said Gilbert.

"You *don't* love America," Bonnie persisted. "You're just afraid to admit it. They made you say the Pledge of Allegiance one too many times in elementary school and now you can't see things clearly. " She forked an olive from the jar and carefully carved out the pit. "Can you honestly tell me you love your country, Arnold Brinkman?"

"I'm grateful for the privileges I have as an American," said Arnold.

"That's not the same thing," she answered.

Arnold had never given much thought to whether or not he loved America—but now it seemed pretty obvious to him that he didn't. Not in the way Nathan Hale had loved America. Or even in the way his late father, a Dutch-Jewish refugee, had loved America. In fact, he found the idea of sacrificing his life for his country somewhat abhorrent. Moreover, it wasn't that he disliked abstract loyalties in general. He loved New York, for instance: Senegalese takeout at three a.m., and strolling through the Botanical Gardens on the first crisp day of autumn, and feeding the peacocks at the Cathedral of St. John the Divine. If Manhattan were invaded—if New Jersey were to send an expeditionary force of militiamen across the Hudson River—he'd willingly take up arms to defend his city. He also loved Sandpiper Key in Florida, where they owned a time-share, and maybe Brown University, where he'd spent five years of graduate school. But the United States? No one could mistake his qualified praise for love.

"I like my country as much as the next man," said Arnold.

"No offense, Arnold," said Bonnie. "You wouldn't

know the next man if he bit you on the ass."

Judith stood up. "That's my prompt to serve the fish."

"I'll come with you," offered Gilbert.

Card followed Arnold's wife into the kitchen.

Arnold found himself suddenly alone with Bonnie. This always made him feel slightly nervous. It wasn't that he didn't both respect and trust Gilbert's wife, but that he was never quite certain what she might say or do next. She possessed just the right irreverence to do a person serious damage.

Bonnie leaned forward. Too close. (She'd never learned to modulate personal space properly.) Although Gilbert's wife didn't smoke, Arnold suffered an irrational premonition that she was about to puff a cigarette into his eyes.

"Do you know what your problem is, Arnold?" asked Bonnie.

"I have friends who think too much."

"You're risk-averse. You create these wonderful opportunities for yourself, but then you don't have the courage to follow through on them."

"I suppose you wouldn't have stuck out your tongue."

"That's water under the bridge," answered Bonnie. "It's what you do *now* that matters. You should call the newspapers and defend yourself. Announce that you *don't* love America—that patriotism is a refuge for scoundrels and all that."

"Talk truth to power," said Arnold.

"Talk common sense," said Bonnie. "But you won't do that. I know you too well. You'll offer some lukewarm apology, something about stress or nerves or whatnot, and you'll go about your business."

Gilbert entered carrying the platter of sizzling fish.

"You two still going at it?" he asked.

"I'm saying he should capitalize on his celebrity," answered Bonnie. "He has a moral obligation to denounce the mob."

"Celebrity," scoffed Judy. She held a tureen of homemade couscous. "This will all blow over. In a couple of days, nobody will remember."

"Do you think so?" asked Arnold.

"I hope so," said Judy.

"Me too," Arnold agreed. "I wasn't destined to be remembered."

"A toast," proposed Gilbert. They all raised their wine glasses. "To not remembering."

"Not remembering," Judith chimed in. "The national pastime."

And they drank.

CHAPTER 3

They stayed up with the Cards until well past midnight, talking politics and neighbourhood gossip, polishing off a second bottle of wine, but Arnold was out of bed before the sun rose above the mansard roof of the community playhouse. The morning glories around the drainpipe still kept their blossoms clenched shut against the dew. On the fire escape, sparrows flitted among the terracotta pots. Otherwise, the predawn was grey and still and silent, punctuated only by the periodic rumbling of sanitation trucks. Arnold *loved* the first hour of a spring morning in Greenwich Village. Wandering through the rows of antebellum townhouses—on their second date, Judith had taught him the difference between federalist-style and Greek revival architecture—Arnold could fool himself into believing he'd stepped back into the previous century. One could easily imagine running into Edith Wharton on a street corner, or exchanging greetings with Walt Whitman, or sharing a stroll with that pioneering American botanist, Nathaniel Lord Britton, who'd live on West 11th Street while he taught at Columbia. Even Britton would have admired the all-indigenous community gardens tucked into the numerous hidden courtyards. What the great naturalist would have thought of the recent horticultural efforts of the block association, the oversized marigolds and snapdragons suffocating the hawthorn roots along the avenues, was another matter entirely—but one couldn't deny these rings of floral invaders *were* beautiful.

Arnold retrieved his *New York Times* from the front steps. He flipped through the Sports pages, then the Metro section. Nothing about tongue-thrusting. Not a word. The incident didn't even make the article about the game itself, which the Yankees had won on a grand slam in the fifteenth inning. Arnold dabbed his forehead with his sleeve. He wasn't famous! What a wonderful way to start off the work week! There'd been a small story on the local television news the previous evening—he knew because Guillermo had phoned him—but mercifully Arnold's social circle did not watch the local news. Most of their friends didn't even own television sets. If he were lucky, a few weeks would pass before anyone actually made a positive ID on him; by then, some other fool would have lit a match during a gas leak, or bathed his children at an automated car wash, or stuck his penis in an electric citrus peeler, and nobody would care that Arnold had ever been born. His sister-in-law would also be home by then, and Ray would be back in Connecticut, and life would have returned to normal. Or at least to baseline. Normal might be pushing it.

That morning, Arnold lost half an hour clearing crushed beer cans out of his newly-planted caladium. His neighbour's son—recently expelled from Binghamton—

had been discarding his trash over the fence. The neighbour was Ira Taylor and he had some foggy connection to Taylor & Taylor Securities, the bond firm, but it didn't appear to involve much in the way of office work, because the man answered his own doorbell at all hours of the day. Arnold found his neighbour abrasive and overbearing. When he complained about the litter, Taylor told him not to "blow his doughnuts." It would be taken care of, the securities trader assured him. But you had to cut the kid some slack. "Tell me you never tossed an apple core out a car window or put out a cigar on the pavement," said Taylor. "Let it go, old man. Let it go." Arnold hated being called "old man" by a guy his own age. But he had cut the son slack. Twice. And the problem, as evidenced by the pizza boxes full of cigarette butts, had certainly not gone away. It was the kid's lucky morning, thought Arnold. He'd let him have a fourth strike. After standing up to all of Yankee Stadium, Arnold had no hankering to duke it out with his neighbour.

Once he'd gathered up the candy bar wrappers and the Doritos bags and what appeared to be the strap from a woman's brassiere, Arnold plunged headlong into his weeding. No new tares were actually visible on the surface. He'd been over this ground too many times for that. But he made a point of churning the soil, particularly the moist earth beneath the Japanese maple, because prevention was the best herbicide. First he worked with a spade, then with a short-handled hoe. He lost himself in the labour. Gardening provided him with the same high that long-distance runners found in marathon training and actors discovered on the stage. The rustle of footsteps in the butterfly hedges took him by surprise. Arnold spun around, brandishing his hoe.

"Jesus, Mr. Brinkman," said the trespasser. "You look terrified."

The voice belonged to an unfamiliar young woman. She was pudgy, with wide-set eyes and the upturned nose of a German peasant, but she was still of the age at which every girl is gorgeous by default. It was an ephemeral beauty. All long hair and smooth skin. You couldn't compare it to the high cheekbones and perfectly curved brow that would keep Judith stunning into her seventies. But the girl was eye-catching. Not so different from the hundreds of other large-breasted, bare-armed graduate students and aspiring artists who rolled their eyes at Arnold every day on the streets of Greenwich Village—except that this young woman was standing in his yard. She wore a cream-coloured tank-top and carried a canvas bag over her exposed shoulder.

"Could you put that down?" she asked. "I'm not a burglar."

Arnold tentatively lowered the hoe. He still feared this might be some sort of elaborate con-game or blackmail scheme—he knew they enlisted teenage girls for just such rackets—but at least she didn't appear to be violent.

"Explain yourself," he ordered.

"I figured you wouldn't remember me," said the girl.

"I know you?"

Arnold tried to place the intruder's face, but couldn't. Had he taught her? Had she worked at the nursery? At some point, all of his former students and employees had blended into each other. Common wisdom said that when you died, you passed through a tunnel of bright light and encountered everyone you'd ever known. Nobody said what would happen if you couldn't recognize them.

"I interviewed you for the N.Y.U. newspaper," said the girl. "About five years ago. When you gave that talk on 'living off the land' in Central Park."

"Five years ago," echoed Arnold. "I think I do remember you." The truth was he'd not only forgotten the interview, but he couldn't even remember the lecture.

"See, I'm not a burglar," said the girl.

"Okay, but how did you get in here?"

The girl smiled mischievously. "Magic."

"Would you care to be more specific?"

"Ladders."

Arnold looked in the direction she'd come from. Sure enough, the upper rungs of a ladder protruded above the butterfly hedge. On the top step, surrounded by a tangle of black-eyed Susans, a catbird twitched its long dark tail.

"I set up one ladder on the sidewalk," the girl explained. "I carried the other one to the top and put it down on the opposite side of the fence. Then I just stepped over horizontally. It's a neat trick I learned in journalism school." Arnold must have looked puzzled, because the girl added: "I borrowed one of the ladders from the theatre across the street and the other from the liquor store down the block. I told them you needed them for your garden."

"I'll be sure to thank them."

"I'm Cassandra. Like from ancient Troy."

She extended her pale hand. Arnold didn't take it.

"Well, Cassandra, you still haven't explained what in God's name you're doing in my back yard at seven thirty in the morning."

"You won't be mad, will you? I want an interview."

Arnold tossed the hand hoe into the grass. "An interview?"

"I'm interning at the *Daily Vanguard*. The new progressive paper. And when I told them I recognized the guy from the baseball game, they totally promised me a front-page byline—if you'd agree to talk. How awesome is that?"

"There's nothing to talk about. That's yesterday's news—no need to stoke any fires. You're a weekly, right? By the time you go to press, nobody will remember me."

"We're a daily, Mr. Brinkman. The *Daily Vanguard*." The girl rummaged through her canvas bag. She passed him the local newspapers one at a time. His photograph—tongue protruding—appeared on every cover. In The *Daily*

News, the headline read: "Mystery Man Mocks Nation at War." *Newsday* ran the caption: "Tongue of a Snake." But none was more direct than the *New York Post*. At the angle they'd photographed him—with one arm raised to block the glare—he bore a striking resemblance to Adolf Hitler delivering a Nazi salute. Underneath, they'd printed "THE ENEMY WITHIN" in bold letters.

"Yesterday's news," she mocked . "They've forgotten you already."

Arnold stared dumbfounded at the tabloid cover; they'd even dotted the i's in "WITHIN" with miniature swastikas.

"Don't look so gloomy," said Cassandra. "You knocked the Bare-Ass Bandit off the front page of the *Post*. I think that's pretty fucking cool."

The Bare-Ass Bandit had been terrorizing the city for weeks. This nude, saber-wielding outlaw confronted lone pedestrians and stole their clothing. All of it. Undergarments. Medical alert bracelets. Hairpins. In one instance, he'd even demanded a woman's sanitary napkin. Then he made the victim watch while he tried on their garments. But in recent days, his M.O. had grown odder, providing a wealth of material for the tabloids. In one instance, he'd kidnapped the Greek Orthodox Archbishop of Brooklyn from his bedroom, and left the cleric bound and naked in Prospect Park, with the words "Jesus didn't save me" scrawled across his chest in human faeces. The following week, he'd hijacked a bus of disabled senior citizens returning from Atlantic City and run off with their wheelchairs and prosthetic limbs. Only a libellous rag like the *Post* could think to lump him and Arnold in the same category.

"This is absurd," said Arnold.

"Of course it's absurd. But it *is*. That's why the *Vanguard* is giving you a chance to tell your own side of the story. We're on your side."

"I don't want to tell my side of the story," snapped Arnold. He felt thirsty, dizzy. "*There is no story*."

The girl shifted her weight from one short leg to the other. She looked as though she might pout. "Please, Mr. Brinkman. We'll help each other out. What's that expression old people use? 'You scratch my back and I scratch yours.'"

No, thought Arnold, we won't. And he used that 'old people' expression all the time. He suddenly realized how uncomfortable he felt having van attractive young woman alone with him in his garden. They weren't *that* far apart in age—no further than Rochester and Jane Eyre or Scarlett O'Hara and Frank Kennedy. (Arnold had just finished writing a chapter on the significance of vines in *Wide Sargasso Sea* and was polishing up an article on the role of cotton strains in *Gone With the Wind*.) He knew he hadn't done anything wrong with the girl—he hadn't even wanted to do anything wrong—but the notion that Judith might suspect him of wanting to do something wrong was enough to make him uneasy. "You shouldn't be here. My wife will be downstairs any minute now."

"Cool. Do you think I could interview her too?"

Arnold looked down at his feet. He toyed with the keys in his pocket. Where the sprinkler hose was leaking, a thin stream of water fizzed anaemically. Clouds of vapour rose from the hot flagstones. The day was going to be a scorcher.

"Look, Cassandra," said Arnold—in the same voice he used with his nephew. "You have to leave. This is not a good time." He decided he hadn't sounded forceful enough, so he added: "This is private property."

"Come on, Mr. Brinkman. You'll to have to talk to the press eventually. So why not me? I was here first."

"Enough. I'm going inside to have my breakfast. You can let yourself out the way you came in."

"Don't be stupid, Mr. Brinkman. You need all the friends you can get."

Arnold walked toward the tool shed. "I have plenty of friends."

That's when the pandemonium erupted on the other side of the fence.

Arnold and Judith had purchased their brownstone from a paranoid ex-Weatherman who'd gained twenty-seconds of fame for founding a Caucasian Auxiliary to the Black Panther Party. "Hurricane" Cohen's one remaining legacy was an elevated stone platform at the corner of Arnold's yard that the radical had used to keep watch. Standing on the three foot ledge, the observer had a clear sight of the front steps and both sidewalks as far as the avenue. A carefully constructed blind kept it a one-way view. In Cohen's day, there had also been an escape tunnel that connected the yard to the vacant lot behind the sex toy museum, but the city had covered the exit with a storm grating. Arnold later filled in his end of the burrow with cinderblocks. He'd kept the platform as an ornamental piece and surrounded it with ferns. When the first shouts and sirens rose over the fence, he climbed onto the moss-coated ledge to take a look.

Television vans lined the entire far side of the street. CBS. NBC. FOX. Some of the news crews were already broadcasting. Others lounged against parked cars, sipping coffee from Styrofoam cups. A crowd of pedestrians and local merchants had also ventured down the block to watch. Arnold spotted Darmopolis, the blind proprietor of the liquor shop, scratching his bushy moustache. Also the Chinese barber who spoke with a French accent, and the homeless poet, and the identical twins from behind the dairy counter at the Gourmet's Paradise. The twins wore matching red bandannas around their necks; they took turns whispering into the blind Greek's ear. Lots of the other faces were unfamiliar: random pedestrians who happened to be cutting between avenues at that moment. In the centre of all of the mayhem stood Ira Taylor, looking far too comfortable in only a dressing gown and slippers, being interviewed simultaneously by several reporters. The bond seller was practically conducting a press conference. He occasionally pointed in the direction of Arnold's townhouse and made animated gestures, but it was impossible to hear his words over the ebb and flow of sirens.

The police department had commandeered the near side of the street. Two patrolmen flanked Arnold's stoop like the guards at Buckingham Palace. Another team of officers hurriedly erected a cordon of blue sawhorses along the pavement. Fire engines sealed off both ends of the block. There was also an ambulance on the scene. The EMTs were posing for photographs with a conclave of Asian tourists.

At one level, Arnold understood that he'd been the cause of this frenzy. At another level, the entire business was so implausible, so unreal.

Cassandra had climbed onto the ledge behind him. He regretted having filled in the Weatherman's escape tunnel.

"Okay, Mr. Yesterday's News. Why don't you go out there and tell *them* there's no story?" asked the girl.

"What am I going to do?" muttered Arnold. "Judith

is going to murder me."

"Not if they get to you first," Cassandra shot back.

Arnold didn't have a chance to respond. From the avenue came a thunder of voices that slowly separated out into chants of "Shame! Shame! Shame!" Then the motley parade of patriots rounded the corner.

The protesters numbered several dozen. Some were clad in military fatigues; others wore red-white-and-blue. Placards read: "A Friend of Osama's Is No Friend of Ours" and "Eternal Vigilance is the Price of Liberty," also "Nuke 'Em" and "Jesus Wasn't A Patsy." Two young dark-skinned men were decked out in revolutionary war garb and had muskets slung over their shoulders; they accompanied the demonstrators on fife and drum. Poorly.

At the head of the procession marched an obese black man in a three-piece suit. Reflective sunglasses shielded his eyes. The man held hands with a tiny, withered old woman done up in a lime green church outfit and matching hat. A band of black satin had been wrapped around the hat's crown. The obese man, in his other hand, held a raised American flag. When this ragtag crew arrived at the police cordon, they removed their hats and sang *God Bless America* in several different keys. Darmopolis, the wine merchant, joined in. So did several tourists. Arnold cringed. "Kate Smith is turning over in her grave," he said. The girl just looked at him, puzzled.

"Do you know who *that* is?" she whispered.

"Who *who* is?"

"The guy with the sunglasses. That's Spotty Spitford. As in The Revered Spotty Spitford and his Emergency Civil Rights Brigade."

Arnold vaguely recognized the name. It reminded him of a fifties vocal group. "Black conservatives?" he asked.

"Black reactionaries," Cassandra retorted. "The self-styled front line in the war against homosexuals and abortionists. They call it the Second Abolitionist Movement. You've got to be living under a rock not to know about them."

"I'm neither a homosexual nor an abortionist."

"Make sure you tell them that while they're stoning you."

When the singing limped to a conclusion, one of Spitford's assistants handed the minister a bullhorn. Now the entire neighbourhood could hear him speak. *And did he speak!* Nearly fifteen minutes on the "Fifth Column of Sixth Street" in a voice as heavy as a boulder. Then he turned the pulpit over to the withered old woman. She held up a photograph of her dead grandson. "I taught my boy about service," she said—barely audible, even with the megaphone. "I'm proud of my Lionel. I don't understand how anybody could not be proud of my Lionel. Why can't this man sing to show my boy respect?" The woman's voice rose in anger. "My Lionel deserves an apology. All the boys in the service deserve an apology." The woman glanced at Spitford for reassurance and he nodded his approval. "I don't want no trouble," the woman concluded. "I just want respect."

The protesters cheered. Even a number of the bystanders joined in. Then a chant of "Apologize! Apologize!" swept across the crowd.

"We'll be here," boomed Spitford, "until that dirty yellow coward does the right thing by this gold star grandmother and says he's sorry."

The girl grinned. "It's your lucky fucking day. You've just seen the beginning of the Spitford campaign for mayor," she said. "If there's one thing that can get a black conservative elected in this city, it's a white guy with a red agenda. I guess that's where you come in." Cassandra pulled a camera from her bag and snapped Arnold's photograph. "A souvenir," she explained. "For our files."

Spitford continued his sermon: "We demand that this reprobate acknowledge the error of his ways. We also demand that our elected officials stand with us in our outrage. Where is the mayor this morning? Where is the governor? Where are the people you pay to represent your values at times like these? I'll tell you where. Nowhere. But that does not mean that we're going to go away...."

"You're so screwed," chimed Cassandra. "He's got his political teeth into you. Now there's no letting go."

Arnold resisted the urge to bean the self-ordained

minister with a gardening implement. It was the man's right to protest. But Arnold had no intention of apologizing. He stepped around Cassandra and lowered himself from the platform. "Good luck with your story," he said. "By the way, that's off the record."

The girl said something in response, but it was drowned out by chanting.

Judith was standing at the kitchen window in her dressing gown. She'd fastened her hair back haphazardly, and sandy strands stuck out in all directions. Her feet were bare. When Arnold entered—still in his gardening clothes, he realized too late—she greeted him with a chilling frown.

"We've had fifty phone calls in the last two hours," she said. "I had to disconnect the doorbell before I went insane."

"Shit," said Arnold.

"I was going to get you, but I didn't want to interrupt your tête-à-tête with the queen of the prom."

"Don't start on that. She's a reporter for the *Vanguard.* Her name's Cassandra. The last thing I need right now is you accusing me of things."

Judith squeezed and released her fists. "Nobody's accusing you of anything."

"You were hinting. As though it's not enough that they've practically strung me up for treason. Now you'll have me shot for adultery."

Judith laughed—a short, sharp laugh. "As I said, Arnold, nobody's accusing you of anything. You couldn't cheat on me if you tried. But you'll have to admit now is not the best of times to be gallivanting around the flowerbeds, cavorting with teenaged girls. For any reason."

Arnold opened the refrigerator. He rummaged through the drawers and came out empty-handed. "Look, I'm sorry," he said. "I'm just not sure what to do right now."

"I suppose you should apologize," said Judith. "Maybe that will placate them."

"That's the one thing," answered Arnold, "that I certainly won't do."

Arnold paused to collect his thoughts. The muffled chanting from the sidewalk was audible in the kitchen. It was giving him a headache. He was about to explain that he was too old to apologize, that he didn't want to be remembered as the asshole who apologized—far better to be hated for not apologizing—when Ray came charging down the stairs. The boy was wearing pyjama bottoms.

"Can I ask a question?" Ray demanded.

"No," snapped Arnold.

The boy turned to Judith. "What's going on?" he asked.

"Some people are still angry at your uncle for not standing up at the baseball game yesterday," explained Judith. "Your uncle was about to apologize to them."

The boy poured himself a bowl of sugared cereal. "What time are we going to the aquarium?"

"Oh, the aquarium," said Judith. "I don't know. Uncle Arnold has to apologize first."

"When will that be?"

Judith turned to Arnold. "When will that be?"

"Never," said Arnold. "Let's drop it."

"Then I guess we're never going to the aquarium," countered Judith. "I guess we'll stay prisoners in this house forever."

Ray grimaced. "Can I ask another question, Aunt Judith?"

"Sure, honey," she said.

"What does nigger mean?"

"Nigger," repeated Judith. She lashed Arnold with eyes as sharp as whips—or maybe she was just asking him for help; he couldn't tell. "Well," she said. "Well."

"The baseball game was your idea," said Arnold.

"How was I supposed to know that you couldn't handle it? Fifty thousand other people managed to make it through the game without causing an international incident."

And then—as Arnold's temper approached the snapping point—the phone rang.

"Don't answer it," warned Judith. "The machine will pick up."

"I'll answer it, all right," said Arnold. He nearly

wrenched the receiver off the wall. "What do you want?" he demanded.

"Arnold? Arnold Brinkman? It's Celeste."

"Oh, Jesus, Celeste. I thought you were somebody else."

"I'm not," his sister-in-law answered. "Is everything okay?"

"Couldn't be better. One of these days, I might just drop dead from pure joy. Any minute now."

"I'm glad—that things are going well, I mean. How's my Raymond?"

"Having the time of his life. I even took him to a baseball game."

"Did he use sun block? You have no idea how that child burns."

"Sure, sure," lied Arnold. "And today, we're off to the aquarium. In fact, Celeste, you caught us on the way out the door...."

Arnold rolled his eyes at Judith. His sister-in-law, rather than taking a hint, had commenced relating her own adventures. She and her new husband, Walter The Republican Chiropractor, had island-hopped across the Dodecanese from American hotel to American hotel. They'd "discovered" a McDonalds with clean bathrooms in Rhodes; Mykonos offered the best Jacuzzi. The one disappointment has been Kos, the birthplace of Hippocrates, where Walter had gotten into a heated dispute with a British cardiologist over the merits of non-traditional healing. Celeste presented the altercation—which ultimately had to be settled by what she called "the gendarmes"—as though reading a trial transcript. Several times, Arnold attempted to interrupt. Finally, Judith took the telephone from him and told Celeste that she'd called at an inopportune moment. "I'm having a difficult time hearing you, dear," said Judith. "No, it's not the line. There's some kind of rally going on across the street. About the war, probably. You know how the Village is." Ray was standing at his aunt's elbow, but Judith hung up the phone.

"You'll talk to Mommy later," said Judith. "After Arnold quiets the masses." She turned to Arnold, arms akimbo: "What is wrong with you? Tell them you're sorry and they'll go home."

"Dammit, Judith. That's like pouring gasoline on a fire. If I humiliate myself a little, they'll want me to humiliate myself a lot."

"Please, Arnold. Nobody ever died of humiliation."

He recalled what Bonnie Card had said: *You'll offer some lukewarm apology, something about stress or nerves or whatnot, and you'll go about your business.*

"I love you, Judith. But I can't do this for you."

The child started to sob. He ran into the living room and buried his face in the sofa pillows. Judith followed and cradled his head to her chest.

"You have to do something," she said. Her expression remained placid, but he could hear the tension rising in her voice. "If you don't do something, I will."

"Fine, I'll do something," he said. "But not what you want."

Arnold walked to the front door. He glanced at himself in the hall mirror—he was poorly shaven and his overalls were caked in loam—but it was too late to do anything about that. "I'll be back," he said. "Wish me luck."

Judith said nothing. The boy whimpered. Arnold opened the front door.

When he stepped out onto the stoop, a gust of hot air slapped against his face. Cameras flashed rapidly. Reporters peppered him with unintelligible questions. Yet miraculously, when he held up his hand, the crowd grew silent.

"This is not a news story," he said decisively. "There are children starving in Africa. *That* is a news story." Arnold paused—and it struck him that a provocateur like Spitford might distort this remark into something racially inflammatory. "There are children starving all over Asia and Latin America," he added quickly. "*That* is where you should be focusing your attention. Get your priorities straight."

A reporter called out: "Does that mean you refuse to apologize?"

"I have nothing to apologize for," said Arnold. He

glared at the obese minister, but the sunglasses deflected his gaze. "Therefore, obviously, I won't apologize."

More cameras snapped. Another reporter asked him a question about terrorism.

"I would appreciate it if you all got the hell away from my house," Arnold added. "You're scaring off the bees. The forsythia won't pollinate."

Then he stepped back into the dim foyer and slammed the door.

Judith was still sitting in the darkened living room. She was clutching one of the sofa pillows to her chest like teddy bear.

"Did you apologize?" she asked. "Please tell me you apologized."

"I told them to get their priorities straight."

Judith squeezed the pillow tighter. "I'm fifty-one years old, Arnold. I can't handle this."

"I'm not going to apologize for something I didn't do."

"But you *did* do it, Arnold. That's the point."

"Well I didn't do it the way they say I did it."

Arnold shook his head in the hope of clearing his thoughts; his brain remained murky. He sat down beside Judith on the edge of the couch and rubbed her shoulder.

"Don't touch me right now," she snapped. Then she added: "Change your clothes. You're trailing mud."

Arnold examined his path. Crumbs of caked earth

speckled the tile in the foyer.

"Dammit," said Arnold. He walked toward the kitchen door. "I'll be outside if you need me. If you want to talk."

In the garden, the sun had burnt off the last of the haze. Brown creepers and nuthatches worked their way down the tree trunks. Wasps buzzed among the hollyhocks. A chipmunk darted across the stone wall beneath the linden. Only the oppressive din from the sidewalk distinguished this morning from any other—from a moment that might otherwise have belonged to a previous age.

Much to Arnold's consternation, the girl had left her ladder behind the hedges. He'd have no choice but to return it as soon as the crisis blew over. He was about to remove it—no need to invite in a real burglar—when a shadow darkened the flagstones behind him. It was the girl.

"Looks like your first run-in with the media was a real hit," she said. "You had them eating out of your hand."

"What the hell are you still doing here?"

"I can hear them packing up their gear and running off to Africa this very minute. Who can blame them? They might miss breaking the next case of dysentery."

"I thought I ordered you to leave."

"I disobeyed."

"You have to leave. I need time to think." Under different circumstances, he would have kept his cool.

He'd even have invited the girl in for a cold drink before expelling her. But when he wasn't getting along with Judith, everything in Arnold's life stopped working. "I'm not joking anymore. I'll call the goddam police."

"We're you joking before?" asked the girl.

"Fine, stay," he snapped. "I'll leave."

That's when the idea struck him. "Wait a minute," he said. "Do you still have that other ladder?"

"It's lying against the fence."

"So I could leave without going through the front door."

The girl smirked. "If I let you."

She stood between him and the ladders. He considered attempting to get past her—to use force, if necessary—but he didn't like the idea of wrestling with a girl in her twenties. Besides, she might scream. The last thing he wanted was Spitford & Company coming around the back of the house.

"You give me an interview," offered the girl, "and I'll lend you my ladders."

"That's bullshit."

"That's my best offer. Only offer, really. Take it or leave it."

Arnold remembered why he'd left academics. Too much negotiating. In business, ironically, nobody ever haggled. It just wasn't worth it.

"You drive a damn hard bargain," said Arnold.

She grinned and stuck out *her* tongue.

"Deal?" she asked.

"Deal. Now let's get out of here."

CHAPTER 4

The Blue Rose Plant & Garden Centre occupied an entire city block on the far side of Seventh Avenue in a gap between two historical preservation districts. Until the late-1960s, the site had been home to Baumgarten's Poultry Yard, the last *glatt* kosher slaughterer south of 14th Street. One of Arnold's first memories was of his father's grandmother, whom everybody called the Baroness, taking him to Baumgarten's to pick out chickens for the Passover *seder.* He'd never overcome his fear of the old widow. Her hands had been mangled in a childhood carriage accident, and she spoke only Yiddish and Dutch, not English, so she communicated with her great-grandchildren by gesticulating with the stump of what had once been her index finger. Arnold had watched in a combination of fascination and horror, but mostly horror, as she'd used the same disfigured digit to pass judgment on three caged hens. In the seconds that followed, the butcher—a cheerful and robust young *chasid*—roped the birds around the legs, as though wrapping a pastry box, and severed their heads on the wooden chopping block. The Baroness had made Arnold hold the carcasses in his lap on the subway ride home.

It was easy, maybe too easy, to trace a line between that visit to Baumgarten's and the botanist's subsequent life choices: abandoning Judaism for secular agnosticism, giving up red meat and poultry for edible flowers, marrying the blue-eyed daughter of a Norwegian laundress, herself the collateral descendant of baronesses, or their Scandinavian equivalent, although this connection came with neither fortune nor privilege. If the Baroness had known that her own great-grandson would wed a lapsed Lutheran, an artist who brewed tea from dandelion stalks, and a poor girl at that, the old refugee would have dropped stone cold dead on the sidewalk—which was what she did anyway, that same Passover, from a blood clot to her brain. What amazed Arnold wasn't that he'd forsaken his heritage—Judith joked that the only roots they had were carrots and sugar beets—but that he'd ended up in business. *That* seemed implausible. As his father had always said, they were descended from an ancient and venerable line of hourly employees: bricklayers, pieceworkers, clerks. Arnold's first foray into capitalism, a sixth-grade carwash, had run two hundred dollars in the red—not including the restitution his father kicked in when he forgot to seal the roof of a convertible. From that point forward, the Brinkman's only son had seemed destined for university life. In the academy, it didn't matter how peculiar or incompetent you were, whether you couldn't tie your own shoe laces or believed the earth was flat—provided you contributed to the intellectual advancement of your field. Arnold knew of one prominent botanist, for instance, who also published self-help books on the therapeutic benefits of drinking one's own urine. But in Arnold's case, his scientific articles hadn't proven terribly valuable. In the words of his tenure committee, they were "perfectly competent, but uninspired." He couldn't have agreed more. Who in their right mind would be inspired by the crosspollination genetics of winter wheat? What he'd wanted to do was to study edible flowers—but *that* wasn't considered serious research.

While Arnold had searched for another teaching post, a senior colleague of his, Hans Overmeyer, probably because the middle-aged professor had an unspoken crush on Arnold, had suggested they purchase the foreclosed poultry yard from the city and use the space for experimental botany. Overmeyer was interested in transplanting animal DNA into plants. He dreamed he might someday be able to produce blue roses from dolphin genes, or pink rice from flamingo feathers, but his first project—breeding glow-in-the-dark crocuses with the help of firefly chromosomes—struck pay-dirt in the mid-70s. For several months, while the rest of the nation grappled with stagflation and gasoline lines, it seemed everyone within walking distance of Sheridan Square had a crocus nightlight in their bedrooms. Arnold owned fifty percent of the proceeds. The following autumn, when Overmeyer's second ex-wife gunned down the older botanist in his Barnard office, a shocked Arnold inherited the entire operation. To that point, he'd done nothing to contribute to the nursery; he hadn't even cleaned out the rusted chicken cages from his designated office. The entire summer had been spent house-hunting with Judith and searching for specimens in Central Park. Yet somehow the glow-in-the-dark crocuses had led to an organic flower market, and then a catalogue bulb-and-seed business, and eventually a multimillion dollar enterprise—albeit one where, for many years, elderly out-of-towners continued to come seeking live ducks and guinea fowl. On the lecture circuit, young horticulturists frequently examined Arnold's curriculum vitae and noted how well all the strands of his life had come together. That was because they possessed the power of hindsight, he warned. A man doesn't list his setbacks on his résumé.

Arnold had always prided himself on taking an interest in the community—not just writing annual checks to City Harvest and the West Village Green Thumb Society, but setting aside time to get to know his neighbours, even though his neighbours changed frequently and his own time grew increasingly precious. Usually, nothing pleased him more than exchanging early-morning greetings and chitchat with his fellow merchants: the chain-smoking Israeli locksmith, the Ethiopian restaurateur who always addressed him as *my cousin*, the elderly transvestites who ran a combination costume shop and internet café. He had even befriended the lizard-tongued kid who pierced nipples and genitals on 13th Street. Arnold called the young man

"The Specialist." But that morning, after his confrontation with the media, Arnold dreaded the prospect of running into anyone he knew. He walked rapidly, steering a broad rectangular course that avoided his usual morning route, so that he approached the nursery from the opposite direction. The girl struggled to keep pace. Several passers-by appeared to recognize him—either from television or the newspapers—but he ignored their stares.

"Can you slow the fuck down?" Cassandra pleaded. "Wouldn't it be easier if we got you a paper bag to put over your head?"

"This is how I normally walk," said Arnold. "If you can't keep up, we can always do the interview another day."

"I think you'd look awesome in a paper bag," continued the girl. She had the habit of following her own train of thought, independent of his interruptions. "We'll cut you some eyeholes and draw you a moustache."

Arnold picked up his pace. He wasn't in the best physical shape—he'd given up jogging years earlier when he'd ruptured his Achilles'—but he was still surprised to discover how easily he winded. Sweat trickled down the back of his neck and under his collar. Somehow, he blamed this flagging breath on the girl. "Did anybody ever tell you that you're a pain in the ass?" he demanded.

"All the time," retorted the girl. "Some guys like that."

Her tone was overtly playful—possibly flirtatious.

Even racing down Sixth Avenue in a condition approaching panic, Arnold couldn't help noticing. But how was he supposed to respond? Ordering the girl to "stop flirting" was somewhat presumptuous. It might even come across as coy encouragement. On the other hand, engaging her in a battle of teasing repartee might give her ideas. So Arnold said nothing. He let her fire off her barbs, but refused to shoot back. Besides, he was out of practice. He hadn't flirted with anyone in thirty years. *He hadn't wanted to flirt with anyone.* Even before that, verbal jousting hadn't been his strong suit.

They crossed the park, cut along the new jogging trail where the city's gardeners had recently set down a bed of asters and heliotrope. "Where the hell are you taking me?" demanded the girl. "We're spinning in goddam circles."

"Squares," retorted Arnold.

Soon they emerged opposite the Plant Centre. Arnold was relieved to see that Guillermo had the place up-and-running in his absence: Display trays of African violets and New Guinea impatiens lined the sidewalk; the heavy iron gates had been drawn open and festooned with wandering jews. Arnold also noticed several unfamiliar decorations: an American flag taped under the "Summer Sale" sign and two dozen plywood boards leaning against the brickwork. Inside, the air smelled pungently of pine sap and pollen. There were only a handful of customers:

an old man with a beagle, an unkempt girl walking her bicycle through the aisles. The nursery generally did very little business before noon in the warmer months. What surprised Arnold was that there didn't appear to be any staff on duty. Where were all those muscular, interchangeable youths—Ecuadorians, Peruvians—whom Guillermo hired "to do the heavy work"? And where were the salesgirls? He finally spotted Maria reading a tabloid behind the last checkout counter. *Soap Digest.* At least he wouldn't be in that.

"Morning, Mr. Brinkman," said the saleswoman.

"Where is everybody today?"

"They're in back, Mr. Brinkman. They're watching television in Mr. Zambrano's office."

"Are they?" Arnold muttered.

Cassandra smirked. "You run a tight ship, don't you?"

He ignored her. "Maria, go outside and take down that flag."

"But Mr. Zambrano said—"

"I don't care what Mr. Zambrano said. Take it down. When Mr. Zambrano owns his own nursery, he can fly any damn flags he wants."

"Yes, Mr. Brinkman."

"And Maria—"

"Yes, Mr. Brinkman?"

"For the last time, do not call me Mr. Brinkman.

Arnold. *Please.*"

"Yes, Arnold."

The middle-aged saleswoman looked at him as though he'd ordered her to call him "Attila the Hun" or "Mary Poppins," but she shuffled outside to remove the flag. Arnold led Cassandra through the cactus-filled hothouse, then between the pyramid displays of wheelbarrows and power saws, to the far corner of the enormous hangar. That's where Arnold and Guillermo had their adjoining offices. The manager claimed the larger of the two, the one that had once belonged to Hans Overmeyer. It was the only room in the nursery that didn't contain any plants.

Arnold found his employees gathered around the portable television on Guillermo's enormous steel desk: a dozen broad-shouldered, copper-skinned men in white t-shirts; several salesgirls in green blazers; the portly Jamaican woman named Lucinda who did the books, the Korean high school student whom Arnold had hired as part of the city's Young Entrepreneurs Program. At first, the botanist hoped they might be watching a soccer match. But they weren't cheering.

When he entered, they stepped away from the television in obvious discomfort. They'd been watching *his house* on the news.

"Good morning," said Arnold.

A chorus of muttered greetings arose—some in English, some in Spanish.

"Time to go back to work."

Several of the men nodded. None moved. Only the Korean boy retreated around Arnold into the nursery.

"What are you waiting for? I'm not going to show up *there*," he added, nodding toward the TV. "I'm already *here*."

Slowly, in twos and threes, the workers departed. Eventually, only Guillermo and Lucinda remained. On the television screen, they'd cut to an interview with the Bronx District Attorney. "It's not clear that any crime has been committed," said the female prosecutor. "But we're looking into the matter closely." *Among the charges Mr. Brinkman could face*, added a fast-talking reporter, *are disturbing the peace and contributing to the delinquency of a minor.* Then they cut back to Arnold's house—first a still shot of the front door, next Spotty Spitford and his protesters, finally more commentary from Ira Taylor. The broker now sported khakis and a Hawaiian shirt. "I grew up with old-fashioned values," he was declaiming. "Not just hard work, but also a sense of communal spirit—of taking one for the team. If someone accidentally drops a cigarette on your lawn, you lump it. No big deal. But this Brinkman's a real stickler, the sort of fanatic who'll sue you over a dirty look. From the start, it was always his way or the highway...."

Arnold stepped forward and shut off the television.

"Well?" he demanded. "Don't you two have work to do?"

Lucinda heaved herself off the sofa. She wore a heavy dress with lace frills to the Plant Centre every day, even during heat spells. It wouldn't have surprised Arnold if the woman's outerwear concealed a whale-bone corset and a starched petticoat.

"I've got to say what I've got to say, Arnold," said the Jamaican woman. "If you fire me, you fire me. But I don't approve of what you did."

"Nobody's firing anybody. But get to work. Please. I don't know—go audit something."

The bookkeeper grunted and toddled out of the office.

Guillermo looked up gleefully at Arnold. He sported his trademark pink shirt, hand-stitched, the collar open so tufts of grey hair protruded over the cusp. Elaborate tattoos covered the entirety of his upper body.

"So?" demanded Arnold. "What's so goddam amusing?"

"Nothing," answered Guillermo, beaming. "Absolutely nothing."

"Then why are you smirking."

The Venezuelan shrugged. "You know how it is with the working class. We can't help laughing at the quirks of the bosses."

Guillermo liked to rib Arnold about their relationship. It was funny because Guillermo was far more the capitalist than Arnold would ever be—and had made quite a killing from his side investments.

"Damn you and your working classes, Willie. You could open your own greenhouse tomorrow if you wanted to. Probably your own chain of greenhouses."

"Maybe," said Guillermo.

While they spoke, Cassandra had settled onto the couch. The girl was scribbling in her tiny notepad. When she leaned forward, the tops of her breasts were visible.

"What's with the goddam flag?" Arnold asked.

The Venezuelan leaned back in his chair, his meaty arms locked behind his neck. "I hoped you wouldn't notice."

"I noticed. What's the deal? And why all that plywood?"

"Better safe than sorry. The plywood's to board up the windows at night so nobody puts a brick through."

"You've got to be joking!" Arnold paced back and forth beside the filing cabinets. The floors were cluttered with stacks of folders and sun-faded invoices. "Weren't you the one who insisted we dump the steel gratings?"

They'd had one of their periodic squabbles the previous winter when Guillermo insisted that they adopt a more modern, "new millennium" look. According to the manager, the steel security gratings gave the place an unwelcoming 1970s feel, "like something off the *Barney Miller* show," and did little to prevent property crime—because there was no longer any property crime to prevent. The squabble ended as all of their squabbles ended: Arnold gave in. They replaced the metal bars with plate glass. Business picked up dramatically.

"Are you telling me not to put up the boards?" asked Guillermo.

"I'm just saying that I can't imagine anyone vandalizing the nursery as a result of what was a *minor, inconsequential* incident." Arnold scowled. "Do whatever you want."

The Venezuelan pressed a button on his phone. "Maria," he said. "Put the flag back up. Mr. Brinkman changed his mind."

"How did you know—?"

Guillermo's eyes twinkled. "That's why you pay me the big money."

It was possible the saleswoman had phoned Guillermo while Arnold and Cassandra were trekking through the hothouse. Or it was just as likely the Venezuelan had anticipated Arnold's response. The two of them shared a long history—back to when the Venezuelan and Hans Overmeyer were selling glow-in-the-dark crocuses out of a pick-up truck. Before that, Guillermo had managed delivery for the poultry yard.

"Trust me on the flag," said the Venezuelan. "It reassures people."

"Okay," said Arnold. "Keep the flag up. But I don't like it."

The girl continued writing. It struck Arnold that

she was transcribing their conversation. "All of this is off the record," he said.

"You *so* can't do that," answered Cassandra. "That's like announcing the Kennedy Assassination is off-the-record. You can't say a public conversation with another person present is off-the-record. That's whack." She sounded upset.

"Fine. Put it back on the record," said Arnold. "But now I'd like to have a *private* conversation with Mr. Zambrano. Why don't you wait for me in my office?"

The girl rose sullenly. She packed her belongings into her bag one at a time—notebooks, pencils, water bottle. Then she tied each of her shoes.

"Down the corridor and to the left," Arnold said.

Cassandra tossed her bag over her shoulder and walked out.

The Venezuelan lit a cigarette. "Quite a charmer," he said. "Looks like she's got a thing for the boss."

"Don't get any ideas," said Arnold. "Cassandra's a reporter for a small newspaper. It's a long story."

"I'm not the one getting ideas."

"Lay off. Judith knows all about her." Arnold ambled over to the Venezuelan's mini-fridge and appropriated a can of Coke. "So what do you really think?"

Guillermo blew smoke out of the side of his mouth. "About what?"

"Give me a break, Willie. You know what about." He pulled up a folding chair opposite Guillermo's desk and sat down. "Was I out of line?"

"You know what I'm going to tell you," said Guillermo. "I'm going to tell you that I don't have an opinion. I am *without politics*, Arnold."

"You always say that."

"And I *mean* it. You wonder how a gay Venezuelan who survived the FALN and Ronald Reagan can be without politics. But that is by far the safest way. If I were not without politics, I would not be....as well-off as I am."

"I just don't get you, Willie."

Arnold confided in him secrets that he didn't even dare reveal to Judith—such as his relief that they couldn't have children. At the same time, he never understood what made the manager tick. Other than financial security and buff men half his age. He'd once asked the Venezuelan if he had any long-term dreams or ambitions; Guillermo had responded: "I'm too old for dreams. At my age, I try to avoid nightmares." Guillermo had equally clever rejoinders for questions about his family, his finances, even his hobbies.

The Venezuelan stubbed out his cigarette. "People are always asking me what I think of the regime in Venezuela," he said. "Am I in favour of it? Am I against it? That's like asking a priest what he thinks of baptism. It's not something I'm going to change any time soon."

"So do you have any wisdom at all?"

"I subscribe to the old Arabian proverb: 'The husband of my mother is my father.' Words to live by."

The manager walked to the doorway and paused.

"Give Lucinda a raise," Guillermo said. "And buy more plywood."

Arnold found Cassandra seated on the swivel chair behind his desk. He sensed she'd been rummaging through his drawers, but when he entered, she was filing her nails nonchalantly with an emery board. Her long, tawny hair glowed pink under the fluorescent lights. "Done with your man-to-man talk, Mr. Private Conversation?"

"You're sitting in my chair," said Arnold.

"I know," agreed the girl. "Do you want to trade places?"

"Honestly, I don't care," Arnold answered. He perched himself on the splintering stool he used to water the pothos and syngonium. "Let's just get this over with."

The girl removed a cassette player from her bag. "You okay if I record our conversation? It's easier this way...."

"Actually—" said Arnold.

"Come on, Mr. Brinkman. Chill out," she said. "It will go much quicker with the recorder. Otherwise, it's going to take me all day to write down what you say."

"Fine, dammit. Use the tape-recorder."

"Awesome," said Cassandra. "Say, you sure have a fucking lot of plants in here."

The room was crammed with pots of succulents, tomato-germinating tubs, even basins full of water lilies. Most of the plants were overgrown, abandoned relics from Arnold's experimentation in floral-based dieting and nutrition. He'd heard several times on the radio that celery was the lowest-calorie solid food available, but this wasn't strictly true. Several common garden blossoms, including primroses, were far less caloric. Many of these species were edible; some contained a host of essential minerals. But most of Arnold's low-calorie flower snacks were either entirely flavourless, like calendula, or strikingly bitter, like daisies. Unlike Guillermo's office, Arnold's shelves didn't contain any business documents. He probably didn't even have a writing implement—other than a wax pen he'd used to prop up a pea stalk. On the desk lay a handful of field guides, birds as well as plants, and a bevelled display case of photographs from his honeymoon.

"I have a lot of plants," said Arnold, "because *I like plants.*"

"More than you like people?" asked the girl.

"I like plants *and* people," answered Arnold. The truth was that he liked people individually, but preferred plants collectively. Who wouldn't prefer a primeval forest to a packed sporting arena? "The two aren't mutually exclusive," he added. "Some people like both children and animals."

"Your friend doesn't have any plants in his office," prodded the girl.

"Mr. Zambrano doesn't like plants. He likes other things."

The girl gnawed the end of her eraser. She examined him closely—and for a moment he thought she might ask: *And do you like other things?* Instead, without taking her eyes off of him, she said: "Your wife was very beautiful when she was young. A total babe."

It was hard to tell whether she was paying him a compliment or taunting him.

"My wife," said Arnold, "is *still* very beautiful."

Cassandra smiled. "How does she feel about what you did?"

Arnold noticed the cassette recorder was turning. The girl had started the interview without telling him.

"You'd have to ask her that," said Arnold.

"Are you telling me you haven't talked to her about it?" persisted the girl. "She hasn't expressed an opinion? You really expect me to believe that…."

"I don't like to put words in my wife's mouth."

"Can you at least tell me whether she approves or disapproves?"

"That's rather complicated," answered Arnold. "I suspect she both approves *and* disapproves."

The girl reached forward and stopped the tape player.

"You're *so* not keeping up your end of our bargain," she said. "You're cheating."

"I agreed to be interviewed," Arnold answered, "and I'm being interviewed."

"You're totally avoiding the questions."

"I can't speak for Judith," he said. "If you have questions about *me*, I'll be glad to answer them."

Arnold waited while Cassandra gathered her thoughts. He was surprised how attractive he found her—especially since, by objective standards, she was far from pretty. He was also surprised how little he cared about the difference in their ages. If he'd had a daughter of his own, he imagined, the disparity might have troubled him more. *But he did have a wife of his own.* He resolved to get rid of the girl as quickly as possible. Meanwhile, the air-conditioner hummed in the window box and pigeons thrashed about on the ledge. From the street rose the muffled honking of taxicabs. Cassandra glowered at him, drawing her thick eyebrows together, toying with her heart-shaped silver locket; the ornament reminded him that she really was just a young girl—with her own young girl's music and young girl's parties and young girl's lack of perspective. Without accepting or rejecting Arnold's terms, she pressed the record button on the cassette player.

"Can you tell me how this all happened?" she asked. "Was it something you'd been planning for a long time or was it more of a spontaneous protest?"

"I didn't intend it to be a protest. I just didn't want to stand up."

"But *why*? Were you protesting the war, Mr. Brinkman? Or the performance of a religious song at a secular event?"

The answer was both. And a whole lot more. In hindsight, he wanted his protest to have been directed at anything and everything—against all of the perversions of justice that passed for decency. But how could he explain this to a young woman who insisted upon boilerplate answers in black-and-white? "I was protesting against the mistreatment of Native Americans," he said decisively. "Wounded Knee, the reservation system, Leonard Peltier."

The girl looked up, her appetite whetted.

"I'm also quite upset about slavery," continued Arnold. "And rural poverty, and the lack of national health insurance, and the imprisonment of Lisl Auman. Then there's the invasion of Panama, and the bombing of North Vietnam, and the entire Spanish-American War. I'm disturbed that they tore down Penn Station, and that gay couples can't adopt children in Texas, and that Washington D.C. isn't a state. Not to mention what happened to Sacco and Vanzetti and the Scottsboro Boys and the Rosenbergs. Especially Ethel. Then there's the two million people in prison—probably half of whom didn't do anything wrong, only nobody knows which half anymore—while all the people who actually belong in prison are enjoying liquid lunches on Wall Street and in the Pentagon. You want to know what I'm protesting? I'm protesting the Salem Witch trials and the blacklisting of Dalton Trumbo and every goddam time Lenny Bruce got arrested. I'm still mad that they stopped delivering mail twice a day, and that Roosevelt dumped Wallace for Truman, and that McGovern dumped Eagleton, and that Victoria Hager dumped me for a football player in the eleventh grade. Son of a bitch! And I'm enraged that Ronald Reagan became President for playing best supporting actor to a monkey while Orson Welles didn't even win a goddam Academy Award. But what I find most frustrating in this Bible-thumping, gun-slinging, sexually-repressed, intellectually-stunted and utterly backwards country of ours is that you can no longer send live plants through the mail. Shall I go on?"

"No," said Cassandra. "Don't bother."

She snapped off her tape recorder and stuffed it into her bag.

"I can't believe I trusted you," she added. "You're a total asshole."

"What's the problem?"

"You're the problem, Arnold Brinkman. I did you a favour and now you're making fun of me. I thought we had a deal."

"I'm sorry," answered Arnold. "I shouldn't have agreed to an interview. You want me to connect what I did to the larger events of the world—to make me into the Rosa Parks of anti-Americanism—while the reality is that I was hot, and tired, and I had to go to the bathroom."

"That's a real awesome story," Cassandra answered bitterly. "Man sticks tongue out because his bladder is full."

"See my point? There really is no story."

The girl examined him closely; she wiped her eyes with her fingers. "What am I supposed to tell my editor?"

"I don't know," answered Arnold. "Anything you want. Tell him your paper is too conservative for me—that I only grant interviews to anarchists."

Arnold grinned. The girl looked up at him puzzled, biting the knuckle of her index finger, as though trying to figure out whether he was joking. She appeared so vulnerable, so close to tears, that the botanist instantly regretted his sarcasm. He wished he had some profound statement about patriotism to offer her—but he couldn't even remember the stock platitudes that Gilbert Card had shared over dinner. He had absolutely nothing useful to say. He resisted the instinct to let her cry against his chest. Then the girl's jaw stiffened and her hands balled into fists. "You're screwing with me, Arnold," she snapped. "I can tell."

"Excuse me?"

How quickly she'd gone from *Mr. Brinkman* and *pretty please* to *Arnold* and *screwing*...

"I'm not a moron," she seethed. "I know you're

thinking I'm just some dumb girl reporter from some second-rate paper, but at least have the guts to say it. You're pathetic, Mr. There Is No Story. You don't think I can tell you're holding out for one of the big-time magazines."

"I had to go to the bathroom," Arnold insisted.

"*Bullshit!*" The girl rummaged through her bag and slid a business card onto Arnold's desk. "If you feel guilty for treating me like shit, here's how to find me. I doubt you will—but deep down you'll have to live with knowing it was *my* interview. It *is* my interview, goddammit, whether I get it or not."

She was gone before Arnold could stop her. He picked up the card.

CASANDRA BROWARD

The phrase "Reporter, *Daily Vanguard*" had been scrawled in red ink beneath her name. There were also a handwritten address and phone number.

Arnold pocketed the card. He was feeling mildly pleased with himself—as though he'd withstood a brutal cross-examination—when he remembered that nothing outside his office had changed. His home was still surrounded by journalists; his wife still had him in the dog house. And to the Spotty Spitfords of the world, he was still Public Enemy Number One.

Once Arnold was certain that the girl wasn't going to return—that her departure wasn't part of some complex ploy to catch him by surprise—he tried to phone

Judith. He wasn't particularly ready to talk to her—usually, if they fought in the morning, they both stewed through the workday and then made up in the evening—but these weren't ordinary circumstances. Besides, he realized that he owed *her* an apology. Not for his antics at the baseball game, or his refusal to prostrate himself before the mob, but because he hadn't explained to her *why* he couldn't do what she wanted. Not adequately. In the heat of the moment, he'd probably just sounded obstinate. Besides, until now, he hadn't even fully understood himself. The girl's questions had helped him see things better: He wasn't merely protesting for the right to protest or for some abstract principles. In a way, as peculiar as it sounded, he *was* protesting against all of the injustices he'd enumerated to Cassandra. Scottsboro. The Chicago Seven. Matthew Shepard. Bonnie Card had a bumper-sticker pasted to her office door that read: "If you're not outraged, you're not paying attention." If he could only find a way to communicate these feelings to Judith, he thought it might resonate with her too. He hoped it would. But Judith didn't answer the phone. Neither did the machine. After twenty rings, he had to accept that she'd unplugged the console or pulled the wire out of the jack. It was possible she didn't even realize he was gone, that she thought he was still blowing off steam in the garden. He slammed down the phone and stormed out into the corridor.

Guillermo had gone up front to supervise the

morning deliveries, but the manager had left open the door to his office. Arnold stepped inside. The Venezuelan relied on the skylight for illumination, and preferred an oscillating fan to air-conditioning, so the warm, shadowy room felt like a government building in Havana. White bands of cigarette smoke still floated on the stagnant air. Arnold considered phoning Judith for a second time. But what would he say? That he'd suddenly realized the world was an outrageously unreasonable place? Then he couldn't apologize because he was standing up for Sacco and Vanzetti. He knew Judith. She was far too practical—too reasonable—for all that. He didn't phone. Instead, he flipped on the television.

They were conducting another interview, this time with a nasal-voiced young attorney from the American Civil Liberties Union. "We're not in the business of forcing ourselves on people," she said. "If Mr. Brinkman would like to retain our services, this is certainly the sort of case we'd take a serious look at. But that's entirely up to him. Trust me, there's no shortage of work for us these days." Arnold flipped to another station. Spotty Spitford was speaking to a different reporter, demanding that the mayor and the governor condemn "this insult to our boys in uniform." On a third channel, the governor's spokesman explained that Yankee Stadium was a private venue and that the Yankees were certainly entitled to ban Mr. Brinkman from future events. He hadn't voted for the governor—in fact, he despised the governor—but if the governor could get him banished from Yankee stadium forever, that would be enough to earn his vote.

Arnold changed stations one final time and found himself watching cartoons. The roadrunner charged off a cliff; the coyote followed. Then the coyote looked down. But the coyote halted mid-plummet as the broadcast switched to a "Breaking News" bulletin.

Suddenly, he was watching the front of his own house again. This time, the door opened. Cameras snapped; protesters chanted. Gilbert Card stepped out into sunlight. The immigration attorney wore a modest pinstriped suit and carried an attaché case. When he raised his hand, like the Pope blessing St. Peter's, the crowd went silent. Then Gilbert stepped to the edge of the porch and read from a prepared statement.

"My name is Gilbert Card. I am a spokesman for the Brinkman family."

Someone shouted a question at the lawyer.

"Card. C-A-R-D. I'm an attorney with Willoughby & Throop."

"Willoughby. W-I-L-L-O-U-G-H-B-Y," he said. "And Throop. T-H-R-O-O-P."

When the onlookers quieted down, Gilbert continued.

"First, let me thank you all for being here. These are difficult times for our nation and especially for New York City, where we live in the perpetual shadow of the horrors of September 11th. That is what makes Mr. Brinkman's behaviour at yesterday's Yankees game all the more unfortunate. I've known Arnold Brinkman for thirty years and nobody is more sorry about what happened yesterday than he is. He did not mean to show disrespect to anyone, least of all to our heroes in the armed forces. Mr. Brinkman has been under a lot of stress recently. As difficult as it may be for many people to understand, he thought he was doing something patriotic by refusing to stand. He now recognizes how mistaken he was and apologizes wholeheartedly." Gilbert looked up at the audience. "Thank You," he concluded. "God Bless America."

A murmur of approval spread through the crowd. Shouts of "Amen!" and "Hallelujah!" drowned out the journalists' follow-up questions. The two protesters clad in Revolutionary War garb struck up a festive duet on their fife and drum. *If you're just joining us from an affiliate station,* the fast-talking reporter explained, *the so-called Tongue Traitor has apologized...* Arnold flipped the channel.

"—and we're getting breaking news of an apology from the Tongue Traitor—

"—so I asked, when exactly would you perform CPR on a fish?—"

"—Traitor's attorney has issued a plea for forgiveness —"

"—disguised as an onion—"

"—actually said, 'God Bless America'—"

"—the other sister, the one who looks like a hedgehog—"

"—has apologized—

"—an apology—"

"—at only $99.99—"

"—rather moving statement from a lawyer representing the Tongue Traitor. It appears to represent a complete change of heart...."

How dare he?! His own best friend on his own front lawn serving him up to the lions. This was worse than Nuremberg; this was like the Politburo officials who read aloud the confessions from Stalin's Purge Trials. He'd be remembered forever as the man who apologized for sticking out his tongue. Even though he wasn't the slightest bit sorry—even though he'd do it again and again and again.

Arnold was about to turn the TV off—or bash it in—when a commotion erupted behind the fast-talking reporter. The camera quickly focused on Spotty Spitford, who stood in the centre of the street with a bullhorn in one hand and what appeared to be a Bible in the other. "We will not accept no surrogate apologies," the minister declared. "We will not accept no statement from a paid mouthpiece. You can't buy no substitute, Mr. Brinkman. This ain't no Civil War. We are the people and we ain't gonna accept nothing less than a personal and unconditional plea for forgiveness." Spitford raised his arms—the megaphone in one, the Bible in the other—as though the heavens might open and summon him up to duty. No such luck. "Let the coward speak for himself," the minister shouted. "We want Brinkman."

The mob took up the chant of "We want Brinkman!" and carried it along the block like a hearse.

They were still shouting, "We want Brinkman! We want Brinkman!" when Arnold came charging up the street. The protesters now numbered in the hundreds. Not just professional agitators, but ordinary people who'd come to "defend their country." There was even a contingent of World War II veterans from the American Legion. A smaller counter-demonstration occupied the opposite sidewalk: Fewer than a dozen college students and down-at-the-heel ex-hippies who could easily have passed as a reunion of the Chicago Seven. One waved a Soviet flag. Another wore a rubber Richard Nixon mask. Their posters read: "Free Palestine" and "Fur is Fratricide." When Arnold passed through their ranks, none of them recognized him.

Arnold pushed his way toward his porch, where the two officers still served as sentries, and the front door stood slightly ajar. Adrenaline and anger carried him forward. When he mounted the steps, the masses stepped back—as though fearing violence or contagion. "I'll be brief," he said.

"Be sincere," shouted Spitford.

"I'll be brief and sincere," answered Arnold. "I do *not* apologize. I am *not* sorry. That man had no authority to speak on my behalf." He took a deep breath. "It is *you* who should apologize. I wouldn't stand during a goddam song. You murdered Sacco and Vanzetti. You tell me who has blood on his hands?" Then he stepped into the house and slammed the door behind him.

Judith was sitting on the piano bench. Her face was streaked with eyeliner and her hair hung down unevenly. "Sacco and Vanzetti?" she said. Her voice was hardly audible.

"Where the hell is Card?" shouted Arnold.

"He thought it was best—"

"He knew I'd kill him."

Judith shook her head. "Please, Arnold. It's not Gilbert's fault. *I told him* you wanted to apologize. If you're going to kill anyone, you're going to have to kill me."

"Godammit, Judith. You had no fucking right...."

"And you had a right to run off on me like that?" cried Judith, rising to her feet. "I couldn't find you. I had no idea where you went. Do you know what it's like to be all alone with that going on outside?"

The chanting started again. Louder. Swelling with rage.

"Is that all you have to say to me?" asked Arnold.

"I don't think I have much of anything to say to you right now," said Judith. Then she walked up the stairs and left Arnold standing alone.

CHAPTER 5

They lived the next five days as though prisoners in a city under siege. Arnold actually knew a considerable amount about sieges—or he'd thought he had. He'd always taken an interest in the botanical ignorance of the besieged, the malnourishment that arises from prejudices against edible shrubbery. In Vicksburg, for example, the Confederates exhausted their energies brewing coffee from cardboard when they might have grilled up steaks from their honeysuckle and verbena. When Henry IV lay siege to Paris, the locals stewed their own furniture to stay alive while embankments along the Seine sprouted enough purslane to feed the entire city. Even the mass starvation at Leningrad could have been eased, if not prevented, had the Soviets fished for edible marsh plants beneath Lake Ladoga. At one point, Arnold had considered writing a book, *The Epicurean's Guide for Famines and Embargos*, but he'd intended this as a serious project, a self-help volume of the life-saving variety, while every editor he'd consulted had hoped to market it as a novelty item. Now Arnold realized how poorly he'd understood the experience of the besieged. He'd always thought of sieges solely in terms of captivity and deprivation—but neither of these conditions applied to him and Judith. He continued to go to work every morning. Judith could have taught her classes at St.

Gregory's, if she'd wanted to. They endured no shortages of food or electricity, no periodic barrage of artillery shells. Yet their days were living hell. No matter where he went, Arnold couldn't escape the feeling that he was surrounded. His deed followed him through the workday like a personal rain cloud. It was the psychological battery of the siege, rather than any physical blockade, that tormented him.

Not that the demonstrations didn't continue. Every morning, at precisely eight o'clock, the singing protesters paraded around the corner and manned their picket lines. The news media estimated their number at nearly five thousand—far larger, it was frequently pointed out, than the group who'd marched against a Ku Klux Klan rally on the steps of City Hall the previous year. Of course, at the time, the media had initially reported the anti-Klan protesters to number 30,000. The pro-Arnold forces didn't grow nearly as rapidly as did his opponents. Occasionally, on his walk to work, a stranger offered Arnold moral support. The greying transvestites at the costume shop promised they were praying for him. But none of these sympathizers had the time, or possibly the nerve, to join his ragtag band of defenders, which on Tuesday afternoon temporarily dwindled down to two pot-bellied motorcyclists handing out Mardis Gras beads on his behalf. By Thursday, his "followers" had been infiltrated by the radical Spartacist League and had turned against him. While Spitford's thousands condemned Arnold's lack of patriotism, dozens of anti-government leftists denounced him for his "petit-bourgeois" business dealings and his apparent unwillingness to renounce his citizenship. Spitford's "Abolitionists" recruited three bagpipe players to accompany their fife and drum team. In response, the Spartacists banged tambourines and kitchen pans. The only sound more unnerving than the chorus of *God Bless America* that disrupted Arnold's weeding each morning was the lacklustre rendition of the Internationale that followed. On the second day of the protests, Arnold incorporated a pair of earplugs into his gardening outfit. This tactic succeeded in filtering out the protesters, but also blocked out the songbirds, the crickets, even the flutter of the breeze through the hemlocks. It more or less defeated the purpose of living.

While the protests grew larger and more aggressive, Arnold's relationship with Judith deteriorated. Initially, he'd hoped her attitude might mellow. He had made meaningful sacrifices *for her* in the past Like placing his mother in that hyper-sterile nursing home when he'd have preferred that Mama come to live with them. Yet now she couldn't accept that his apologizing didn't matter as much to her as his not-apologizing mattered to him. Judith wouldn't even give him the opportunity to argue his case. After he'd disowned Gilbert's statement, she refused to speak to him at all. When Arnold entered a room, she left it quickly. If he tried to touch her, she swatted his hand away. One afternoon, she took Ray to the aquarium. Arnold suggested they leave by ladder. Instead, Judith walked straight through the front door and down the block, past the hooting demonstrators, without turning her head. Otherwise, she didn't leave the house. She phoned in sick at St. Gregory's. Her painting materials collected dust on the dining room table. Arnold's wife spent her evenings ensconced in front of the television, watching their private lives being dissected for public outrage and amusement. A conservative cable network was running "24-hour Tongue Traitor" coverage that included interviews with a disgruntled former student whom Arnold had failed for cheating, although the news broadcast didn't mention the cheating episode, as well as with the father of the nine children from the baseball game. "My daughter was scared," the man said. "She's had nightmares." The media also burrowed deeper into Arnold's past: his draft deferment during the Vietnam War, his summons for being in a public park after hours as a teenager. (Nobody explained that he'd been in the park hunting for moonflowers, which blossom only at night.) A digital counter at the corner of the television screen calculated exactly how much time Arnold had gone without apologizing. The counter was shaped like an alarm clock, but with horns and a forked orange tail. Judith called out the number of hours periodically. "I thought we were on the same side," Arnold pleaded with her. "Can't you try to see things my way?" In response, she shut off the television and locked herself in the upstairs bathroom. At night, she slept in her studio. She could have kept this silent treatment going for weeks or months. Judith was capable of just such intransigence. But even a siege does not relieve a household of its minor crises, such as the daily crush of domestic challenges. It was one such episode, on the third morning of the protests, that finally forced them to speak.

Arnold had just come inside from the garden, where he'd been slicing a fallen sycamore with a chainsaw. He'd earlier put off this task for several months. Truthfully, the saw blades always scared him. But that morning he'd been in the mood to hew something—or someone—limb from limb. Chopping up the tree trunk presented fewer negative consequences than dismembering the Reverend Spitford. Besides which, the whir of the implement had helped drown out the chanting from the street. Arnold had thrown himself into the sawing with full force, working up a sweat, and when the task was done, he actually found himself disappointed that there was nothing else left to cut. On the way to the tool shed, he snipped at a few stray wisteria vines, gumming up the blades. Back in the townhouse, he ran the tap in the ground-floor bathroom and splashed his face in the sink. Then he took a swig of cool water from a paper cup. What he really wanted was a tall glass of orange juice, but Judith was preparing the kid's breakfast in the kitchen, and Arnold didn't want to drive her out of the room. Even though *she* was being unreasonable, "forcing" her to relocate made *him* feel guilty. So he sprawled out on the living room sofa to kill time.

Arnold had been resting only a few minutes, his eyes closed, when he was startled by pounding at the door. Like a watchman's nightstick or the back of a flashlight. At first, Arnold feared the protesters had overrun the police sentries—that his house was about to be stormed by the mob—but the hammering was too methodical for a stampede. The masses would have broken the door down or set the entire building aflame. Instead: Thump. Thump. Thump. Then an authoritative voice shouted: "City Marshal. Open up." Arnold's stomach tightened. Were they actually going to arrest him? Was this the beginning of the end? All that could be hoped for from the authorities was that they might keep him separated from other prisoners for his own protection, as they did with Charles Manson and child molesters. Better to run. Arnold retreated toward the kitchen with the intent of fleeing over the back fence, but Judith inadvertently blocked his escape route. She stepped past him and opened the front door, sending Spitford's army into a frenzy.

The city marshal held the screen door open with one hand. He was a squat, red-faced officer whose long, craggy head was capped with a conspicuous toupee. "I have a special delivery for Arnold Brinkman," he said.

"I'm his wife."

"More than I need to know," said the city marshal. He handed Judith a small beige envelope. "A pleasure doing business with you," he said.

Judith shut the door and held out the envelope toward Arnold. He motioned for her to open it.

"You're not going to believe this," said Judith. Whatever the contents of the envelope, they were enough to override her silence.

"I've been drafted?"

"You've been subpoenaed."

Arnold's muscles relaxed. "It's better than being arrested."

"This is just too perfect," continued Judith. "You're being subpoenaed for creating a public nuisance. Apparently, darling, it's your fault that those John Birch hooligans are out there shouting all day."

"Not just the John Birch Society," said Arnold. "Also the Daughters of the American Revolution, the Knights of Columbus, even the goddam Young Americans for Freedom. I didn't know there were any more Young Americans for Freedom."

"Maybe they're having a reunion," answered Judith. She was still reading the contents of the envelope.

"Doesn't that make them the Old Americans for Freedom?"

Judith didn't smile. "Would you like to know *who's* suing you?"

"Let me guess. That woman whose dog kept tearing up the dahlias."

Several years earlier, Arnold had complained to the neighbourhood association about a rottweiler with a penchant for tubers; the owner, a mousy English nurse, still crossed the street whenever she spotted him approaching.

"Much better," said Judith. "You're being sued by our dear neighbour Ira Taylor."

"You're serious?"

"Better than being drafted," said Judith. "I think."

"That's outrageous! *He's* the one creating the nuisance. He's been out there holding court every morning."

"Are you going to tell that to a jury?" asked Judith. "Who has more credibility? A retired banker whose ancestors probably bankrolled the Mayflower? Or the Fifth Column of Sixth Street?" She slapped the court papers against his chest. "Chickens coming home to roost, my dear. I warned you to press charges over the soda cans."

"What good would that have done?"

"At least there'd be a written record," said Judith.

"It wouldn't matter," answered Arnold. "Those are facts. This has gone far beyond facts." He crumpled the subpoena and tossed it onto the marble tiles. "Can we talk for a couple of minutes? Please?"

Judith didn't answer directly. Instead, she crossed into the living room and sat down beside the bay windows. She peeled back the drapes, just enough to peek into the street. A thin sliver of light danced across the opposite bookshelves. The protesters must have noticed the movement behind the glass, because their chanting suddenly rose in intensity. Judith let the curtain fall shut. "I'm very unhappy," she said.

Arnold had prepared a speech to win his wife over to his side. He'd rehearsed it hour after hour at the nursery. But now, faced with the overwhelming simplicity of Judith's declaration of unhappiness, he found himself at a loss for words. All he could muster was: "I'm sorry that you're unhappy." In case this wasn't enough, he added, "I'm unhappy too."

"My sister called again this morning. While you were playing Paul Bunyan," continued Judith. "It seems the Tongue Traitor is even newsworthy in Greece."

"You mean she knows?"

"She went through the roof, my dear. I've never heard her like that before. Some of it may have been for the effect—you know how Celeste is, and I think Mr. Republican tight-ass was in the room with her—but the bottom line is that they're cutting short their trip. She's booking the first flight out of Athens."

"But that's totally unnecessary."

"She'll be here tomorrow afternoon," said Judith, "to pick up Ray."

"But she can't—"

"Of course, she can," Judith cut him off. "Ray's

her son."

It surprised Arnold that he cared so much about losing the boy. He hadn't particularly enjoyed having his nephew around. If anything, Ray's presence had impinged upon his social life with Judith, kept them from enjoying the theatre and the ballet. Besides, if not for the damned kid, he'd never have ended up at Yankee Stadium. But Arnold took his sister-in-law's intentions as a personal affront—like being dis-invited from a party that one didn't wish to attend. He also understood that Judith was being unfairly punished for his own actions. This made him feel even worse.

"I'm so sorry," he said.

Judith shook her head. She stood up and circled around the room—past the new cherrywood end-tables and the newly upholstered armchairs and the newly hung prints of the Sandpiper Key lighthouse at sunset. For her fiftieth birthday, Judith had redecorated the townhouse. That had been her present to herself. It had left her personal imprint on each room, much as Arnold had left his on the yard. Arnold hadn't cared. Interiors weren't his thing. Besides, he didn't spend very much time inside—except when he was writing or socializing. But now that they were fighting, he suddenly felt as though he was conducting his struggle in alien territory. "It's hard to believe I spent so much time redoing this place," Judith said. "As though anybody cares what colour wallpaper we have. As though anybody gives a damn about us at all."

Arnold followed her across the room. "Can I hold you?" he asked.

She let him hug her—but only for an instant. Then she pushed him away.

"I want to have a baby."

The words hit Arnold without warning, but they came more as a confirmation than a surprise. "Now?" he asked.

"I know it's not rational. It's completely irrational. But it's what I want." Judith spoke rapidly, as though afraid she might lose her mettle. "If you don't want to apologize, don't. Let's just sell this place and move far away and raise a child."

Arnold had considered leaving New York until the situation blew over, maybe renting a bungalow in the Catskills for a few weeks. Or going on a cruise—turning the getaway into a second honeymoon. Nobody ever criticized dissidents for fleeing China or Iran. Or Einstein for leaving Nazi Germany. But the more Arnold thought about it, running away seemed as bad as apologizing. In either case, it was giving in. Moreover, he'd envisioned a temporary escape. It had never crossed his mind that they might relocate permanently—that they would end up refugees like his ex-brother-in-law in Fiji. Arnold could imagine only one fate worse than permanent banishment from New York: Being permanently banished from New

York *and* having to raise a child in exile.

"I don't want to leave New York," said Arnold. "And you don't want to leave New York either. You're not thinking straight."

"Why not?"

"Please, Judith. In the first place, you're fifty-one years old. You'd be seventy when the kid graduates from high school."

"I've been reading a lot about older parenting. On the internet," insisted Judith. "It's far more common than you think. Look at Tony Randall. Or Saul Bellow. Or Anthony Quinn."

Arnold recognized this as one of Judith's traps, that she wanted him to say was: *But they're all men*—so she could dismiss his objections as sexist. What he'd actually thought was: *But they're all dead.* He knew enough not to say this either.

"And how exactly do you propose to have this baby?" he demanded.

Judith paused in front of a long walnut sideboard covered in knickknacks and photographs, picking up a hand-carved wooden stork that they'd purchased on a trip to the Canary Islands. "There are ways," she said. "I don't care about *having* the baby. Or even that it's a baby. We can adopt a ten year old from Africa or a little girl with Down's syndrome....*But I want a child.*"

"I thought we were on the same page about this,"

pleaded Arnold. "I thought we'd decided...."

"I've changed pages," snapped Judith. "I'm glad you wouldn't apologize. If you'd apologized, everything would have stayed the same. I'd have gone on listening to Bonnie Card and her bullshit about the indecency of motherhood until I really was too old to raise a family. It all seems so horrifically obvious to me now: I'd have ended up one of those pathetic old widows who pesters strangers with photographs of her nieces and nephews." She slammed the wooden stork against the sideboard, snapping off its bill. "Well I'm not going to let that happen! Bonnie Card can go fuck herself."

"Okay, okay," said Arnold. "We'll figure something out. But can't we deal with one problem at a time? I don't think this is really a conversation to have while the Black Nazis are camped outside our door."

"This is precisely the time to have this conversation, my dear," answered Judith. "I want to know what I can expect from the rest of my life."

"What's that supposed to mean?"

"It means I'm going to have a child, Arnold. One way or another." Judith's voice was suddenly calm. "I love you and I'd like you to be part of that experience. But whether you want a child or not, I'm going to have one. All you have to do is decide whether you want to share that with me."

"But I love you..." said Arnold.

"I'm not bluffing."

"I know you're not," he answered. "Let me think about it."

That was the wrong answer. Arnold realized his mistake as soon as the words left his mouth—that a "maybe" was as good as a "no." Both suggested that he'd consider leaving her, or letting her leave him, that the status quo wasn't an inevitability.

Judith stared at him blankly. Then she knelt down on the carpet and gathered together the pieces of the shattered stork.

Later that afternoon, at the nursery, a second incident reinforced the sudden fragility of Arnold's marriage. He'd ordered Guillermo to make sure that he wasn't disturbed, and then he'd sat in his office, the door bolted, munching on cornflowers and pitying himself. Dozens of pink phone messages lay on his desk blotter—mostly from various news outlets, but also from at least two progressive law firms who'd volunteered to take "his case" *pro bono.* His aunt had also phoned from her summer cabin outside Santa Fe in order to let him know that she'd seen him on television. "Just wanted you to know; no need to call back." At least his parents were dead. And Judith's too. That was some solace. If Arnold had had to listen to his father describe the bombing of Rotterdam, or the three years he'd spent concealed under the floorboards of the baboon cage at the Utrecht Zoo, stinking perpetually of primate shit and surviving on monkey rations smuggled to him by a devout Catholic keeper, he'd have lost his resolve. Pieter Brinkman was the sort of man who loved the Statue of Liberty as much as his own wife and who experienced a chill down his spine when he saw the American flag draped at half-mast. He'd volunteered to fight in the Korean War, but his age and severe asthma had rendered him unfit for service. Eleanor Brinkman had also been a fierce patriot in her own way—a social worker who spoke of "my" President, as though he belonged to her personally, and who'd insisted upon mounting a portrait of FDR on her wall in the nursing home. How odd that none of this had rubbed off on Arnold. He balled up the pink slips one at a time and lobbed them at the wastepaper basket. Three of them were from Cassandra Broward at the *Daily Vanguard.*

Arnold considered returning Cassandra's calls—but to what end? No matter how many times he assured himself that his intentions were purely professional, that he'd have done the same for any reporter who shared his politics, the fact remained that he hadn't phoned back the other periodicals whose messages now lay crumpled around the trash can. And several of these, like *The Nation* and *The Village Voice*, had run editorials in his defence. If he phoned Cassandra, no good would come of it: Some itches weren't meant to be scratched. Instead, he flipped on the television set that he'd commandeered from his manager's office—nominally, because the staff had been sneaking into

Guillermo's quarters on breaks to watch the news updates, but really because he was growing addicted to the coverage of himself. He was constantly a bit on edge about what else they might reveal of his past, but also curious that they might uncover something even he didn't know. They'd already tracked down Judith's estranged brother, to whom nobody in the family had spoken in twenty years. (The man ran a pawn shop in Bethel, Alaska, with his Yupik wife, and kept referring to Arnold as "Alfred.") But that afternoon—the third since the baseball game—the cable networks were merely rehashing the week's events. On the right-wing station, the camera panned across the demonstrators, many of whom had brought along umbrellas and trench coats to ward off the drizzle, so that the mob now looked slightly more civilized, like FBI agents attending a funeral. Four men held a green-and-black canopy above Spotty Spitford to keep him dry. The minister looked so pleased with himself, like a cat who dined on canary at every meal. Then the camera pulled back and surveyed the opposite side of the street: the bored cops chewing the fat under the sassafras tree, the octogenarian who lived on the other side of Ira Taylor, and her centenarian mother, relaxing in lawn chairs on their stoop. That's when Arnold caught sight of Gilbert Card. The immigration lawyer was wearing a trench coat with the collar turned up and walking rapidly. Not unusual behaviour, considering the weather, but it gave Arnold pause nonetheless. He watched helplessly as

Gilbert waited on his porch—his back turned to the jeering throng—until Arnold's wife opened the door. In the brief interval when the door stood open, Arnold caught sight of Judith in the entryway. It looked to him as though she'd been smiling.

Up until that moment, it had never crossed Arnold's mind that Judith might have a secret love interest of her own. They'd always been far too happy with each other, their lives far too intertwined, for infidelity to gain a foothold. Judith was constantly saying that if he were to die first, she'd never remarry. Not because she objected to a second husband in principle—that was probably the psychologically healthy choice—but because she just didn't have it in her to start over again. (He'd admitted that he probably would remarry eventually, that anything was better than growing old alone.) It was hard to reconcile the Judith who criticized unfaithful wives *in movies*, the sharp-tongued creature who had no compunction about telling a dinner party that "Emma Bovary got what was coming to her," with the Judith who was bonking his best friend on the sly. But, in hindsight, maybe the woman had protested too much. If he could have a crush on Cassandra Broward, Judith might as easily have a thing for Gil. After all, the lawyer was good-looking, personable, easy-going—and it didn't take too much reflection for Arnold to realize that Bonnie Card wasn't giving Gilbert what he needed in bed. She couldn't be. Which meant that all of those references to national borders might have been a secret code that referred to other, more personal barriers. Maybe Judith's baby was just a symptom, not the underlying problem.

Once the ugly idea took root in Arnold's thoughts, it wasn't too difficult to rethink his entire past. All of those dinner parties with the Cards now acquired a sinister meaning: Gilbert *was* always wandering off with Judith to look at her paintings or to offer her wisdom on interior decorating. Arnold had always just been pleased that they'd gotten along so well. How many evenings had he listened to Bonnie criticizing Western Civilization's irrational censure of bestiality, or our culture's peculiar reverence for corpses, or insisting that chimpanzees be given the right to vote? He imagined listening to her declaim on the moral equivalence of golf and genocide, as he had done only last month, while her husband was going down on his wife in the linen closet. For all he could tell, Bonnie might have been in on the arrangement. Arnold could imagine her saying: *There's nothing natural or preferable about monogamy. It's just an arbitrary choice, like monotheism.*

He could easily return to the house and confront the pair, disrupt their lovemaking and drive Gilbert naked from his bedroom. But what if he were wrong? And worse, what if he was right—but the affair was taking its natural course and would soon be water under the bridge. The last thing Arnold wanted to do was to force his wife's hand, to transform an unfortunate transgression into a marriage-breaking calamity. Under the circumstances, maybe not knowing was best.

He picked up the phone, intending to call Gilbert's cell. All he wanted was to hear the lawyer's voice—to see if the man admitted where he was. But Arnold's entire hand shook as he lifted the receiver. What would he do if Gilbert lied to him? What could he do? Instead, he dialled Bonnie's number at home. The machine picked up:

You've reached Gilbert and Bonnie. Please leave a message. Beep.

"It's Arnold and I'm leaving a message," said Arnold. "I just wanted to say hello and to tell you two how much we enjoyed dinner the other night and—"

"—Arnold. Hey, it's Bonnie."

"You're there."

"Can't be too careful. You wouldn't believe the sorts of phone calls I get," answered Bonnie. "On second thought, I suspect you're getting your fair share."

"Judith pulled the phone out of the wall."

"Been there, done that," said Bonnie. "So how is notoriety treating you?"

"You've been through this, Bonnie. When will it end?"

"I'm surprised it's lasted this long. I was sure you'd have given in by now."

Arnold was suddenly struck by the realization that he didn't like Bonnie Card—that he'd *never* liked Bonnie Card.

"I'm not giving in."

"Why not?" asked Bonnie. "Why do you care what a bunch of total strangers think about you? And particularly if they're right-wing lunatics?"

"I'm not giving in," Arnold repeated. "*You* didn't give in," he objected. "Why did *you* care what all those cystic fibrosis people thought of *you*?"

"I'm not a good role model, Arnold. In the first place, I'm an ethicist. I have to worry about my professional credibility. Nobody expects the guy who sells them vermiculite to stand up for civil liberties." Bonnie paused—probably to let the vermiculite jab sink in. "But what you're missing, Arnold, is that I *enjoyed* being under attack. Don't get me wrong. I'm not saying it was a picnic. Let me tell you: There are few experiences less pleasant than finding a dead foetus nailed to your front door. But, on the whole, I relish the good scrap. A battle-royal. It keeps my blood flowing. Gilbert's the same way. So what if we have to call out the bomb squad every once in a while to open our mail? When strangers send us white powder, we sweeten our tea with it. You and Judith, on the other hand, you're not fighters. Quite frankly, you're made of softer stuff. What do you hope to achieve by resisting? Will it really be worth it….?"

Arnold had reached his saturation point with Bonnie Card. Only five days earlier, Bonnie Card had been urging resistance to the last—and now she wanted him to roll over. It was all a game to her, just an endless series of questions that led to more questions. If he took one stance, she'd choose the opposite—merely to demonstrate that the opposing side also had merit, that our social universe was entirely constructed and no philosophical principle was truly sound. For a professor of ethics, Bonnie Card was utterly amoral. But no sane person could lead his life like that, and Arnold wasn't going to let the woman twist his thoughts in circles. *Not this time.*

"Thanks for the wisdom," answered Arnold.

"Any time."

He drew a deep breath.

"How are you and Gil?"

"Busy, the usual chaos. He's been working long hours." Arnold detected a hint of derision in the woman's voice—but he wasn't sure whether she was merely complaining about Gil's schedule, or hinting at something more. "He's really sorry about the other day," added Bonnie. "He thought you *wanted* to apologize."

"No big deal," Arnold answered. "Just a misunderstanding."

His entire existence felt like an enormous misunderstanding, a colossal failure to make himself understood. He was fifty-five. Far past the halfway mark. Far too late to hope for a breakthrough.

He said goodbye quickly and hung up the phone.

That evening, Arnold stayed late at the nursery. He ambled around the greenhouses, pinching chrysanthemum shoots and peeling dead leaves off dieffenbachia stems. The botanist was no stranger to the Plant Centre at night: At the height of his experiments with flower recipes, he'd often crashed on a cot in his office. But in those years, he'd felt so alive among his blossoms, sheltered in his little botanical oasis and yet simultaneously a part of the city. Iron gratings kept out vandals without dampening the sounds of Village nightlife. In contrast, the plate glass windows, now boarded over with plywood, kept the outside world entirely at bay. Arnold felt as though he'd been sealed in a tomb. He assured himself that he was staying late to think matters through—that he wanted to avoid making any rash decisions—but he knew what he was actually doing was giving Gilbert time to leave his house. He didn't want to stumble upon the two of them in some obscene state of undress, to listen to the lawyer quote George Bernard Shaw on adultery. Better to hide among his rose bushes until he was certain the coast was clear. It was nearly ten o'clock when he finally arrived home.

The protesters had packed up for the night, so there was no need to climb over the fence on the ladders. It was a pleasure to walk up his own street and climb his own front steps without being compared to Saddam Hussein. He said good evening to the police guards, but they remained as stock-still as cigar-store Indians. No matter. As Bonnie

Card said: *Why did he care what a bunch of total strangers thought about him?* It was *his* home and *his* garden—his private space inside that stockade fence—and no amount of public scorn could take that away from him.

Arnold's key was only halfway in the lock when Judith pulled open the door. His wife wore a threadbare bathrobe and a pair of pink socks. Her face was pallid as a bed sheet. Her eyes were bloodshot. For the first time ever, she didn't look stunning to Arnold—merely worn out. "Something happened," she said.

So it was true. Even though he'd expected it, it didn't seem possible.

"I don't want to know," said Arnold. "Let's just put it behind us."

Judith didn't seem to register his words. "I don't know how to say this," she continued. "I sent Ray out with Gil Card for the afternoon—to get him away from all this madness—and I was taking a nap…and then I came outside…there were the ladders…and…and…" She raked her fingers through her hair. "I'm so, so sorry."

"What are you talking about?"

Arnold's heart quickened. He could hear his pulse in his temple, could sense the perspiration seeping through his palms. Judith's expression told him that no amount of anxiety would prove sufficient for what came next.

His wife didn't answer him. Instead, she stepped aside—and instinctively, Arnold crossed through the kitchen into the yard. "What have they done?" Arnold appealed to the cool night air. "Good God! What have they done?"

The garden hadn't been vandalized. It had been razed.

The perpetrators had lopped the heads off every tea rose and gladiolus, torn the lilacs from the arbour, sheared apart the rhododendrons with the chainsaw. They'd done even more damage with the annuals, scooping pansies and phlox from the soil as though they were weeds. An uprooted forget-me-not hung from the Japanese maple like an epiphyte. They'd also raided Judith's studio, arming themselves with enamels and varnishes that they'd sprinkled liberally across the grass. Whole swaths of lawn had been stained the colour of mahogany. The air that yesterday smelled of fragrant pollen now stank pungently of oil paint and turpentine. Not even the lily pads in the birdbath had been spared—the innocent leaves had been plucked from the water and ground up under the tires of the wheelbarrow. What it had taken Arnold three decades to build had required only several minutes for a stranger to destroy. To Arnold, it was a holocaust—the scorching of the very earth beneath his feet. The Romans sowing salt in the fields of Carthage had done no worse.

Judith came up behind him. She placed her hand on his elbow to comfort him, but he could feel her fingers trembling. "I know there's nothing I can say," she said.

"I've had enough," said Arnold. "It's over."

"Please don't do anything rash, darling." Judith tightened her grip on his arm. "Let's call the police. They'll take care of it."

"*Like hell* they'll take care of it." Arnold wrested free of his wife's grasp. "I'm going to take care of it."

Arnold charged up the steps into the kitchen. "Where the fuck do we keep the phone books?"

"Please, Arnold. I'm begging you…."

He searched the magazine rack, then inside the utility cabinet behind the toaster. Rolls of duct tape and industrial-strength twine toppled onto the counter. A light bulb fell to the linoleum and shattered. "Goddammit," cursed Arnold. He finally found the white pages on the floor of the pantry.

"What are you going to do, Arnold? Talk to me."

He sat on the un-swept spruce floorboards of the storeroom, the musty air lit only by a low-watt hanging bulb, and turned over the brittle pages. *Spitelli, Spitfire, Spitfish, SPITFORD!* "Spitford," Arnold said aloud. "Spottsylvania Otis."

"You don't know it was Spitford."

"I *know* it was Spitford."

"Take a few seconds to think about what you're going to do," pleaded Judith. "It's a lot easier to do things than to undo things."

"I'm done thinking. I've been thinking too

much already."

"You're not going to do something violent, are you? You wouldn't hurt anyone?"

"Of course not. Nothing violent," said Arnold. "But I think it's about time to beat Mr. Spitford at his own goddam game." The botanist tore the page out of the phone book and stuffed it into his pocket. "He's going to protest outside my house, is he? We'll I'm not the only one with a house."

CHAPTER 6

The quiet Upper Manhattan cul-de-sac that housed both Spotty Spitford's home and his church was located on a rise overlooking the Hudson River. Ornamental wrought-iron gates guarded the block's entrance, where one sign warned PRIVATE WAY, WALK YOUR HORSES and another marked the site of General Washington's headquarters during the retreat from the Battle of Harlem Heights. The street was still cobblestone, shaded by an avenue of venerable beech trees. Most of the row houses displayed carefully-tended, if unimaginative, window-box gardens: geraniums, columbines, hosta. Spitford's own residence, a three-story structure in the renaissance revival style, was sheltered by a hedge of Queen Anne's lace. The hedge wanted trimming. Arnold recalled the lines from *Richard II*: *Noisome weeds which without profit suck the soil's fertility from wholesome flowers.* Yes, Spitford was one of those. But seeing his dishevelled shrubbery, his overgrown pachysandra, Arnold fought the urge to lecture the agitator about the need for periodic pruning.

Spitford's neighbourhood was only a twenty-five minute subway ride from Arnold's townhouse, but it had taken the botanist nearly three hours to get uptown. He didn't dare ride public transportation, and two cabbies had refused to drive him, before he'd found a third, a white-bearded Sikh, who clearly had no idea who he was. But then the taxi had been pulled over for a broken taillight, and he'd had to negotiate the final fifteen blocks up Broadway on foot. Luckily, it was well past midnight, so the streets were nearly deserted. Anyone who was still awake had sidewalks to hose down, or Chinese food to deliver, or prostitutes to manage—in short, business to attend to that left little time for recognizing or harassing Arnold. When he finally reached Spitford's street, nearly all of the homes were already dark. A solitary lamppost illuminated a small corner of sidewalk, where an obese raccoon rummaged among aluminium trashcans. Farther up the block, although it was mid-spring, one file of second story windows remained framed by multi-coloured Christmas bulbs. Beyond that stood the gargoyled church, its imposing gothic silhouette rising above the river. The night was overcast and muggy, punctuated by gusts of warm wind. In Spitford's residence, a light glowed in an upstairs window. Arnold double-checked the address from the phonebook against the brass numbers posted on Spitford's front door. He mounted the steps and pressed the buzzer.

Arnold's temper hadn't calmed since discovering the garden massacre—if anything, his anger had increased on the trip uptown. But now, listening to the groan of distant stairs, he second-guessed himself. Why did challenging Spitford at the man's own residence suddenly seem unreasonable to Arnold? Wasn't that what the minister had been doing *to him* all week? But it *was* nearly one o'clock in the morning. Something about the hot, stagnant spring night reminded Arnold of the Klansmen who used to waylay black ministers outside their homes. Then another concern struck Arnold: What if *Spitford* turned violent? For all he knew, the man might keep a shotgun at his bedside. He scanned the stoop for anything he might use as a makeshift weapon, but except for the welcome mat and the milk bin, the area was bare. And then it was too late. The door opened—not a crack, but all the way, and swiftly, as though in defiance of any lurking danger. Spitford loomed in the doorway. The minister was fully attired in his double-breasted black suit, with the gold chain of his watch poking out of his pocket. His reading glasses sat perched on his flat nose and he held a book under his arm. Without his sunglasses, he looked much older.

"Yes?" demanded the minister.

"It's Arnold Brinkman," retorted Arnold. "The man you've been harassing."

Spitford tucked his glasses into his breast pocket. "So?"

"So this has to stop," said Arnold. "You're going to pay for my garden and you're going to get your goddam goons away from my house."

The minister raised his eyebrows. "I'm afraid that's not going to happen, Mr. Brinkman," he said. He spoke politely, almost sympathetically, as though the matter were well beyond his control. Nothing in his tone suggested the least displeasure at having been summoned to the door in the middle of the night. He'd probably have displayed the same mildly intrigued expression if he'd been purchasing Girl Scout cookies. *But it was one o'clock in the morning!* The man had no right to equanimity—his very reasonableness seemed unreasonable to Arnold.

"Don't you 'Mr. Brinkman' me," shouted Arnold. "It took me thirty years to build that goddam garden."

Arnold's voice was far too loud for the street; his words echoed in his ears. At the same time, a door creaked behind Spitford. The minister ducked his head inside and said, in the gentlest voice, "It's nothing, Mother. Just business. Please go back to bed." When his gaze returned to Arnold, it was not nearly as friendly.

"This is neither the time," said Spitford, "nor the place—"

"—You leave me alone and I'll leave you alone."

"As I was saying, Mr. Brinkman, this is neither the time nor the place. However, since you've come all this way, I can spare you a few moments. But why don't we step over to the church? You possess a very loud voice, Mr. Brinkman, and my mother is not a heavy sleeper."

The minister drew the door shut behind him and led Arnold twenty yards down the sidewalk. They stood directly in front of the Church of the Crusader, where a black and white sign read: "God Hates Sin." Another banner, proclaiming IT'S NOT A CHOICE, IT'S A HOLOCAUST, hung above the towering stained glass windows.

Spitford flipped open his watch and noted the time. Then he stuffed his fleshy hands into his trouser pockets. "Here's how it is, Mr. Brinkman," he said. "You've made some terrible mistakes and the only thing to be done is to ask for forgiveness. That's what the Lord wants. That's what *I* want. Too many men have died for America to let you mock their courage. If you don't make amends, I'm afraid you're going to have to face the consequences."

That's what it was all about to Spitford: consequences, a simple matter of cause and effect. As though the universe were an enormous billiard table under the supervision of a Newtonian deity, some celestial engineer who managed the human drama with mathematical precision. The minister's confidence irked Arnold. "Don't you have anything better to do with your time?"

"The truth is, Mr. Brinkman, I *do* have better things to do with my time." Spitford's voice was deep and resonant. "We live in a culture of death, where radical homosexuals are corrupting our children and bloodthirsty abortionists are committing a genocide that makes the African slave trade pale by comparison. Every day that I'm compelled to squander outside your house, waiting for an apology, is one more day lost to unnecessary distraction. But what am I to do? This is what the Lord has asked of me and I have no choice but to obey."

Arnold tried to keep his cool. "The Lord wants you to ruin my life?"

"The Lord wants you to apologize."

"Well He's going to have a long wait," snapped Arnold. "Next time you speak to Him, tell Him to go screw himself with a chainsaw."

Spitford remained unflappable. "You're a very angry man, Mr. Brinkman."

That was *too* much. "Wouldn't you be angry if a pack of Black Nazis—that's right, the goddam Black Gestapo—tore up your garden?"

The minister shook his head. "I want to give you fair warning," he said softly. "It has come to my attention that you did far more than insult *the flag* at that baseball game. I have four witnesses willing to swear that you were teaching racial epithets to a child. I doubted these young men as first—quite honestly, you didn't strike me as the type. But what I've heard tonight confirms my fears, rather than my hopes. Tomorrow morning, Mr. Brinkman, I'm going to have no choice but to expose your views. All I can say is that I hope you'll take this as an opportunity to get right with God."

"The kid asked a question," objected Arnold. "I was just trying to explain...."

He looked up into Spitford's hard glare and stopped speaking. What could he possibly say? Spitford was far too certain, far too persuasive, to be outmanoeuvred verbally. A few more exchanges and he'd probably have Arnold convinced that his actions were indeed clouded by prejudice—that the botanist had discriminated in hiring, or locked his car doors unnecessarily, or masterminded the assassination of Malcolm X. People who professed to know everything were always perpetrating that sort of "instant brainwash" on people like Arnold. He thought of what Spitford's goons had done to his garden—the decapitated dianthus, the mangled viburnum branches—and, for the first time in his adult life, he truly hated another human being.

"Do you own a copy of the scriptures, Mr. Brinkman?" asked Spitford. "If you don't, why not take mine? Maybe it will soothe some of your bitterness." The minister clasped Arnold's hands and folded them around the Bible, his own fingers warm against the botanist's clammy flesh. "Even the most hardened racist can mend his ways."

This last accusation jolted Arnold alert. How dare this priggish homophobic Neanderthal—this Uncle Tom—call him a bigot? "I was trying to explain to my nephew what a nigger was," shouted the botanist. "Well, you're a goddam nigger. And I don't mean the colour of your skin. I mean the content of your character."

Spitford stepped backwards, apparently nonplussed. His eyes bulged; a vein in his forehead pulsed ominously. He started to speak several times, but all he managed to produce was a short choking sound. When he reached into his jacket pocket, Arnold feared the man might draw a pistol—but instead he produced a paisley handkerchief and dabbed at his temples. "Good evening, Mr. Brinkman," he said.

"The evening's not over yet," responded Arnold. "Not by a long-shot."

He raised the book above his shoulder and hurled it across the churchyard. It slammed into the decorative window, shattering the stained glass.

"You show up at my house again tomorrow," shouted Arnold, "and I'll cut you in half with my chainsaw."

The botanist turned on his heels and walked swiftly into the darkness.

Once he'd left Spitford's, Arnold wasn't sure why he'd ever gone. To threaten the minister? To annoy him? If so, he recognized he'd failed on both counts. It was now apparent to him that the minister was one of those fatalistic men who could *never* be annoyed, not by anything, because every inconvenience and aggravation was part of a divine scheme to draw him closer to Jesus on the cross. If that meant martyrdom, so much the better. Just as the followers of Calvin had once measured their heavenly value in earthly goods, the Spitfords of the world used pain as a benchmark for human worth. The more they suffered, the happier they were. Which made Arnold's threats utterly futile. Not that he was actually going to attack the minister with a chainsaw—but even if he did, Spitford would count each missing limb as a special gift from God. *Or would he?* In his gut, Arnold still harboured doubts. He sensed a certain shrewdness, even guile, behind Spitford's indignation. A servant of the Lord, maybe, but not one above cutting corners. The man would certainly crack a few innocent eggs to make an omelette for Christ. For whatever reason, he'd apparently decided to make Arnold into one of those eggs.

But what troubled Arnold the most about the encounter—even more than the minister's intransigence—was his own anger. He had levelled a racial slur at the man and tossed a Bible through a church window. Neither of these were capital offenses, and both had been provoked, but now he understood how otherwise decent people could explode on occasion and gun down their co-workers or their in-laws in cold blood. If *he'd* had a gun, he could easily have lost his temper enough to take a shot at Spitford. Which meant what? That hot-headed people shouldn't be issued gun licenses? Or that the enemies of hot-tempered people ought to be issued bullet-proof vests? Maybe that anybody accused of a violent crime should be sent to an anger management course and given a second chance. That sounded like good social policy—but it didn't excuse Arnold's outburst. On the other hand, there was no epithet too harsh for a man like Spitford. Even if Arnold had thrown a thousand Bibles through a thousand church windows, or burned Notre Dame to its foundations, it wouldn't have squared the score with the Bible-thumpers after what those Black Nazis had done to Arnold's garden. In other words, what he'd done to Spitford had been both highly justified and utterly inexcusable.

Arnold braved the subway ride to the Village. It was nearly four o'clock on a Friday morning and the odds of extensive human contact were low. The only other person on the platform was a shirtless, disfigured African-American wino strumming a broken ukulele. It sounded like the guy was attempting to sing *O Susannah!* but he had few teeth and his mouth was far too misshapen to articulate the words. Arnold generally didn't give to the homeless individually—he preferred to send his donations to reputable, high-profile organizations of the sort that offered complimentary return-address labels—but a sudden yearning to demonstrate that he wasn't a racist, maybe even to prove that he was a decent human being, took hold of him. He fished in his pockets and handed the man a ten dollar bill. The man growled what might have been a "thank you." So far, so good. But then a gleam appeared in the guy's eyes, a burst of sudden lucidity, as though the universe had been clarified for him or his crooning had conjured up a private vision of the Virgin Mary. The man opened his engorged mouth and stuck out a large diseased tongue. "God bless!" he cried. "God bless!" After that, he chased Arnold across the platform as though he might lick him, his tongue hanging from his foaming mouth like that of a rabid hound. Fortunately, the train arrived a moment later and the botanist darted into the final car as the doors closed. Unfortunately, he'd been so aggravated by the episode that he'd boarded an uptown train by mistake. At the next station, he'd had to get off and switch directions.

When Arnold finally arrived at Sheridan Square, shortly before five o'clock, he realized that he didn't want to return home. Not yet. Judith would be awake, he was sure, waiting to press him for the details of his encounter with Spitford, and inevitably, against his better judgment, he'd share them. Arnold had never mastered the art of lying to his wife, even when it served their mutual interests. So he shared secrets that would have best been kept to himself—whether a clinically insignificant rise in his cholesterol level, which was bound to cause Judith unnecessary worry, or a colleague's infidelity, which might forever doom the man in her eyes. Once, Arnold had thrown Judith a surprise birthday party—fifty of their dearest friends at the Swiss bistro with the authentic cuckoo clocks—but he'd broken down and confessed on the stroll to the restaurant. He just wasn't wired for dishonesty. Moreover, the problem with deceiving your spouse was that you couldn't tell only one lie. Constant companionship forced you to cover your tracks, weaving more intricate falsehoods until neither of you knew what was true any longer. Arnold wanted no part of that. But he also didn't want Judith raking him over the coals for losing his cool with Spitford. He cringed at the thought of sharing what he'd said about the content of the man's character. It wasn't Judith's reaction only that he dreaded—although his wife, who'd sided with a contingent of St. Gregory's parents protesting the use of the adverb "niggardly" in a school budget report, was unlikely to sympathize with his conduct. He was also sincerely embarrassed, not because he would have retracted his statement, but because language that might have been perfectly suited for a heated confrontation would seem ridiculous when repeated in his living room. And there was another reason Arnold didn't want to return home: He couldn't handle the thought of waking up to tend the garden that was no longer there.

A whisper of light was already visible in the pink-grey sky, and the starlings were scavenging around the mesh garbage cans, when Arnold walked past Sixth Street and headed toward the nursery. The cot in his office might not be the city's most comfortable bed—he'd have to clear the tubs of pepper seedlings off the mattress—but at least he wouldn't be disturbed. That would give him time to prepare for Judith. And to figure out his next course of action. Maybe he *would* sue Spitford over the garden. Wasn't the best defence a strong offense? But all of that planning would have to wait until after a good night's sleep. Or at least a power nap. Right now, he could hardly keep his eyes open.

Much to Arnold's surprise, the showroom lights were illuminated in the nursery. Maybe this was another of Guillermo's security measures, he figured. But then he crossed through the hangar and found the manager himself awake in his office. The Venezuelan was lying on the sofa, staring wide-eyed at the popcorn ceiling. A bag of soy chips and a no-calorie vitamin drink lay on the floor nearby. On the manager's desk, at the opposite end of the room, stood a conspicuous orange sunflower in a bud vase.

Arnold knocked on the open door. Guillermo glanced in his direction, then returned his gaze upward.

"What are you doing here?" asked Arnold.

"Thinking."

"I thought that was my job."

"We do different kinds of thinking. I've been thinking about business."

"Have you?"

"I had Lucinda run some numbers for me," said Guillermo. He sat up and rolled down his sleeves one at a time, fastening the buttons. "Do you know how many individual plants we sold last year during the second week of May?"

"I don't have the foggiest idea."

"Seven hundred forty-eight," answered Guillermo.

Arnold had little doubt the Venezuelan could itemize each sale, if asked. "Do you know how many individual plants we've sold over the last five days?"

"Not as many, I suppose."

"Thirty-nine."

"That's definitely not as many." Arnold hadn't expected the number to be *that* low. "I take it that's not just a glitch in the business cycle…"

The Venezuelan folded his arms across his chest. "It's a glitch in the political cycle, Arnold."

"You mean to tell me people aren't buying my plants because they don't like my politics?"

"That's what it looks like. *Or* they do like your politics, privately, but they're afraid to be seen here. *Or* they just want to stay clear of trouble. Who knows? The bottom line is that we're haemorrhaging cash."

"So you think I should apologize."

"I'm not saying that. I told you I don't go near that stuff," said Guillermo. "What I'm telling you is that if you don't intend to apologize, you'd better come up with a plan B before we go bankrupt."

"And if I don't have a plan B?"

Guillermo removed a toothpick from a tiny see-through case and twirled it between his lips. "I'm not too worried. The bosses always have a plan B."

The Venezuelan stood up. "Time to call it a day," he said. "Any interest in breakfast?"

"Go ahead," said Arnold. "I'm not done thinking yet."

The truth was that he would have loved breakfast—and companionship—but he was afraid to show his face in public.

"Okay, suit yourself. By the way, your wife called looking for you. Twice."

"I had an errand to run."

"She told me all about it," said Guillermo. "I trust you didn't kill the guy."

Arnold didn't say anything.

"On second thought, if you did, I don't want to know." The Venezuelan retrieved his cap from the hat rack. "By the way, aren't you going to ask me about the flower?"

"Sure. What's with the flower?"

"It's for you. From that girl. They delivered it this morning while you were going through your DO NOT DISTURB phase."

Arnold walked over to the vase and examined the miniature card. It read:

CAN WE TALK ON THE RECORD? CASSANDRA

Guillermo chuckled. "Are you going to talk to her?"

"She's off her gourd," said Arnold. "Why in the word would anyone send me flowers. I own a nursery for Christ's sake."

"I think it was supposed to be a joke," said the Venezuelan.

Some joke. He'd lost the garden it had taken him a lifetime to cultivate and she'd sent him a droopy, dehydrated supermarket flower in a pot of lukewarm tap water. A gift that ranked right up there with sending condoms to nuns or lampshades to holocaust survivors. Who the hell did this girl think she was? The sunflower didn't make him want to give her an interview—it made him want to call her and scream at her. To tell her that his life was falling apart, piece by piece, and the last thing he needed was some teenybopper cub reporter sending him gag presents and stirring up trouble. What he really wanted to do was to shout at her until she realized that his life was no joking matter and certainly not a tool for left-wing propagandists. Maybe that had been her intended effect.

"Most people laugh at jokes," said Guillermo, "or at least smile."

"I'm guffawing in my head."

"Whatever, boss," said the Venezuelan. "Don't forget to breathe."

Guillermo departed and Arnold heard the manager's footsteps echoing across the hangar, then the pulse of the door chime as the Venezuelan exited out to the street. The botanist retrieved the sunflower and carried the vase into his own office. He cleared the pepper tubs from the cot, brushing away crumbs of fertilizer, but he was no longer sleepy. Why couldn't the damn girl just leave him alone? He was having a hard enough time as it was. Nothing he'd ever done was so horrific that it merited a supermarket cutting. Arnold removed the sunflower from its stand. He clipped the stem with surgical expertise and set the stalk in a glass of distilled, refrigerated water. He verified the temperature. Thirty-five degrees. Next, he checked the pH. Five. Far too high. So he added lemon juice, bead by bead, with an eyedropper. Florence Nightingale could have done no better. Tomorrow, the drooping stalk might hope for at least a limited recovery. When the first aid was done, Arnold reached across the desk absentmindedly and flipped on the television.

The botanist recognized the voice before he saw the face: the affected English accent, the effeminate lisp, the mouth draw tight as that of a ventriloquist. There was no mistaking that voice—like a gay, aristocratic Charlie McCarthy. And there was its owner, Arnold's ex-brother-in-law, being interviewed beneath a coconut palm. Vince Sprague was one of those rare men over sixty-five who actually looked good in a crotch-hugging swimsuit. Celeste's former husband boasted that he did five hundred push-ups every morning, half of them on his knuckles; at a dinner party, several years earlier, he'd consumed too much port and bench-pressed the host's piano. Sprague's chest was tan and waxed and as defined as a Michelangelo sketch. Even the muscles in his neck were as thick as those in Arnold's legs.

"Of course, I am *quite* disturbed," said Sprague. "If you'll pardon my French, it's bloody outrageous. Categorically despicable. I am not myself an aficionado of American baseball, you understand, nor am I an American citizen, but on the occasions when I have found myself at such a match, I have always risen for the national anthem. I cannot imagine what lapse of judgment allowed my ex-wife to trust our son to such a misguided—if not outright dangerous—influence."

Arnold pounded his fist on the desktop. "You're from Staten Island, goddamit," he shouted at the television. "You're not a citizen because you renounced your citizenship to avoid paying income tax."

"I did not know Mr. Brinkman well myself," continued Sprague. "I tried to avoid him, to tell you the truth. I always thought him somewhat unscrupulous."

Amazing! The man sells thousands of teenage girls into prostitution, abandons his wife and son for a Romanian gymnast one-third his age, flees the country to avoid a federal indictment so long it contains an index, and doesn't even send Celeste a dime of child-support—and now he's calling Arnold unscrupulous. Why didn't they ask Sprague why *he* hadn't taken the boy to the baseball game? Why he hadn't sent the boy so much as a postcard in six years? Because they wanted Arnold to lose, that's why. Because now the object of this game was to see how much dirt they could pile on Arnold before he suffocated. They could discover that he'd spent the last thirty years reading bedtime stories to blind nuns, or that he'd been a POW in southeast Asia, and they'd still find a way to spin the news against him. Even if it were discovered that he were a paraplegic who suffered tongue spasms, that the entire incident had been involuntary, they'd rake him across the coals for not seeking pre-emptive treatment.

"I am consulting with my attorneys," said Sprague. "I intend to take every necessary measure to make certain this blasted outrage does not recur in the future."

"I'm not the outrage, dammit!" shouted Arnold. "You're the outrage!"

He stormed out of the office, carrying the sunflower with him. Never in his life could Arnold recall being so worn down—so close to snapping. Usually, a few hours hoeing in the garden would tranquilize his nerves, but that was no longer a possibility. Nor was a hug from Judith. The only other genuine pleasure the botanist could think of were the hothouses, where they kept the tropical plants and exotics. One of these greenhouses was dry and served the cactus. The other, the wet greenhouse, contained liana-draped banana thickets and Brazil nut trees festooned with orchids. The Garden Centre's stock of bromeliads was the most impressive private collection in the world. Nominally, all of these plants were for sale—which was essential, according to Lucinda, for taxation purposes. In reality, few if any of the rarer specimens ever found a buyer. Even in the West Village, there was little market for $15,000 pitcher plants. Arnold loved the scents of the wet greenhouse: Not just the sweet aroma of bee-pollinated flowers, like mock-orange, or the lemon fragrance of citriodora, but also the pungent stench of the durian fruits and the cadaver-like odour of the Rafflesia. All of it reminded the botanist of the near infinite variety of plant life, the endless promise and possibility. Ornithologists had more or less run out of birds. They might yet discover one or two new species—maybe recover an isolated stand of Ivory-billed woodpeckers every fifty years—but the day to day life of a bird scholar was more like that of a classicist than that of an explorer. But botany! The Amazon basin alone was home to tens of thousands of un-catalogued species, any one of which might cure cancer or taste of ambrosia. Which was why Arnold enjoyed relaxing in the wet greenhouse, as others might savour a Jacuzzi or a sauna, letting the plant world pollinate his lungs. He sat on a wooden shelf with the sunflower braced on his lap.

"Apologize," he said—and he picked a petal.

He plucked a second petal: "Don't apologize."

If only it could be that easy—following the dictates of chance. But of course *it could be that easy.* All he had to do was to beg forgiveness and he'd be off the hook. His life would once again be his own. He might even win public esteem for his confession like those adulterous televangelists, forcing the genie back into the bottle except that was what everybody expected of him. What everybody wanted. He'd apologize, and adopt a kid, and six months later he'd be at a baseball game singing *God Bess America*—and even he wouldn't care anymore.

He pulled out more petals. "Apologize. Don't apologize. Apologize." Soon the blossom was nearly bald. Before the plant rendered a verdict, he dozed off.

Although Arnold slept less than a quarter of an hour, when he awoke, it felt like a new day. What a difference a few minutes made. Sunshine was already streaming through the skylights and Lucinda's Myna bird, which she kept behind the lycopodium and old world ferns, was scratching at the door of its cage. The sunflower lay at Arnold's feet, mutilated, and he'd long lost track of where he was in his plucking. The botanist dropped the remains in the compost bin.

In his office, the television was still playing. But miraculously, the right-wing cable channel was no longer covering his case. Instead, they'd apparently glommed on to a fresh cause célèbre, this one an urban crime scene involving yellow police tape. Arnold was about to shut the machine off when he heard his own name mentioned. *Mr. Brinkman*, said the newscaster, *may be armed and is presumed to be dangerous.* That's when the crime scene came into focus. They were showing the Church of the Crusader with a police searchlight illuminating its enormous windows. Only rather than one broken pane, *all* of the glass was shattered. "He ran from window to window like a maniac," Spotty Spitford explained. "I'd given him a Bible in the hope that it might soothe his anger, but that wasn't the Lord's will. What did he do with it? He used it as a weapon against God. The beast—for it's hard to think of a hatemonger like that as anything else—seemed determined to knock out every window in the tabernacle. I pity a creature who has no love for his own country, but I fear an animal who can desecrate a house of worship." But what amazed Arnold most weren't Spitford's lies, but his clothing. The minister wore a pair of cotton pyjamas and a stocking cap. He'd *changed* out of his suit before phoning the police. "It pains me to say that Mr. Brinkman also chose this opportunity to express himself through racial invective. He called me a word that begins with the letter N that I will choose not to repeat."

So the exploits of the Tongue Traitor grow increasingly deranged, observed the reporter. Not the fast-talker who usually followed Arnold's actions, but a higher-ranking "correspondent at large" from the network. *If you recall, earlier this week the Bronx county prosecutor announced that she might charge Mr. Brinkman with disorderly conduct. That may now be the least of his problems. We have word in this morning from the United States Attorney's Office that, after this latest incident, the federal government is planning to charge*

Mr. Brinkman under the Terrorism Acts. Such charges may include destruction of a house of worship with the intent to incite widespread fear, as well as issuing threats against a public official, because Reverend Spitford is a member of the City Council's advisory panel on religious affairs. Conviction on any of these counts would obviously result in a substantial prison sentence. That's the latest from here in Upper Manhattan, where it appears that the Tongue Traitor will soon officially be known as the Tongue Terrorist.

PART II
Spring-Summer 2004

CHAPTER 7

Prisons, according to Bonnie Card, were highly underappreciated.

They'd had this conversation nearly a decade earlier, in the Berkshires, on the lakefront deck of the Cards' summer retreat. The cottage itself was a clapboard structure constructed from red cedar and bald cypress around the turn of the twentieth century. At first, the choice of wood had mystified Arnold. Why import cedar boards from Ontario, or barge cypress planks up the Connecticut River, when the local forest abounded with white pine and Balsam firs? Bonnie and Gilbert hadn't a clue. They'd purchased the property from a real estate firm in Pittsfield. Enough history for them. But Arnold had made a point investigating the construction. He'd spoken to the former owner of the defunct summer camp across the lake, who'd referred him to the elderly widow of a local dairy farmer. The only answer she'd offered was: "All the houses around here are built like that." Eventually, the proprietor of the local bookshop, where the botanist had led an informal discussion on floral-based dining, had unravelled the mystery: One hundred years earlier, there'd been hardly a tree within a day's walk of the Cards' cabin. Only pastureland. Miles and miles of defoliated brush. So the Brahmin textile magnate who was erecting the cottage as a fishing lodge, forced to cart in his lumber, had splurged on the most lavish softwoods he could find. That also explained the maple floors on the lower level and the tamarack wainscoting in the bedrooms. "It's incredible how you can spend so much time in a place and yet know so little about it," Arnold had mused. Bonnie had responded with her tirade against the penal system.

How often do you think about prisons? She'd asked. *Not often, right? Maybe when you pass a sign on the interstate warning you not to pick up hitchhikers. Or on the rare occasion you hear about a jailbreak or violent uprising on the evening news. But prisons are the defining moral feature of our culture—the atrocity by which future generations will judge us. The Medieval Church had its Inquisition. The South had Negro slavery. We have two million men and women behind bars. Which is something we never think about, on a daily basis—though it's far more important than wondering about how our homes were built or with what sort of wood.* Arnold recalled insisting that *he* thought about prisons all the time: Hadn't he even taught a workshop on gardening for juvenile offenders at Riker's Island? That had just whetted Bonnie's appetite. *You think about prisons in the abstract,* she'd said. *Incarceration is a misfortune that happens to other people. Occasionally, when you feel a human connection to one of those people, let's say Nelson Mandela or the Birmingham Six, you find the concept of imprisonment unsettling. Because it could have been you. That's the reason Kafka's* The Trial *is so disturbing. But the truth of the matter is that you never reflect upon what it means to spend thirty years in a small padlocked cell. You don't* appreciate *the horror. And I mean whether for a crime you didn't commit or a crime you* did *commit, because if imprisonment is torture, whether or not the prisoner is guilty is beside the point.* Bonnie had later expanded this sermon into a highly controversial article for a British magazine in which she referred to American prisons as "concentration camps for the poor." That had provoked outrage from Holocaust survivors and public prosecutors, but also leading prisoner rights groups, which weren't exactly thrilled to find themselves allied with Professor Babykiller. Now, a terrorism charge hanging over his head, Arnold couldn't shake Bonnie's final words on the subject: *People like Arnold Brinkman don't think about prisons because people like Arnold Brinkman don't end up in prisons.* Maybe people like him might spend a few months in a country club jail if they misappropriated other people's money, but these institutions were like boarding schools for recalcitrant adults, wall-less facilities surrounded by chalk lines, not *real* prisons where rape and isolation defined the daily routine. That Arnold might be sent to a run-of-the-mill locks-and-bars federal penitentiary—for many years, if not forever—was absolutely unthinkable. He refused to let that happen.

But what then? Arnold wasn't exactly capable of holing himself up in the basement of the nursery with a stockpile of ammunition, a là Butch Cassidy and the Sundance Kid—nor was he foolish enough to try. He certainly wasn't ready to call it quits with a cup of hemlock. The wisest choice would have been to follow Vince Sprague to Fiji—or some similar island sanctuary, because one atoll probably wasn't large enough for the two of them—but that sort of escape required planning and connections and time. Arnold had none of these. He wasn't even sure where he'd put his passport. Moreover, he couldn't possibly hope to make it past airport security. That was the difference between Arnold and his ex-brother-in-law: Celeste's husband was just another obscure white-slaver, not even a footnote on the crime-blotter. The Tongue Terrorist was a household name. Which meant, ironically, that Gilbert Card had been right. It *was* all about borders. And Arnold was on the wrong side of them. He'd end up spending the rest of his life in a 8' x 10' cell, another darling of the Left like Mumia Abu-Jamal or Lisl Auman, because he happened to be standing on one side of an arbitrary political boundary, a line as imaginary as the equator. In some countries, sticking out his tongue at the American flag would have made him a hero. He could have been elected mayor of Havana or Tehran. But that did him little good in New York City after 9-11. Even the so-called liberals would offer a half-hearted, apologetic defence: *We deplore his actions, but we believe in the principles of free expression. Because* we *do love America.* He had hundreds of "free-thinking" friends, but not one couple he could call upon who would let him hide out in their cellar while the FBI hunted for him. Not if that meant jeopardizing their own freedom or compromising their grandchildren's chances of preschool admission. He also had a rolodex full of college classmates and hiking partners, every last one of whom, he sensed viscerally, would have handed Anne Frank over to the Germans. Even Bonnie and Gilbert would urge him to turn himself in. Only Judith might help him—if she could. And Guillermo. He didn't doubt the business manager would shield him from a hail of bullets, if necessary. But loyalty and utility were not one and the same. Where could the Venezuelan possible conceal him that the authorities wouldn't think to look? What Arnold needed was a new friend: an instant Sancho Panza. Or a sure-shot mistress of the Belle Star-Calamity Jane variety.

That's when he thought of the girl. Why not? They shared no common past, no mutual acquaintances. She wasn't enough part of his life that the powers-that-be would ever think to trace him to her. Maybe he could offer the girl a trade: He'd do the damned interview *her way* if she'd let him hide in her closet. Not forever—just long enough for him to gain his bearing. Long enough to arrange for a more permanent escape. Even Judith couldn't reasonably fault him for contacting the girl under these circumstances. Arnold knew enough not to return home: As much as he longed to see his wife, to discuss this crisis like any other family emergency, he imagined the FBI was already ensconced at their townhouse—lifting fingerprints from their glassware, scanning their computer for pornography, exploring their basement with a Geiger counter. So he'd have to take the initiative and grant himself Judith's permission to contact the girl. They were a nation at war, right? Well, war made strange bedfellows. *Metaphorically speaking.* If his only friend turned out to be a radical reporter half his age, Arnold was no longer in a position to turn down any offer of assistance. He was even willing to eat crow and concede that he needed Cassandra's help desperately, an admission he sensed that the reporter would relish. Luckily, he'd kept her handwritten business card. Where he'd stashed it, of course, was another matter entirely. He rummaged through his desk drawers, finally turning them over on the blotter in frustration. The contents still smelled of sweet tobacco from his pipe-smoking days. It amazed him what junk he'd collected over the years: matchbooks from upscale restaurants, insects preserved in amber, his mother's old address book—which he'd used to telephone her surviving friends on the night she'd died. He had contact information for dozens of retired social workers. But no handwritten card. Of course not. Because the card, he recalled, was in the pocket of his overalls, and his gardening outfit was hanging on the hook in his tool shed.

On the television, they were showing a taped interview with two college kids who'd begun marketing "Tongue Traitor" paraphernalia. T-shirts and caps. The shirts featured gargantuan mouths with protruding tongues and captions like: "The Tongue Traitor: From His Lips to Osama's Ass" and "Loose Tongues Topple Towers: Keep Your Mouth Shut." Arnold swept his elbow across the desk, knocking the television to the carpet. The set emitted a flurry of sparks, but continued broadcasting. He didn't unplug the device—no need to risk electrocuting himself. That would just be more headline fodder for the tabloids. The disabled television reminded him that what the situation called for was level-headed thinking. Before his employees started showing up for work or a SWAT team surrounded the building. Arnold scoured the nursery in search of a phone book. In his haste, he accidentally overturned a bin of exotic bulbs, but didn't bother to retrieve them. Fifty dollar tulips rolled under glass display cases. The only directory Arnold managed to find was a set of Staten Island yellow pages from the mid-1980s that had been used as a doorstop. Lucinda most likely had white pages for all five boroughs in her cabinets, probably for the surrounding counties as well, but she'd locked her office door. Guillermo possessed the spare keys, not Arnold. Which meant he'd have to dial the operator and risk having the FBI trace the call. No, that wouldn't do. That's exactly how second-rate crooks got caught. They figured the police would overlook one minor clue—like leaving the blood-stained knife in their freezer or the getaway car parked in their driveway—as though the authorities didn't have the sense to trace a 411 call and find out which address he'd requested. Or maybe he was paranoid. In any case, there was no point in hanging out at the nursery. Far better to make a go of it on the streets. Arnold raced down the rear steps of the loading dock and darted across the back alley, nearly toppling over the auburn-wigged transvestite from the costume shop. The old woman was perched on a milk crate, reading a fashion magazine and smoking a cigarette through a holder.

"Goodness, Mr. Brinkman," said Gladys. "You startled me."

"Do you have a phonebook?" he asked.

The drag queen folded shut her magazine and blew a perfect ring of smoke. She massaged her forehead as though Arnold's request required deep reflection. "I remember when you didn't need a phonebook," she said. "All you did was ring up the operator and tell her who you wanted to speak to. That was outside Laramie, Wyoming, of course. We had a party line when I was a boy."

"Please, Gladys. This is an emergency. Can I borrow your white pages?"

"Heavens. I really don't know if we have any. You'd have to ask Anabelle and she's still upstairs." The transvestite scooped a plump Abyssinian cat onto her lap and began stroking its coat. "I wish I could sleep half as many hours as Anabelle does. A good night of Z's works wonders for the complexion."

"Can we wake her?" pleaded Arnold.

"Wake Anabelle?" Gladys appeared genuinely shocked—as though he'd suggested axe-murdering the old woman rather than rousing her. "You've clearly never seen my sister without her ten hours."

Arnold usually got a kick out of the 'sisters' and their idiosyncrasies. Anabelle, the older of the pair, was a Korean War veteran. Gladys had been a star of the longhorn rodeo circuit in the late 1950s. Both were practicing Catholics—"the most devout cross-dressers south of 14th Street"—and they'd actually met at Sunday vespers on the weekend after the Stonewall riots. The pair enjoyed a cat-and-mouse relationship with the young Polish priest at St. Felix's, Father Stanislaw, who allowed them to take communion but insisted on calling them Andy and Gary. Since the transvestites lived above their shop, and Gladys suffered severe insomnia, she often greeted Arnold in the early morning with anecdotes about "poor Father Stan" and his adventures in cognitive dissonance.

"I'm afraid my sister doesn't do mornings, Mr. Brinkman. They take such a toll. But if you'll stop by later in the day, I'm sure she'd love to see you. She is always saying that we should invite you over for tea one of these afternoons." Gladys smiled genially. "My, my, Mr. Brinkman. You look out of sorts."

Arnold held back the urge to grab the old woman by the shoulders and shake her. "I don't have time for this now, Gladys" he said. "I'm in desperate trouble."

"We know that," answered Gladys. "Poor Father Stan mentioned you in his homily. He was warning us against the sin of irreverence."

"I need your help."

"We've been counting the Rosary for you every night."

"Goddam it, Gladys. You're not listening to me. If I don't find this address, I'm going to end up in jail. You've got to help me."

Gladys looked distressed. "You want an address?"

"That's right, Gladys," said Arnold. He spoke slowly, articulating every word. "I need you to wake up Anabelle so we can look up an address in the telephone directory."

"Oh, is that all?" Gladys answered with apparent relief. "Why not find the address on the Internet?"

"Can you do that?"

The transvestite smiled. "You truly are an odd duck, aren't you, Mr. Brinkman? Come inside and we'll have you your magic address in a heartbeat."

She led him up the iron stairs into the long, narrow shop. Costumes blanketed every inch of wall space. These included the standard assortment of Halloween and disguise-party fare—clusters of Elvis masks, Che Guevara masks, masks of pop-culture figures whom Arnold didn't recognize—but also several full sets of medieval armour and a phalanx of vintage nativity outfits. Above the counter hung sizeable photographs of each Pope since Pius XII. There were the harried Paul VI, the genial John Paul I, a beaming John Paul II and a solemn Benedict XVI facing each other in an eternal game of good cop – bad cop. But the 'sisters' had reserved the place of honour for a larger portrait of John XXIII blessing Jackie Onassis. Beneath the pontiff, they'd written: GOOD POPE JOHN, ONE OF US. What exactly they meant by this, whether to suggest that the late Cardinal Roncalli had possessed the common touch, or had worn women's clothes, wasn't clear. In addition to the papal gallery, there were posters of Mother Theresa, and St. Francis, and Tony Curtis and Jack Lemmon in *Some Like It Hot.* A stringy spider plant hung beside the cash register. The internet terminals, which had been added one-by-one over the course of a decade, ran along both of the side walls. None of the computers matched. Gladys settled down in front of the newest model and asked for Cassandra's full name.

"What kind of name is Cassandra?" asked Gladys.

"It's Trojan," answered Arnold.

The transvestite plugged the name into the machine. "It's a gorgeous name. I thought it might be from the Caribbean."

"It means, she who entangles men," said Arnold.

Gladys stopped typing. "Well, it looks like she does her entangling in Brooklyn." She printed the address on a post-it note. "I'll admit you've peaked my curiosity, Mr.

Brinkman. I thought you were already spoken for."

"Purely business," Arnold answered—too defensively. "But please don't tell anyone I asked you. Not even Father Stan."

"I can't keep a secret from Anabelle."

"Of course not. But nobody else," said Arnold.

"Discretion is one of my two virtues," Gladys assured him. "My other virtue is indiscretion."

"I owe you," he answered.

Arnold examined the address, penned in the daintiest script. He was about to ask the old transvestite for a map—*the girl lived in Brooklyn, for Chrissake!*—when he heard the first wail of sirens. They were at a distance, but approaching. In a matter of minutes, they'd have the nursery encircled. If Arnold started running now, he could easily avoid that particular vice—but how to get to Brooklyn without being recognized? Every toddler old enough to speak could pick the Tongue Terrorist out of a line-up. Mickey Mouse's face was less familiar. Which meant he'd have to travel by night, possibly through underground sewers, or——. That's when he stumbled upon his plan B.

"Say, Gladys," he said. "I think I'd like to buy a mask."

"You're better off waiting until the autumn stock comes in. There's a much wider selection and the rubber will be fresher."

Arnold scanned the walls. "I need something now. As quickly as possible."

"Well, let's see. First, I'll have to measure your head."

"I don't have time for that. How about one of those pirate masks?"

"It will only take a moment," said Gladys. She shuffled over to a cabinet and returned with a tape measure. "All of our costumes are custom fit."

"Don't you have anything one-size-fits-all?"

"Heavens, no!" retorted Gladys. "My 'sister' would sooner die."

She wrapped the measuring tape around Arnold's skull and whistled. "Twenty-six inches!"

"Is that good or bad?" asked Arnold.

He'd never given much thought to the size of his cranium.

"That's enormous. It's the equivalent of a size nine hat." She returned the tape measure to its drawer. "I don't know if we have much in that size."

"Please, Gladys. Before the cops get here."

The old transvestite ducked into a walk-in closet. She reappeared several minutes later with two masks. "I'm afraid your options are limited. It's either going to be Mr. Nixon or Mr. Reagan—but Mr. Reagan is only a size twenty five and seven-eighths. He may chafe a bit around the ears."

"You really don't have anything else?"

"You're lucky we have these, Mr. Brinkman. We generally don't stock anything over a size twenty-four."

"Okay. I guess you have what you have. Which do you think is less conspicuous?"

Gladys held one palm skyward in a half shrug. "We sell ten times as many Nixons. Even when he was President, we didn't sell many Reagans."

Arnold held each mask in one hand. He suspected he'd get a harder time for wandering around Greenwich Village disguised as the cowboy. People still despised Reagan in downtown New York. *He despised Reagan.* Nixon's offences had been so long in this past, so much part of a different era that he now seemed more like some lovable but bigoted uncle you tolerated at Christmas and Thanksgiving.

He drew the rubber mask over his head. It was tight-fitting and very warm. Arnold's nostrils filled with a pungent, synthetic aroma that had to be carcinogenic—and with his luck, he feared he might develop an acute-onset carcinoma of the nose. But his choices, it appeared, were either rubberized air or iron shackles.

"So tonight, to you, the great silent majority of my fellow Americans," Arnold said in his best Nixonian voice. "I ask for your support." He held up his fingers on both hands in a pair of victory signs.

Gladys sighed. Outside, the sirens rose in intensity.

"That bad?" he asked.

"You look fine. It's me that needs the help. I honestly can't remember whether or not Reagan and Nixon ran against each other."

Arnold passed the morning rambling about the city. He left the Village quickly, afraid his acquaintances might recognize his gait, and squandered a good deal of time sampling mushrooms on the Great Lawn of Central Park. In the afternoon, he rode the subway up to the Bronx and strolled about the Botanical Gardens. The poppies and yarrow were just starting to bloom—and when he was certain nobody was looking, he snacked on a bouquet of dogbane. Although he was wearing his Nixon mask, nobody paid him very much attention. That was one of the great pleasures of New York City;; he could have wandered around the streets in his bathrobe and slippers, like one of those mob bosses feigning insanity, and most people wouldn't have batted an eye. It wasn't the "live and let live" spirit you might find in Alaska or the Mountain West. He'd learned that the hard way at the baseball game. It was more of a collective immunity to the unusual, an acceptance that in a city of eight million people, many of them refugees from various forms of orthodoxy and tradition, one was bound to run across one's share of nutcases. Passers-by relegated Arnold into that category—and thought of him no further. Only in an Italian section of the Bronx, where he'd gone for a cup of espresso, did his costume draw anything other than amusement. A retired Sicilian shoemaker buttonholed the botanist outside a café and explained why he'd voted for Nixon: in '60, '68, '72, and as a write-in candidate in '76. "You stand up for what you believe in these days and everybody comes down on you," complained the pudgy, red-faced man. "They gave Nixon a raw deal. Just like Mussolini."

He finally set out for Brooklyn in the early evening. There was no point in showing up at the girl's place any sooner—she'd still be at work, churning up propaganda for the neo-Trotskyites, and he might appear suspicious if he spent too much time hanging around outside her building. On the way, he ducked into an appliance shop and watched the network news on the floor-model televisions. The war was still the lead story, but his disappearance was a solid number two. A Deputy Attorney General stood at a podium in Washington and outlined a series of charges that Arnold would face, noting soberly that none of these offenses made the botanist eligible for the death penalty. The Justice Department was offering a $50,000 reward for information leading to Arnold's capture; Spotty Spitford's organization had sweetened the pot with $25,000 of its own. The bank of televisions showed footage of Gilbert Card, standing on the steps of Arnold's townhouse, pledging his friend a vigorous defence if he turned himself in. Even the mayor weighed in with a somewhat diplomatic statement about the importance of maintaining public order. Yet Arnold learned the most crucial information from the network's terrorism consultant, a retired Air Force colonel, who speculated on the ways in which the FBI was conducting its search. "They're probably tracing his electronic footprints," said the gravelly-voice officer. "Credit cards, calling cards, ATMs. When he runs out of money, he'll turn to plastic. Then it's just a matter of time." Up until that moment, it hadn't even crossed Arnold's mind that he could be traced through his bank cards. He checked his billfold. Less than eighty dollars. Eighty dollars wouldn't go very far in New York City—not even in the outer boroughs. That meant another long subway ride over the East River. Cab fare was out of the question.

He arrived in Brooklyn after dark. The girl lived in a converted warehouse several blocks from the waterfront in what had once been a Polish-Ukrainian neighbourhood. According to an exhibit on the subway platform, these early inhabitants still maintained a foothold through nearly a dozen churches—half-Catholic, half-Orthodox—including one that offered Latin masses and the old liturgy. There were also diners serving up blintzes and kielbasa, a twenty-four hour "borscht bar" internationally renowned for its cabbage rolls, a pan-Slavic credit union, and a handful of merchants who advertised in Cyrillic script. But the area had turned over three times since the initial influx of Eastern Europeans—first Dominicans arrived in the '80s, then Bangladeshis and Egyptians in the '90s, and now recent graduates poured in from the liberal arts colleges of New England. The panels in the exhibit generously referred to these underemployed twenty-somethings as "up-and-coming writers and artists." Cassandra's building showcased the community's ethnic mix. The ground floor housed an Iranian furniture wholesaler, a Ghanaian hair-braider and a Moroccan butcher shop, but out front a team of Hispanic men were examining the engine of a battered Pontiac, and across the street a portly Black woman was hanging laundry on a clothesline. Arnold was relieved that the girl's name was the only one on her mailbox. No roommate. No live-in boyfriend. Yet he felt genuinely nervous, as jittery as a teenager anticipating a date, as he pushed the girl's buzzer.

"Come on up," called the voice through the intercom. The door unlatched electronically and Arnold entered. He found himself in a small vestibule that smelled pungently of urine and cleanser. A cracked mirror hung opposite a teapoy stacked with unwanted advertising circulars. The staircase was narrow and highly uneven, its wooden steps and canvas-draped railing practically screaming "Fire Trap!" Arnold wondered which was preferable: Life behind bars or death by burning? The botanist knocked on the girl's door. It opened instantly and the girl's eyes appeared through the crack.

"What do you want?" she asked sharply. A dog snarled behind her.

That was when Arnold realized he was still wearing his mask. "Give me a second here," he said. He pulled the disguise over his head—letting his face breathe for the first time in hours.

"Oh, it's you," said Cassandra. "The intercom's gone haywire. I can speak out, but I can't hear anything at this end. Some good that does. I thought you might be some sort of push-in rapist with a Watergate fetish."

"I'm not nearly that imaginative."

She closed the door to unlatch the chain and then opened it again all the way. "You've really become something of a celebrity since last time I saw you."

"Lucky me. Can I come in before somebody sees me?"

The girl looked him over. She was wearing a button-down men's shirt and loose-fitting jeans. "Okay, you can come in," she agreed. "But just for a minute."

She stepped aside and Arnold found himself in a studio apartment that reminded him of a college dormitory room. Cardboard bookshelves lined two of the walls, while a pink dresser and a futon ran along the third. One window sill supported a jar of seashells and a stunted hedgehog cactus; a snug kitchenette separated from the main room by a waist-high plaster divider. Above the futon hung a reproduction of Wyeth's "Christina's World"—that haunting image of the crippled farm girl dragging her broken body across a field. This was more-or-less how Arnold had felt since his encounter with Spotty Spitford. On the futon, its head cocked alert, sat a massive

German shepherd.

Arnold smiled at the dog. The animal growled back. "It's alright, honey," soothed Cassandra. "It's just an old friend of mine." The girl shut the door behind her. She settled onto the mattress and scratched the beast behind her ears. "Son of a President's not used to visitors, are you girl?" she explained.

"Son of a President?" asked Arnold.

"Because in America, even the son of a President can grow up to be President. And if we can elect this guy, why not a German shepherd?" Cassandra kissed the dog on the top of its wet nose. "But you'll have to forgive her. She's a bit overprotective."

"That's good to know," said Arnold. "If I ever open a prisoner-of-war camp, I'll be sure to call you."

The girl scrunched up her face at him and stuck out her tongue. She retrieved a beer from the table, but didn't offer Arnold anything to drink. "So what have I done to deserve such an honour?" she asked. "You know it's not every day I get a visit from a notorious criminal."

Arnold looked around the room. There were no chairs. He didn't dare sit on the futon without permission. Instead, he walked to the window and gazed down at the stone courtyard. Ailanthus trees poked through the cracks in the pavement. On the fire escape sat a long, low trough full of compost in various stages of decay. It let off an earthy, but not unpleasant scent. He reflected that if he were ever to cheat on Judith—which, of course, he wouldn't—it would have to be with a woman who composted her biodegradable waste.

"I need a place to stay," he said. "Just for a few days."

"Until you figure out how to flee the country?"

Arnold nodded. "Something like that."

"I was just discussing you with my boss," said Cassandra. "I was saying how ironic it is that it's easy for terrorists to get into the country, but it's a million times harder for them to get out."

"I'm *not* a terrorist. Spitford provoked me."

"*I know that,*" retorted Cassandra. "I'm on your side, remember."

"So you'll let me stay?"

The girl smiled at him sympathetically. "Let me see…." she said. "No."

"No?"

"You screwed me over completely. It was totally humiliating to tell my boss that you'd backed out on our interview. And then you didn't answer my phone calls for, like, three days. And now you want to crash at my place?"

She'd folded her arms across her chest. Arnold couldn't tell if she was bluffing.

"I'm sorry I didn't call you back. It can be a bit distracting when you're being harassed by Black Nazis."

"Whatever. I'm not risking prison for harbouring a terrorism suspect. I'm an idiot even to let you be here. If

I had any common sense, I'd turn you in for the reward money."

"You wouldn't?"

"No, I wouldn't. But you have to go."

This wasn't going according to plan. It hadn't crossed Arnold's mind the girl might actually turn him down, but she sounded sincere.

"I was one hundred percent in the wrong about the interview," he said. "I promise I'll make it up to you. Why don't we do another interview?"

"And like what am I supposed to do with it? If I print it, I'm basically admitting I've been talking to the most wanted fugitive in the country. I'm not looking to be the next Judith Mitchell."

"They let her out eventually."

"Because she was really on their side. Screwing over Valerie Plame is not the same thing as screwing over God and apple pie."

"You can print it as soon as I leave. You can say you interviewed me last week. You *were* at my office....You even have witnesses."

The girl appeared genuinely torn—not nearly as enthusiastic as he expected. Her thick eyebrows came together in absorbed reflection. Then she stood up suddenly, crossed over to the bureau and retrieved a tape recorder from the upper drawer. "Fine, you can stay," she said. "But a couple of days, tops. So don't get too comfortable."

"Deal," he agreed.

"And we do the interview right now," she added. "I'm not trusting you and any farther than I can kick you."

"Throw you. The expression is 'farther than I can throw you.'"

"Fuck off. You say things your way and I say things my way. It's called evolution."

Arnold had been wandering the city all day wearing a hot rubber mask. He was thirsty. His calves ached. His hair felt heavy and matted. The last thing he wanted at the moment was an argument about linguistics. Or almost the last thing. The only thing he wanted less was a grilling on complex political issues.

"Can I at least take a shower—?"

"Now," snapped Cassandra. "Before you screw me over again."

"Once bitten, twice shy," mused Arnold.

"I don't let myself get bitten," retorted the girl. "And I'm never shy."

"I didn't mean anything...." he said—but it wasn't worth apologizing.

She lit a clove cigarette and made room for him on the futon. "Have a seat," she said, patting the mattress. "I don't get bitten, but I also don't bite."

"How about the dog?" asked Arnold.

"Son of a President? She only bites when I tell her to," answered the girl.

"How reassuring," he muttered—but he settled hesitantly onto the corner of the bed.

Cassandra poked her head into a mini-fridge in the corner. "You want a beer before we start?"

"No thanks. I put my foot in my mouth enough when I'm sober."

"Suit yourself."

She returned to the futon with one beer and took a swig. Then she turned over the cassette and pressed the record button.

"Interview with Arnold Brinkman. Monday, May 21," the girl said into the machine. It was actually Friday, May 25. "So, Mr. Brinkman," she continued, "Can you tell me how this all came about? Was it something you'd been planning for a long time or was it a spontaneous protest?"

Arnold took a deep breath. "I'd been planning it for a long time," he said. "I've been terribly disturbed by the events of the last four years....of American's increasingly bullying role on the world stage...and this was my way of showing my opposition." Total bullshit—but exactly what the readers of the *Daily Vanguard* wanted to hear. Not a word about the Scottsboro Boys or Sacco & Vanzetti. "I'm a bit surprised at how much publicity I've inspired. Surprised, but also pleased. It's because I love America—with all of my heart—that it pains me to see her drift so far astray."

The girl grinned. She flashed him a thumbs-up. "So

the war must have been a major motivating factor for you?"

"How couldn't it be?" answered Arnold. "I have such deep respect and admiration for our boys—and girls—in uniform. But the flag no longer belongs to ordinary patriotic citizens like them. It's being held hostage by the military-industrial complex, by Big Oil, by a right-wing conspiracy of greed. That's why I wouldn't stand up—not to dishonour the flag, but to honour the principles it stands for."

He mouthed the word "bullshit" at Cassandra. She glared back at him.

"And how does your wife feel about your one-man protest?"

Arnold squeezed and un-squeezed his fist, letting the knuckles crack. "Judith is a very independent-minded woman," he said. "So I'm very reluctant to speak for her.... But I do know that she's also deeply troubled by the gross injustices perpetrated in the name of the American flag."

"Injustices," prodded Cassandra. "Would you say atrocities?"

"Sure," agreed Arnold. "Atrocities. Carnage. Mayhem. You can trace it all back to the massacre of the Native Americans."

The girl pounded her fist on the railing of the futon.

"I'm just saying...."

"—That the United States is currently committing atrocities abroad."

Arnold cupped his fist in his palm. "Yeah. I guess I'm saying that."

"Good," answered Cassandra. She shut off the machine. "You pass."

"With flying colours?"

"In a manner of speaking. I wish I could ask you about that manager of yours, but then they'd know I did the interview after his arrest."

"What arrest?"

"The feds finally caught up with him."

"What the hell are you talking about?"

"You really don't know, do you? That office manager of yours. Sambarino—?

"Zambrano. Willie Zambrano."

"That's him. Well he's actually Willie Vargas. As in: Willie Vargas, Castro's man in Caracas. He blew up a Peruvian jetliner in the early 60s."

"Who told you that?"

"Nobody fucking *told* me. I heard it on the radio on the way home."

"Willie? Apolitical Willie?"

The girl took another swig of beer. "I can't tell if you really didn't know or if you're snowing me. But in any case, it's amazing what secrets people have. Right now, we're doing a story on a big name conservative politico—I can't tell you his name—who has a second family living in Florida. I mean children, grandchildren. He's even served on the P.T.A. down there a number of years ago. His wife in New York doesn't have a fucking clue."

"But you're going to do her a favour and tell her."

Cassandra shrugged. "We just report the news. We don't *make* the news." She hoisted her bare feet onto the bed and settled into the lotus position. "Everybody's pretty screwed up, when you get right down to it. You can live with someone your entire life and not know the first thing about him."

"I can't believe this. Willie doesn't have a political bone in his body. He doesn't even vote."

"Maybe he reformed," answered Cassandra. "Not that it will do him much good now. He'll probably face a firing squad in Peru."

"You think?"

"This administration's taken such a tough line on terrorism, they don't exactly have much wiggle room. If he's lucky, he may get a straw pallet next to Lori Berenson. In my humble opinion, he's probably better off being shot." The girl set her empty beer bottle on the window sill. She retrieved another pair of beers from the refrigerator and passed one to Arnold. "I'm sure he's glad you generated all this publicity for him. If not for your tongue antics, they'd never have caught him."

"I'm aware of that."

"I've got to hand it to you, Mr. Foot-in-your-Mother," said the girl. "It's starting to look like a conspiracy."

"What do you mean?"

"You don't think it strikes anyone as a bit weird that a wanted terrorist has been employing another wanted terrorist for the last thirty years....I bet they'll sock you with a conspiracy charge too."

"Shit," said Arnold. "Shit. Shit. Shit."

"You're not good luck, are you?" asked the girl. "But you *are* famous. The Bare-Ass bandit abducted two federal judges this afternoon and ran off with their robes, but not before making them sing *We are teapots, short and stout* stark-naked in a five-star restaurant, and you're still the lead story on the news. Or you and Willie and the rest of your henchmen."

"I'm starting to feel like Job," said Arnold.

"You're starting to look like Job too," said the girl. "You might want to think about shaving. And, for what it's worth, you stink."

"Thanks. Anything else?"

The girl took one of the pillows from the futon and handed it to him. "You sleep on the floor," she said. "You also *wake up* on the floor."

"I wake up on the floor," he repeated.

It hadn't crossed his mind that he would wake up anywhere else. But something in her tone of voice suggested that *she* had been debating other possibilities, so much so that he kept waiting for her to add the words: "For now." She didn't. Instead, she took a shower while Arnold listened to the news on the radio. The media was indeed speculating that he'd conspired to cover up Willie's past. They'd raised the bounty on his head to $125,000. That meant he was worth two school teachers, five convenience store clerks. As a fugitive, this terrified him. As a taxpayer, it raised his gall. Who in hell's name would pay that kind of money to apprehend an unpatriotic botanist? He turned off the radio and tried to find a comfortable position on the floor. In the morning, after she'd gone to work, he'd shower and shave at his leisure.

When Cassandra emerged from the bathroom, she was wearing only an apricot towel. A second towel was wrapped around her hair. Arnold tried to keep his gaze off her bare, dripping thighs. This was particularly difficult as she rose on her toes to pull shut the heavy curtains, letting the towel inch up her body.

"It's good for your back," she said.

"What is?"

"Sleeping on the floor."

Arnold grunted. By that logic, he might as well sleep on a bed of nails—they'd be good for his character. He looked up at the dog, still perched on the futon. The animal glowered at him as though preparing to pounce.

"He's not going to maul me in my sleep, is he?"

Cassandra laughed. "He is a *she.* And she'll leave you alone—as long as you stay on the floor."

"But *she* gets to sleep on the bed," observed Arnold.

"That seems fair."

"Do you know why she gets to sleep on the bed? Because I trust her."

Then Cassandra flipped off the lights and the room went black—but not before the girl winked at Arnold. Or at least he thought she'd winked at him. It had happened so fast, he couldn't be certain.

CHAPTER 8

Arnold woke the following morning to the scent of wet dog. The German shepherd, covered in lather, was tracking suds around the apartment. Great balls of foam covered its pointy ears. When the animal noticed that Arnold was moving, she lunged at him and rubbed her wet coat across his face.

"We went for a walk," the girl explained. "Son of a President found a skunk."

Cassandra grabbed hold of Son of a President and pulled the dog toward the bath. The sound of splashing water soon filled the apartment. Here was yet another advantage of Manhattan that he and Judith had taken for granted: You didn't have to worry about skunks. Or rabbits. Or woodchucks. In contrast, Brooklyn was a jungle of herbivorous pests just waiting to sink their canines into burgeoning flowers.

Arnold wiped the soapy dog-froth from his lips. "You need ketchup."

"What?"

"Don't waste your time with soap or shampoo. Cold water and ketchup works wonders."

"Are you for real?"

"I had a Fulbright to Italy a couple of years ago. I came up with the ambitious notion that I was going to do for tomatoes what George Washington Carver did for peanuts." Arnold stood up and stretched; his muscles ached from sleeping without a blanket on the cold floorboards. "Dried tomato paste is also an excellent adhesive. Not to mention a very efficient source of automotive fuel. If I ever find a way to show my face in public again, I'd love to market a tomato-powered car."

"You call that ambitious?" answered the girl. "I call that wacko."

She shut the water off in the bathroom and set about preparing breakfast. It struck Arnold how easily they'd settled into a domestic routine—as though they were a married couple. As peculiar as it must be for this girl to have a stranger twice her age sleeping on her floor, and a fugitive on top of that, she acted as though it were nothing out of the ordinary. Arnold glanced at his watch. It wasn't yet six o'clock. When he pulled open the heavy damask curtains, the sky was still grey.

"I like to get up my ass up early," said the girl. "Otherwise you lose half the day."

Cassandra sliced a mango with a pocket knife and ate a sliver directly off the blade—a sin for which Arnold's great-grandmother, The Baroness, had once fed him castor oil. Then the girl handed a morsel to Arnold. The fruit tasted perfectly sweet. For their main course, Cassandra prepared granola and blueberry pancakes—a far cry above the botanist's standard fare of orange juice and toast. It was impossible to imagine Judith labouring over a frying pan early in the morning unless she were arranging a still life. He could never forget the first meal his wife had cooked for him. She'd baked eggplant lasagne, but she'd forgotten to boil the pasta before she put it in the oven. The end-product had displayed the consistency of birch bark. Judith had learned her way around the kitchen over the last thirty years, but she was a one-meal-a-day chef—and that meal was dinner. So it was a treat it was to wake up in an apartment that smelled of sizzling butter. As soon as he made the comparison, though, the botanist hated himself for it. How could you weigh three decades of companionship against a stack of organic flapjacks? Besides, he'd derived more pleasure from cracking the birch-bark lasagne with Judith than he ever could from a five-star meal. Arnold's thoughts drifted to his life with Judith, to the memory of one morning when he'd ducked out of a symposium on "Environmentalism & Diet" to meet his wife for breakfast at McDonalds, not because they enjoyed fast food—they probably ate it a total of two or three times in thirty years—but because sometimes a healthy serving of hypocrisy was just what the doctor ordered. When Arnold looked up from his reminiscences, the girl was examining him intensely.

"So, Professor Tomato Cars," she asked. "How exactly do you intend to go about showing your face in public again?"

"I'm working on that."

"The way I see it," continued the girl. "You've got three choices."

"Do I now?"

"Yes, you do. You want know what they are?"

Her matter-of-fact tone struck Arnold as smug. "Enlighten me," he said.

"First, you can turn yourself in right now and face the firing squad. Or death by hanging. Or whatever it is they do to accused terrorists these days. Maybe they'll even tear your tongue out as a symbolic gesture—a warning to other would-be traitors."

"Sound like a great choice to me."

"It wouldn't be my top choice," said the girl, feeding batter scraps to the dog while she spoke. "But at least it would all be over with. I imagine they'd put you out of your misery pretty damn quick."

"Or subject me to slow torture. What's my second choice?"

"You could try to escape. While you were sleeping, I printed out a list of countries that don't have extradition treaties with the United States. You actually have quite a selection. You could probably become a leading botanist in Uzbekistan or Kazakhstan or Tajikistan. Assuming they have plants in those places."

It amazed Arnold what odd prejudices ordinary people had about vegetation. How could you possible have a country without plants?

"The Uzbeks actually have a first-rate botanical garden in Tashkent," he observed. "Persimmons and Magolepian cherries come from the Caucasus."

"Well, I'll be damned," she mocked. "But I guess that's a good thing for you. There's only one problem with your escape to who-knows-where-istan plan."

"Getting there."

"Bingo," said the girl. She began clearing the plates. "So much for those leprous cherries."

"Magolepian cherries."

"Which leads us," the girl continued, "to choice three."

"I'm not going to like this, am I?"

Cassandra stacked the dishes on the drainage board. "You can lay low until the furore subsides," she suggested. "I don't mean for a few weeks. I mean years. Like the Weathermen or any of those Puerto Rican nationalists from the 1950s. When you eventually do poke your head out again, you'll still draw a prison sentence, but it will be much lighter—maybe a couple of years and a long parole."

"You're suggesting I go underground for years?"

"It's an option," said the girl. "It's an amusing one too, you have to admit. You're *so* not the sort of person who usually jumps to mind when people think about underground fugitives."

"What's that supposed to mean?" demanded Arnold.

He didn't relish the prospect of life on the lam—but that didn't mean he wasn't capable of it. Nobody had any business questioning his adequacy as an outlaw, at least not until he'd had a chance to show his mettle. "I'm more resourceful than you think," he insisted.

"Yeah, whatever. That's why you're crashing on my floor."

She sat down opposite him at the table and lit a cigarette. The smoke smelled both toxic and inviting. Arnold said nothing. It was amazing how easily this damn girl got under his skin.

"Can I ask you something?" asked the girl. "Off the record."

"That's a first."

"What I mean is, I'm not asking you for my article. But I *am* curious. Would you do it again?"

"You mean not stand up?"

"All of it. Not stand up. Stick out your tongue. Refuse to apologize."

Arnold hadn't really thought about this before—not in such explicit terms. He'd been too busy dealing with the consequences of his actions to consider the desirability of undoing them. Moreover, he sensed the girl was delving beyond the specific incident. She wasn't asking: 'Do you regret not standing up at the baseball game?' She was asking: 'Do you really think you can possibly make a difference?' That wasn't a fair question, because you could ask the same thing of almost anybody who defied the rules. The big rules. Arnold realized he might indeed be one of those rule-crushers, one of the rare few who are actually *part of history.* He might even have it in him to murder a lout like Spitford to make that happen. But he wasn't prepared to share these thoughts with his hostess.

"I really don't know what I'd do," he said. "My brain is a bit addled these days."

"Well, you'll have a long time to think about it," said the girl. "I should be home around six-thirty."

"Say hello to the Revolution for me," said Arnold.

The girl tossed her canvas bag over her shoulder. "By the way, I hope you weren't planning on wandering the neighbourhood in that mask of yours."

"Why not?"

"You've got to stay on top of things," answered the girl. "They've detained your two transvestite friends. There's a manhunt on for a fugitive in a costume."

"They've arrested Gladys and Anabelle?"

"Detained," said the girl. "As material witnesses. But they haven't specified what sort of costume—so it looks like they're keeping your secrets. For now."

"This is outrageous. They haven't done anything. Anabelle wasn't even awake...."

"The noose tightens," observed Cassandra. "Being friends with you comes with all sorts of advantages, doesn't it?"

Arnold thought of the two old 'sisters' being carted off in handcuffs and his entire body surged with anger.

"I totally have a death-wish for letting you stay here," added the girl. "If I had half a brain, I'd take the $125,000 and turn you in."

Cassandra was right: Arnold did have a lot of time to think about what had happened at the baseball game. During the initial phase of his captivity—for during the workday, when the girl was gone, her tiny, nearly plantless apartment did feel like a prison—Arnold thought principally of Judith. He wondered what his wife was doing, what she was thinking. In moments of weakness, he contemplated surreptitious ways to contact her. He could ask Cassandra to act as an emissary, at least to let Judith know that he was safe. Or he could have the girl post a letter for him. Or, if he felt particularly daring, he might even telephone the townhouse from a nearby payphone during the middle of the night. But all of these plans came with substantial risks. Moreover, he wasn't sure what he would say to Judith. She'd held a press conference two days after his disappearance, in which she begged him to return home. Gilbert Card had stood behind her, sober and erect. The pair didn't look at all like lovers—but looks meant nothing. Many couples who appeared happily married stood on the brink of divorce. Moreover, Judith was still Judith. She'd still want him to apologize and to raise a child. It was difficult to see the point of risking his neck for a conversation that would change nothing. Better to lay low. He reconsidered only once, when they arrested his wife as "an accessory after the fact," but the authorities quickly released her to home confinement, pending trial. Arnold doubted she'd ever face a jury. Or that the elderly transvestites would remain in custody much longer. This was just the police-version of the hard sell: They were harassing his loved ones in the hope of pressuring him into surrender.

Unfortunately, Guillermo's fate was another matter. The Venezuelan appeared on the front page of the *Times,* the morning after his arrest, wearing a restraining belt and an orange jump suit. He appeared wan and disoriented. On public radio, family members of the plane-crash victims expressed their relief and gratitude at his capture. The Cuban government issued a statement accusing the United States of a double-standard when it came to terrorism—but Havana offered nothing that might exonerate Arnold's office manager. Within days, he'd been turned over to the Peruvian authorities for trial. When Arnold heard the news, he sat on the fire escape and wept. He'd have done anything to help the Venezuelan—even have turned himself in—but, in this case, there was nothing to be done. Guillermo Zambrano *was* Willie Vargas. He *had* blown up all of those innocent people. Producing a fugitive botanist as a character witness wasn't going to do the poor man any good and the NPR story on the plane bombing had shaken Arnold. It crossed his mind that his friend had done something horrific, something that *did* deserve to be punished. Bonnie Card could say all she wanted about "one man's terrorism being another man's freedom-fighting," but at the end of the day, one hundred forty-two innocent people had died. That was the heart of the problem: every choice made sense from some vantage point. Like butchering Spitford. Several nights Arnold woke in a cold sweat, having dreamed that he was squeezing shut the clergyman's windpipe.

The botanist's first days at Cassandra's were marked by an intense interest in the world outside the apartment. Denied access to the city, he longed for its bustle. He suffered cravings for vegetarian paella and crepe suzette and oven-hot anchovy pizza from Sal & Joe's—in short, for anything that would be difficult to bring back to his isolated quarters. But what he longed for most was news, the details of the daily life that he'd abandoned. He sent the girl to check out the nursery, in the wake of Willie's deportation, and he'd suffered acutely when she reported that the Plant Centre had been closed indefinitely "Due to Unforeseen Circumstances." He endured another blow when Spitford announced a boycott of "All Things Brinkman," and several major retailers responded with immediate announcements that they were pulling his books from their shelves. Arnold stewed over this treachery and ranted about suing them from absentia. But then his entire "business empire"—as the media called it—was seized by the government. According to the F.B.I., their HAZMAT team had discovered traces of castor beans at Arnold's office. These plants were the principal ingredient in the bio-toxin ricin. The authorities described their find as "a weapons-grade cache" that "could be transformed into a mass poison in a matter of weeks." Which applied to all castor beans. And to every nursery and green grocer in the country that carried them. All through Arnold's childhood the Baroness had hand-made her own castor oil—and had tortured Arnold with its properties in the name of digestive health—but nobody had ever accused *her* of being a terrorist. "Next thing you know they'll brand me a terrorist for growing water lilies," he told Cassandra. "People can drown in water, you know."

As one afternoon drifted into another, all of these setbacks seemed increasingly abstract, as though they'd happened to someone else. Which wasn't so far from the truth. Arnold the Fugitive felt little connection to the happily married and successful entrepreneur who'd refused to stand up at a baseball game. Maybe this was a psychological necessity, a coping mechanism. Like the women who'd shared the nursing facility with his mother, for whom a few dingy corridors and a sterile recreation centre became an entire universe, Arnold grew more and more focused on his immediate surroundings: the apartment, the wall-to-wall books, the cramped courtyard where the superintendent's teensy Filipino wife, a mail-order bride, raised ornamental cabbages. That first day, as a gag, the girl bought him a bag of tomato seeds and a tray of soil, but he enjoyed the present so much that soon he was cultivating half a dozen tins of plantlets. Never have garden tomatoes been so carefully tended. His trove included beefsteaks, currants, plums, and a marvellous patch of cherry tomatoes that the dog accidentally kicked off the fire escape. Arnold's days were spent tending these plants, and reading from Cassandra's philosophy library, and, as the spring bled into summer, thinking about his relationship with his new roommate.

Cassandra Broward was, by any standard, an odd creature. The girl appeared to live an entirely hermetic existence. She didn't have one visitor during Arnold's first two weeks in the apartment: her only phone calls came from her boss at the *Vanguard*; once from a telemarketer pitching industrial carpet cleaner. Other than work, and the weekly chores of shopping and laundry, she didn't spend much time outside the tenement. It was possible that she'd altered her routine on account of Arnold's presence, but the botanist didn't think so. Her studio apartment lacked the postcard-dappled refrigerator and photo-clad bedside tables that suggested a network of kith and kin. No, she appeared to be on her own in the world. Yet what amazed Arnold was that the girl didn't seem to mind at all. She spent most of her evenings reading high-end philosophy—

Marx, Schopenhauer, Heidegger—or, later in the week, completing the *New York Times* crossword puzzle. There was no point in trying before Wednesday, she explained. The Monday and Tuesday puzzles were designed for halfwits—Judith had felt the same way. Arnold loved the first puzzles of the week because they were the only ones on which he could make any headway. He wondered how he kept falling for women who were gifted at word games. Because, in spite of himself, he was developing an unhealthy romantic attachment to his hostess. Arnold recalled an old expression: "Give a man a hammer and he will view all problems as nails." He told himself his feelings for Cassandra were of a similar nature—he liked her *because she was there.* 'Stockholm Syndrome'. But increasingly, he wasn't so sure that was all there was to it….

One night, after supper, Arnold asked her about her social life. They were sitting on the fire escape, between the tomato trays and the compost bin, enjoying a fine cool mist that had settled over the city. Cassandra had lit a handful of scented candles, perfuming the night with a pleasant, wax-tinged aroma. Her cigarette smoke also hung in the damp air. The shades were drawn in the opposite apartment, but it didn't matter, because the girl had draped towels over the upper steps and railing to create a protective screen for Arnold. He took a drag from Cassandra's cigarette—Judith would have killed him—and watched the girl cobbling together a response.

"I don't have a social life," she finally said.

"That's my point," answered Arnold. "Why not?"

She reclaimed her cigarette. "Why?"

Her response wasn't what the botanist had expected. "Most girls your age like to hang out with friends. Maybe even go on dates." He regretted the words as soon as they left his mouth—they sounded so *parental*—but the girl didn't appear to mind.

"I'm not most girls my age."

"I don't understand," Arnold pressed. "Don't you get…lonely?"

Arnold had been in her apartment for only ten days and already *he* felt lonely. He didn't confess this, of course, because he didn't want to appear weak.

"I guess I'm a Calvinist at heart. That sounds totally pretentious, doesn't it? But it's true," answered the girl. She took a deep drag on her cigarette. "The way I see it, life is going to give you what it's going to give you—and there's not a fucking thing you can do about it. If someone wants to be my friend, I'm glad to be friends. But I *so* don't see the point of going out and trying to make friends. Take you, for instance. I'm fine hanging out with you because you showed up. On the other hand, I'm not going to put up signs around the neighbourhood advertising for fugitives to crash on my floor."

"That's extremely passive, don't you think?"

"But I don't mind, really," said the girl. "The pathetic

truth of the matter is that most people don't have any friends once they reach a certain age. Sure, they make friends in high school or college—but then they give them up when they have children. So why bother putting in all that effort when you end up right where you started?"

"Why bother waking up in the morning when you eventually end up dead?"

"I *like* waking up in the morning," retorted Cassandra. "I don't care about friends."

Arnold gazed up at the orange-tinted sky of Brooklyn. He could make out one solitary star pulsing through the glow. Or maybe it was a planet.

"I know you don't believe me," continued the girl. "But it's true. Socializing is just not my thing. I've always been like this, even before my parents died." The elder Browards had owned a seafood restaurant; they'd died of smoke inhalation, during an electrical fire, while Cassandra was in college. "Your problem is that it *is* your thing—for people like you, your whole life is about socializing. Dinner parties and cocktail parties and all that bullshit. That's how you convince yourself that you matter. I bet you go to twenty weddings a year, every time you've got a friend whose kid gets married, and every time, you're bored out of your fucking skulls. Right? But even though you don't actually like all that social bullshit, you still can't handle that someone else—someone like me—doesn't want to buy into it."

She was at least partially right. Arnold did measure much of his own success in terms of his reception by others. He cared deeply whether people liked him—and the more people who liked him, the better. At least with regard to people of his own class and values, of course, not the over-breeding troglodytes one brushed elbows with at sporting events.

"I do value the approval of other people," he conceded. "But I *can* understand why one wouldn't....I guess."

"No, you can't," answered the girl. "But that's okay."

Arnold wondered precisely what she'd meant by "okay": "Okay" for a stranger or "okay" for a companion. He spotted a moth circling one of the candles. It was a large, russet-coloured gypsy moth of the defoliating variety—the sworn enemy of hardwoods everywhere. Arnold usually felt an obligation to destroy these creatures, for the sake of the city's sweetgums and alders, but he was afraid the girl might not approve, so he watched the insect's orbit indecisively.

"Any other burning questions?" she asked. "I don't want you to think I keep secrets."

"Well....," stammered Arnold. "You don't happened to have a boyfriend, do you...? Or a girlfriend?"

The girl grinned. "I happen to like men, if that's what you're asking. And no, I don't have one."

"Do you want one?"

"Of course I want one. Who doesn't? But most of the men I meet are sub-par." The girl laughed to herself. "Okay, *all* of the men I meet are sub-par."

"*All* of them?"

"More or less. When I was eleven, and we lived outside Miami, I was madly in love with an Indian guy in his twenties who sold cotton candy at the amusement park. Not that I knew him—but I could tell he was the sort of guy I'd like. He had the longest straight black hair and he used to sing while he worked. American show tunes. But eleven-year-old girls aren't supposed to fall in love. At least not in this country. If I'd lived in Europe, I might have ended up married to him."

"Are you making fun of me?" asked Arnold.

"I'm dead serious. But I don't usually tell this to people. It tends to make them uncomfortable." The girl stubbed out her cigarette. "Most people have strange hang-ups about age and sexuality."

This was just priceless. He'd set out to discover whether the girl might have a crush on him and they were going to end up discussing the ethics of paedophilia. It was hard to think of a less romantic subject. Besides, this was one of those areas where rational thought and philosophical discourse didn't do one much good. He'd heard Bonnie Card go on for hours about how child molesters were actually victims of a social structure that unfairly stigmatized sex with toddlers—targeted as unreasonably as homosexuals had once been—but Bonnie's conclusion, namely that we ought to live in an alternative universe where young children were taught to enjoy sex, including with adults, *did* leave him nauseous. *And he didn't even like children.*

"I'm making *you* uncomfortable," said the girl. "I can tell."

"No, you're not," lied Arnold. "I was just thinking... So what exactly are you saying? That age shouldn't be a factor in romantic relationships?"

"Oh, no. I wasn't talking about that at all. What I meant to say was that we make a mistake when we deny the sexuality of children. Sure, we want to protect young kids from violence and exploitation....But it isn't always like that."

This wasn't exactly romantic encouragement. Arnold watched the moth as its wings caught the edge of the flame and ignited.

"You look so unhappy," said Cassandra. "Cheer up. I have a surprise for you."

Arnold's spirits rose instantly. "What sort of surprise?"

"I can't tell you yet. I'm sworn to secrecy. But it will happen soon, and you're going to like it a lot."

"Can I have a hint?"

She squeezed her lips together and shook her head vigorously. He asked again several hours later—and once more the next morning—but no matter how hard he pressed her for her secret, she wouldn't reveal it.

"If I told you," she taunted, "then it wouldn't be a secret."

Several days later, while scanning Cassandra's bookshelves for any volume less demanding that the dog-eared copy of Habermas's *The Theory of Communicative Action* that lay on the girl's nightstand, Arnold stumbled across a hard-cover edition of *Please Do Eat the Daylilies.* He was impressed, at first. His readership tended to be older and midwestern—porcine, heartland women who had both pounds and flowers to spare. But then he recalled that the girl had once interviewed him at NYU. She'd probably picked up the cookbook as part of her advance research. The collection of recipes was now nearly twenty-five years old and in its eleventh printing—although Spitford's boycott probably wasn't doing much for sales. Arnold leafed through the yellowed pages of the old volume: daffodil salads, magnolias au gratin, two different recipes for hollyhock pie. He'd nearly forgotten how much fun it had been concocting these unlikely formulas. There had been a recklessness to it, an abandon—not so different from riding a motorcycle. That night, after Cassandra whipped up a first-rate lobster bisque, Arnold volunteered to take over the dinner duties for a few days.

"My cooking's not good enough?" demanded

the girl.

"Your cooking is spectacular," answered Arnold. "But I'm the one with hours of time to kill, in case you've forgotten."

"Does that mean we're eating grass from now on?" Cassandra snickered.

"You know, for a communist, you're awfully elitist when it comes to food."

"I'm *not* a communist," retorted the girl. "I'm a journalist. I'd write for the *Gestapo Press* if they offered me a lead story."

"You would, wouldn't you?" mused Arnold. That admission made the girl all the more alluring, because amorality was one step above idealism among feminine charms. "And yes, we will eat grass. And daisies. And sweet-william. But I think I'll start us off tomorrow with a warm spiderwort soup."

The girl squeezed lemon onto her lobster. "Spiderwort. Yummy."

"What I'll need from you," he added, "is a half-pound of spiderwort."

He retrieved a yellow notepad from beside the telephone and drew a picture of the heart-shaped violet flowers. Then he explained where in Prospect Park she was likely to find them. "You might as well pick up some bastard toadflax too," he decided. "Toadflax makes excellent seasoning."

After that, Arnold took over the kitchenette. He sent the girl scavenging the city for honeysuckle, bergamot, and trumpet-creeper. These he transformed, with the help of some birchbark and water, into a tepid pink broth that tasted like chicken. He made mock-veal from elecampane and mock-ham from climbing buckwheat stems. On Cassandra's twenty-third birthday, they celebrated with a pie made of strawberries, coconut cream and three-toothed cinquefoil leaves. Their new culinary life was not without mishaps, as when the girl accidentally brought home a poisonous species of buttercup. And Arnold didn't risk having her hunt for mushrooms, though he would have loved to add an umami flavour to their meals. Yet once he got the hang of floral cooking again—it had been several years since his last experimental foray into the kitchen—they ate better than any food critic. He made a conscious effort to impress his roommate. She was supporting him, after all. He'd long since turned over the last of his eighty dollars. The least he could do was send the girl to bed on a full and satisfied stomach. This meant that each night Arnold raised the ante: He fashioned pizzas from mullein and gentian stalks, clover-based yoghurts, a coneflower chop-suey. The lobster bisque that he concocted from nineteen varieties of wildflowers was just at flavourful as the one she'd prepared from shellfish—only cheaper and healthier. Unlike lobsters, most wildflowers came free of charge. The entire experience was empowering for the botanist. He derived the sort of pleasure that he imagined more rugged men might find in shooting a moose or erecting a wooden deck. How many other men in New York could fashion a four course meal for the cost of two hours electrical current and a pot of boiling water? Certainly not Ira Taylor or Spotty Spitford, Arnold thought.

Arnold was in the process of preparing one of his delicacies, a coleus casserole, when Cassandra returned home from work at the end of the week. Her cargo pants were rolled up at the bottoms, exposing an alluring pink ankle bracelet. She'd arranged her hair into intricate cornbraids. In contrast, Arnold was wearing a pink checkered apron and a pair or well-gnawed slippers. "I got a head start on dinner," he announced.

"I like the apron," she said. "Very becoming."

"I stole it off one of your neighbour's laundry lines, the tubby fundamentalist with the blotchy skin," said Arnold. "She'll probably think it was an evil spirit."

This particular neighbour, who Arnold knew only from sight, sold evangelical tracts from a folding table on the sidewalk. Her fire escape, opposite Cassandra's, contained the desiccated remains of what had once been a philodendron. Arnold held against her the double sins of religion and vegecide.

Cassandra frowned. "Don't mess with the other tenants," she said. "I have to live here after you leave."

That was the first the girl had ever said about

Arnold's leaving, at least since the evening of his arrival, and it caught the botanist off guard. He'd begun to believe he was welcome to stay indefinitely. The girl must have seen the alarm on his face, because she smiled in amusement. "Don't worry, I'm not throwing you out," she said. "At least, not yet. I'm actually getting used to you. But absolutely no more screwing with Mrs. Poxly's laundry. Or anybody else's laundry, for that matter. If you want women's clothes, you can buy them yourself."

"Yes, ma'am," said Arnold, relieved.

The girl reached into her canvas bag and produced a bottle of red wine. "Besides," she said. "Tonight, we're celebrating."

"What's there to celebrate? My one week anniversary in hiding?"

"Better than that," she answered. "Have you seen the paper yet?"

"No, I listened to the news at lunchtime."

She uncorked the wine bottle with a dull pop. "Radio is a second-rate medium," she said. "It's like television for blind people."

They'd actually argued about the merits of television over breakfast. Arnold had been anti-TV all of his life—but now that he was confined to one-hundred-forty square feet of floor space, he wanted Cassandra to invest in a portable set. The girl thought that was a waste of resources and brain cells.

Arnold slid his casserole into the oven. "Are you going to tell me?" he asked. "Or do I have to wrap bandages around my face and buy a *Times* at the bodega?"

The girl poured them each a glass of wine. "It wouldn't be in the *Times*."

"Let me guess. It's in the *Vanguard*. You ran my interview."

"It's in the *Vanguard*, all right. But we didn't run your interview. I'm not that stupid." She reached into her bag again and pulled out a copy of the radical broadsheet. "Take a look at that," she said.

"What is it? Has socialism triumphed? Or has Lenin risen from the dead?"

He'd stockpiled a whole slew of sarcastic quips to level at Cassandra's employer, which usually ran articles laced with words like *imperialism* and *hegemony*, but the banner headline brought his mockery to an immediate halt:

THE MINISTER'S TWO WIVES

Far Right's Spitford Spotty on Monogamy.

The exposé covered the entire front page and included photographs of the clergyman with his wife in New York and his *other* wife and five children in Tampa.

"I told you you'd like your surprise," said the girl.

"I should throttle you for not telling me sooner."

"Take a look at the by-line," urged the girl.

There was her name:

CASSANDRA BROWARD, INVESTIGATIVE REPORTER

"A toast," proposed the girl. "To my promotion."

They clicked glasses and drank.

"That should give him a taste of his own medicine," she said. "So much for Mayor Spitford. Now what was that you were saying about Lenin's resurrection?"

"I stand corrected, once again. I guess I should go eat my hat."

"There's no need for anything so drastic," she answered. "You can thank me by pouring me another glass of wine."

Arnold poured them each another glass and they toasted again. Her face flushed from the alcohol.

"I also have something else for you," said the girl. "A present."

"What more could I possibly ask for in life? Don't tell me Ira Taylor also has two wives?"

"Who?"

"An old nemesis of mine. Never mind."

"You have an awful lot of enemies, don't you?" observed the girl. This might have been true—but she didn't give him a chance to think it over. Instead, she withdrew a small appliance from her bag. "But now, at least, you can track their progress from home on your new portable television."

"But I thought you said television was the root of all evil."

The girl's eyes twinkled. "I didn't mean it. I just like

arguing with you."

Arnold was truly happy, practically giddy, for the first time in weeks, so happy that he could have kissed the girl in gratitude—but he didn't dare.

CHAPTER 9

Arnold insisted upon testing out his new television later that evening. They cleared the seashells and hedgehog cactus off the window sill, giving the small twelve-inch set a place of honour more suited for a rare family heirloom. Additional effort was required to adjust the antennae in such a manner that more than waves of snow were visible on the screen. At its best, the picture remained cloudy. But it *was* a picture. He even cooked up a bowl of popcorn for the inaugural viewing. Not bugleweed 'popcorn' or peppergrass 'popcorn,' but the old-fashioned variety, the stuff formed from exploded corn kernels. They also used real butter—of the sort that came not from buttercups but from dairy cows. When Cassandra finally managed to jiggle the machine's static into sound, a feat that required the device be titled upward forty-five degrees, they relaxed on a pair of aluminium lawn chairs and watched the local evening news. It felt as though they were attending a picnic or a drive-in movie.

The lead story that night was Spitford's double life. At first, the anchorman rehashed the article in the *Vanguard.* He also quoted several noncommittal statements from leading African-American political and religious figures. Then came more critical words from white conservatives. Arnold found himself contemplating the larger implications of the black fascist's downfall. If Spitford were discredited, Arnold wondered, might that lead to his own early rehabilitation? It seemed plausible. The media often had a difficult time keeping two villains in their crosshairs simultaneously, particularly if the two evildoers were themselves adversaries. Complexity and nuance didn't rake in advertising dollars. Maybe the tide had turned. Next week, he might be sitting in his own living room while Spitford hid from the authorities. He and Judith would laugh at this entire episode as a minor blip in the otherwise smooth course of their passage into old age. In his fantasy, they even invited him back to Yankee Stadium to throw out the first pitch on opening day—and he had the satisfaction of rejecting their offer. And he'd owe it all to Cassandra and her investigative journalism. Even Judith's attitude toward the girl would have to soften if that came to pass. Arnold smiled at the girl. She winked back—unmistakably. He felt a warm, devoted feeling toward her, he decided, that could just as easily become familial as romantic. Who knew? Maybe Cassandra would become the child Judith so desperately wanted.

The television had cut away from the anchor's desk to live footage of Musty Musgrove, the fast-talking reporter who'd made a name for himself covering Arnold's disgrace. "We're waiting for Reverend Spitford to emerge from his limousine," explained the newsman. "We've been told that he intends to make a brief statement and after that he will take questions from the media. According to our sources inside the Emergency Civil Rights Brigade, Reverend Spitford personally decided to have this late-night press conference, overruling his closest advisors. Whether we'll get the usual voice of defiance, or something more contrite, we'll have to wait and see...." The camera panned across the street to Spitford's black stretch limo, and Arnold recognized the scene instantly. The limousine was parked *on his own block.* The Black Nazi apparently intended to hold his goddam press conference opposite Arnold's townhouse. Yet when the portly minister stepped out of his vehicle, sporting his reflective glasses despite the darkness, the extent of the clergymen's impertinence turned out to be far more greater than even Arnold had thought possible. Spitford, flanked by his dark-suited bodyguards, *mounted the steps of Arnold's home.* He was going to give his valedictory from the botanist's own front porch. Sure, it was private property. But nobody was going to make any effort to stop him.

The minister held up his hand for silence. Then he removed his glasses, dramatically, exposing a set of bloodshot eyes. "May I ask you to dim your lights?" he requested softly. "I have been crying and my vision is quite sensitive."

Several photographers did indeed lower their lights. The minister's broad, flabby face fell into shadow.

"I have been crying," continued Spitford, louder,

"because I have done a great wrong. We are all sinners, but I am a greater sinner than most. I will make no effort this evening to explain or justify what I have done. It is unjustifiable. Unpardonable. No censure is too strong for an abject wretch like me…."

The minister's deep voice resonated along the dark, silent street. Arnold relished the man's degradation, but he felt a growing sense of foreboding. Spitford's words were apologetic, but the minister's tone contained hints of his usual defiance. This was a man who'd been bent, but not broken.

Spitford paused and dabbed his eyes with a starch-white handkerchief. "All I can say in my own defence," he continued, "is that I loved not wisely but too well. I had the grave misfortune of losing my heart to two glorious, God-fearing women, and I am afraid that this love got the better of me. I made the inexcusable mistake of raising two wonderful families—seven children, each of whom I adore more than life itself—and although I owe an apology *to them*, I will never owe an apology *for them.* But I say to all of you, tonight, that I was wrong to yield to my excessive love, and on that account I am terribly, terribly sorry." Spitford paused again—as though trying to compose himself. "What I am *not* sorry for, is crusading against hatred. Given the choice of too much love or too little, I will choose too much love any day. Because of that, I have no choice but to continue with our struggle against prejudice and violence of all sorts. I stand before you at the home of a man whose sin is the veritable opposite of mine: I have far too much love to offer. Arnold Brinkman does not have any. You must decide for yourselves which of those transgressions is worse."

The minister stepped forward toward his audience. On the bottom on the screen, the day's baseball scores scrolled past. The camera panned in for a close-up of the minister's pained expression. "I plead with you to accept my sincerest apologies and not to let my own shortcomings injure my innocent children, jeopardize my work toward social justice, or, most importantly, weaken the security of the nation that I love beyond all else: The United States of America. It is in the name of our homeland—and for its protection from men like Arnold Brinkman—that I get down on my knees and beg your forgiveness." And then Spitford did just that. He fell to his knees, tears streaming down his cheeks. Soon members of the press corps were also crying, and applauding, until someone struck up a chorus of *God Bless America.* When Arnold snapped off the television, the cameras were focused on Musty Musgrove, standing at attention, singing, with his hand over his heart. Arnold had no doubt who the next mayor would be.

"Goddam useless machine," growled the botanist. "What a waste of money."

"I can take it back," offered the girl. "I'm sure if I return the TV, it will change the media's attitude toward your friend Spitford."

"We've already got it," snapped Arnold. "We might as well keep it."

But after the minister's press conference, he didn't turn it on again.

As Arnold took less interest in the news, the news took less interest in him. He still remained on the FBI's most-wanted list, and Spitford continued his vigil outside what had once been Arnold's townhouse, but now a particularly violent day in the Middle East or a celebrity wedding might easily drive coverage of his disappearance to the middle of a radio newscast. Several commentators speculated that he was dead, either by accident or suicide, and that his bloated body would eventually wash up in the East River. An NPR crime consultant quoted unnamed sources as saying the investigation had run cold and that the authorities were diverting resources away from the search. This prompted an angry denial from One Police Plaza. But after four weeks underground, Arnold was beginning to think he was in the clear. And then, one Friday evening, the intercom shattered the tranquillity of their dinner. This was the first time since his arrival that the girl had received another visitor, and the rarity of the event made it all the more alarming. His adrenal glands kicked into overdrive. He looked to Cassandra for wisdom, but she shrugged.

"Are you sure you're not expecting someone?"

he asked.

"Who on earth could I be expecting? I already told you: I don't have any friends. *None.*"

"Acquaintances?" he ventured. "Enemies?"

The buzzer sounded again—seemingly louder, though Arnold knew that wasn't possible. The German shepherd vaulted off the futon and cowered in the corner.

"You're the one with enemies, Mr. I-Value-People's-Opinions," retorted Cassandra. "Not me."

Arnold scanned the apartment for a place to conceal himself. There wasn't one. The futon rested directly against the ground and the teak wardrobe lacked doors. His only avenues of retreat were the bathroom or the window.

"We should have planned ahead," he said. "We should have arranged for a hiding place before tonight."

"Could-have, would-have, should-have," answered the girl. "Go out on the fire escape and lie down under one of the sheets."

Arnold had little choice. He climbed through the open window, prepared to conceal himself under damp bedding, but the linens and blankets that Cassandra had draped along the railing were all missing. There wasn't so much as a tatter of cloth on the entire platform. They'd been robbed.

He glanced over the railing, hoping he might be able to vault himself into the apartment below. That's when he caught sight of the checkered pink apron. It was hanging from the obese fundamentalist's laundry line, just as it had been before Arnold had scooped it up with a hook. And now that damn hag Poxly had paid him back in kind by appropriating their wet bedding. Which meant he'd spent the rest of his life in prison for stealing a woman's apron. Unless, of course, Cassandra opened the door on a troop of girl scouts selling cookies. Let them be girl scouts. If they were, he swore he'd buy every last baked good in their warehouse. Arnold clung to this fantasy for a couple of seconds, and then he watched through the railing as the girl opened the door on a pair of burly men decked out in New York Yankees paraphernalia. One wore a solid navy shirt with an insignia and torn dungarees. The other had his cap on backwards. Both looked dour.

"Can I help you?" asked the girl.

"Federal Bureau of Investigation," answered Backwards Cap, flashing a badge in the girl's face. He spoke with a lisp. Why were these officers wearing baseball outfits? To taunt Arnold? To make the arrest photographs more poetic? Did it matter? The bottom line was that the pair was clearly onto him and he had no way out. Or almost no way. Arnold squeezed his eyes shut and, drawing a deep breath, climbed into the compost trough. The fermented stench of the decomposing produce nearly overpowered him. When he lay flat on his back, only his nose protruded about the mounds of murky, semi-liquid slop. The conversation in the apartment now came to him from a great distance, as though through a long tube.

"I take it you're Yankees fans," said the girl—cool and collected.

"It gets us in the door," answered Navy Shirt. "We used to wear suits. People mistook us for Mormon missionaries."

"I'm sure they're relieved when they find out you're G-men."

"Depends who they are," said Backwards Cap. "And what they've been doing."

"That makes sense," answered Cassandra. "So what have *I* been doing?"

"Maybe you'd like to tell us?" persisted Backwards Cap.

"We could play twenty questions," offered the girl.

A long silence followed. Arnold tried to breathe silently.

"We're investigating the disappearance of Arnold Brinkman," Navy Shirt said eventually in a business-like tone. "We're going to have to look around your apartment."

"And you think *I'm* hiding Arnold Brinkman?"

"*Are you* hiding him?"

"I don't think so," said the girl. "But you'd better check under the futon and in the wardrobe. And if he's not there, the bathroom and the fire escape wouldn't be such bad bets. You have to figure I'm an amateur, so I probably wouldn't have come up with anything all that creative."

The G-men didn't seem to find the girl amusing. Nor did Arnold. Arnold had discovered that policemen, like physicians, enjoyed being treated as though they were better than other human beings. Simply addressing them as "doctor" or "officer" at the end of every sentence was bound to get you better healthcare and a reduced speeding ticket. Arnold didn't imagine that repartee was one of the qualities that J. Edgar Hoover had looked for in hiring.

"Please sit down right there, Miss," said Backwards Cap sharply.

"And don't do anything foolish," added Navy Shirt.

Arnold heard the floorboards squeak in front of the window. He took a deep breath and drew his nose into the mire.

"Are those your plants?" demanded Backwards Cap.

"They're tomatoes."

"You've got an awful lot of them."

"They're essential for the proper balance of yin and yang," answered Cassandra. "And they improve the sex drive."

He was suffocating on rotten sugar beets and the girl was proffering theories on the spiritual properties of tomatoes. Which weren't even true. Tomatoes screwed with your yin and yang. They were totally incompatible with a macrobiotic diet. Drano offered more promise as an aphrodisiac.

"What's that over there?" asked Backwards Cap.

"Compost. Decaying produce. Would you like to try some?"

"Jesus, that stinks," answered the agent. "You *eat* that?"

"I don't," said Cassandra. "But you're welcome to."

Backwards Cap muttered a word that sounded like "bitch" and slammed shut the window, preventing Arnold from hearing the remainder of the conversation. The two agents stayed in the apartment for another hour. Arnold could feel the watery sludge soaking into his shoes and creeping around his groin. His haemorrhoids itched; the waterline tickled his nostrils. He didn't dare move. If the hippie movement were looking for a modern variant of medieval torture, compost dunking was surely it.

Arnold felt as though his entire body had started to decompose when he heard the window squeak open again.

"You still out here?" called Cassandra.

The botanist climbed out of the trough and opened his eyes. Sludge trickled off all of his bodies extremities, even dripping from his hair. Cassandra nearly collapsed in hysterics. "I had no clue..." she gasped between fits of laughter. "How are you feeling?"

"Like a giant pickle. What took you so long?"

"They had a whole series of questions to ask," answered the girl, composing herself. "Not just about you. Also about Spitford. And the Bare-Ass Bandit. They seem to think you and Bare-Ass are in cahoots." Cassandra handed him a towel through the window. "And then I had to give each of those fine officers a blowjob to keep them from arresting you on the spot."

Arnold examined her face closely. He honestly didn't know if she were sincere.

"I hope you're joking," he said tentatively.

"Don't look so shocked," snapped the girl. "If that was all it took to get you out of trouble, you'd be grateful for it."

"That's not true," objected Arnold.

"Yes, it is. You just can't decide whether you're revolted or jealous." The girl disappeared from the window and he heard the bath water running. "Anyway, I'm the one who should be offended," she called out, "that you'd even *think* I was serious."

The incident with the compost trough changed Arnold's relationship with the girl. Before that, he'd made a point of reassuring himself that his feelings toward her might have been base, but at least his intentions were honourable. Yet once she'd made reference to his jealousy, he realized that he was indeed jealous—or that he would have been, had she pursued another romantic interest. This prospect remained highly unlikely, of course, because, except for work, Cassandra hardly left the apartment. But now the botanist took a greater interest in her wants and moods.

He stole glances at her as she lay in bed, reading Habermas by the bedside lamp, and he longed to exchange places with the dozing German shepherd at her feet. He replayed their conversations in his mind, delving for hidden meanings in apparently casual remarks. Her playful insults, which had previously amused him, now stung like darts. And once, when he warned her not to eat off her knife blade and she jokingly called him 'Papa', his face flamed up with fury and disappointment. Arnold's feelings grew so all-consuming that he passed several consecutive afternoons pacing the apartment, for hours on end, contemplating the idyllic life they might live together if he headed the Tashkent Botanical Gardens. But he didn't share his fantasies with the girl. In the first place, he was twice her age. And married. And out of practice. But deep down he knew none of these factors was holding him back. The only impediment was that he was scared of rejection.

Arnold stayed in this state of limbo for six days. He didn't bother to rotate his tomato plants, letting them grow haphazardly toward a stationary light source. He prepared increasingly flamboyant dinners of poppy soufflé and orchid crepes, designed to impress the girl, but he picked indifferently at his own helping. And then, one Friday, he forget himself entirely: Someone knocked at the door and he answered it without thinking. As soon as he found himself staring into the bulging eyes of the obese fundamentalist, he realized what he'd done. It was all over.

But the fat woman didn't seem to recognize him. Or if she did, she didn't let on. She stood at the threshold, her torso larger than the doorframe, resting a plastic tub of clothing on one monstrous hip.

"You are the father of the angel who lives here?" asked Mrs. Poxly.

It took Arnold a moment to realize she meant Cassandra. "I'm staying with her for a few days," he answered noncommittally.

"You will be kind enough to give her these," said the woman. She handed Arnold the basket of laundry. It contained Cassandra's bedding—the bedding the old hag had stolen from the fire escape. "The devil has been at work on our balconies," the woman explained matter-of-factly. "I took her sheets to the church to be washed and blessed. She will find them better now."

"Thank you," answered Arnold.

"Don't thank me, thank the Lord."

The woman looked up at the ceiling as though God might be found among the spider webs and chipped plaster. "Your face is very familiar to me," she said.

"Thank you again for the laundry," replied Arnold.

"I have it now!"

Arnold glanced around the room for a weapon. He didn't have it in him to injure the Bible-thumper harpy, but he could tie her up, if necessary, in order to escape.

"You look like the man who wrote my diet book," she

continued. "Only he's much younger."

Mrs. Poxly lowered her voice to a confidential undertone. "It's a good diet. All flower petals and stems and leaves and whatnot," she explained. "But I add some pizza and ice cream once in a while to flavour things up. You don't think a grown woman can survive on flowers, do you?"

"I imagine not."

"So you *are* the Flower Chef?"

"No," answered Arnold. "But I'm often mistaken for him"

"Too bad for you," said Mrs. Poxly. "I bet he makes a pretty penny off those books of his."

"I'm sure he does," agreed Arnold.

He shut the door, his pulse racing. His body was a tightly-wound ball and not even a cold shower managed to soothe him.

I'm going to tell her, he decided. Tonight. Before it kills me.

While Arnold had been grappling with his feelings, day after day shot by rapidly, like the growth of a kudzu vine, but now that he'd made his decision, he found the hours crept forward at the pace of pea tendrils. He killed the remainder of the morning listening to the radio, where the Bare-Ass Bandit had once against leapfrogged Arnold in the headlines. The saber-wielding desperado, whom Arnold had begun to think of as "the competition," had made a sudden appearance in the nation's capital that morning, stealing the collection of First Ladies' gowns from the Smithsonian Institute. He'd even taken Mary Todd Lincoln's whalebone corset. The Justice Department had issued an all points bulletin for a six foot three inch bald man dressed as Dolly Madison. The same Deputy Attorney General who offered the press morning updates on the Tongue Terrorist now issued a statement describing the Bandit as the Department's "number one priority." He quickly backtracked under pressure—acknowledging that "Osama bin Laden and Arnold Brinkman also remain the subject of intense international manhunts." The official refused to confirm or deny speculation that the three men might be working together. While Arnold listened to the news, he transplanted his tomatoes to a larger tray. He couldn't help wondering what other high-profile fugitives did during their expansive hours of leisure time. Because they must have done something. Macramé. Scrimshaw. Building battleships in bottles. That would have been a fertile subject for a book—the hobbies of outlaws. He suspected even bin Laden, when they found him eventually, would be surrounded by soap-carved figurines or hand-woven plant holders. But that afternoon even gardening proved no match for Arnold's romantic anxiety. He paced back and forth on the narrow fire escape for several hours, chain-smoking Cassandra's cigarettes, waiting for the moment when she would determine his fate.

The girl arrived home later than usual, carrying two large bags of groceries. Her shirt was stained dark with perspiration, and she wore an endearing moustache of sweat above her upper lip. Her tank-top left exposed a sliver of midriff, baring a cute but conspicuous belly. Many men would have dismissed her as chubby. Arnold didn't care how much she weighed, one way or the other, but if she were unattractive to other men, he imagined this might increase his own chances of success. He wouldn't have minded if she were considerably uglier, at least to a degree. There was probably a point of diminishing returns.

"You're still here?" she said coyly.

"No, I'm not," answered Arnold. "You're imagining me."

"Good. Then I want to imagine you putting away these groceries. And changing the light bulbs in the kitchen. Use the sixty watts in the bag, not the one hundreds."

Arnold set about his chores. He climbed onto the stepladder and removed the burnt-out bulbs one at a time. For the girl, this afternoon was no different than any other—that she *hadn't* been thinking about *him* all day.

"How was work?" he asked.

"It's getting exciting. I'm suddenly the unofficial expert on politicians with double lives. Isn't that awesome? We've gotten half a dozen anonymous tips this week." The girl retrieved a beer from the refrigerator. "On the other hand, your friend Reverend Spitford is suing the pants off us for invasion of privacy."

"Invasion of privacy. After what he did to me…."

"I thought you'd get a kick out of that."

But the mention of Spitford gave Arnold a different sort of kick than Cassandra had intended. It reminded him—at some primal level—that he'd once had another life outside of the girl's apartment. It reminded him of Judith. He sensed his wife viscerally, the way a certain scent or season can bring back the memory of a loved-one long dead. When the moment passed—*he forced the moment to pass*—he found Cassandra lounging on the futon with the German shepherd cuddled at her feet. The girl was embroiled in the crossword puzzle. Her bare toes were tinged black, but the nails had been carefully polished—alternating crimson and fuchsia. The evening sun danced off her tousled hair. Arnold settled down beside her on the mattress. It was now or never, he realized. This was another of those definitive moments, like the interlude at the baseball game, which would render the future unalterable.

"I have a confession to make," he ventured.

The girl looked up. "You want me to get my tape-recorder?"

"Not that kind of confession," said Arnold.

"Too bad," answered the girl. She looked around the room suspiciously and asked: "So what did you break?"

"It's not that kind of confession either," said Arnold. He sensed the conversation slowly seeping from his control. "It's more of a secret. You know how you said you can live with someone your entire life and not know the first thing about them? Well, there's something about me that I haven't been able to tell you."

"Let me guess," said the girl. "You're actually a woman—"

"No, I—"

"Or maybe you're black. Got it. You're actually a black woman."

"What I'm trying to say—"

The girl grinned and clapped her hands together. "Okay, I've got it. You really are a terrorist. A black female terrorist."

"Godammit," shouted Arnold. "I'm in love with you."

The frustration in his voice made the words sound ridiculous. He sat sheepishly on the edge of the futon, waiting for her to respond.

"Okay," answered the girl.

"Okay?" he asked. "Is that okay, I'm in love with you too. Or okay, you're allowed to make a fool of yourself."

"That's okay, I figured you might be," said the girl

"You did?"

"Yeah. I am an investigative journalist, remember."

Arnold waited for the girl to say more. She didn't.

"I'm sorry," he said. "That was really stupid of me.

It's just I've been stuck in this apartment for day after day and—"

He was still blubbering when she kissed him on the lips. Hard. He kissed back tentatively, but he didn't dare breathe. The dog started barking. The girl pulled back.

"It's okay, honey," soothed Cassandra. "I'm just having fun." She ran her fingers over the scruff of the animal's neck. "She doesn't understand," the girl apologized. "I guess a few hours in the bathroom won't kill her." She led Son of a President away and returned a moment later. "Now where were we?"

"You were telling me about your investigative journalism."

"Was I?" asked the girl.

She climbed onto his lap and kissed him again, this time letting her tongue explore his mouth. She broke away again.

"I have a confession to make too," she said.

"Shall I get *my* tape-recorder?"

"I'm being serious," she continued. "But I'm afraid you're going to be upset...You've got to promise that you won't hate me."

"I think it would be very difficult for me to hate you," said Arnold.

"I don't know how to say this. It's about your garden....I'm the one who destroyed it."

Arnold's breath caught in his chest.

"I'm so so so sorry." The girl had started to sob. "I was angry at you for backing out on our interview….and not returning my calls….and I don't know what came over me. It *so* just happened. And then it was too late to undo."

Arnold felt the anger surging in his chest—the same rage he'd felt toward Spitford, but ten times stronger. Ten billion times stronger. How easily he could have reached forward and wrapped his fingers around her treacherous neck. What had his roses and hydrangeas ever done to her? Here she was smiling at him over dinner each evening—and a villain all along. Her confession couldn't have repulsed him more if she'd admitted to massacring a village of young children.

He stood up and retrieved his shoes from the entryway. He needed to breathe fresh air before he did to her apartment what she'd done to his garden.

"I'm leaving," he said icily. "For good."

"Where are you going?"

That question just raised his ire, because he had no idea where he was going—he had no place else to go—but he refused to take the bait. If Anne Frank had learned her Dutch protectors had been necrophilic cannibals, she'd have considered leaving her attic.

"I don't know," he said. "Someplace better than here."

The girl looked up at him, her eyes pleading. "Give me a second chance. I'll totally make it up to you. We'll run off someplace and start a new garden."

"What happened to 'life giving you what it gives you'?"

"Life gave me you," said the girl.

"I never want to lay eyes on you again."

He truly didn't. Whatever his feelings, some atrocities were unforgivable.

"I can't believe you're just going to run off like this. What happened to being madly in love with me?"

Arnold tied his shoes, one at a time. "I never said madly."

"Fine, get the hell out of here," she snapped. "You think you know everything."

"Not everything. Just enough."

"Well, just so everything's clear, you can't possibly remember me interviewing you at N.Y.U. because I didn't. I didn't even go to N.Y.U. I just happened to be at the campus store one day when you were signing books."

"It's all water under the bridge," said Arnold. "You got your interview. That's what you wanted. If the Trotskyites take over, I'm sure you'll be minister of propaganda or something like that."

He looked around the room to see if he'd left behind any belongings. The tomato sprouts were all that were truly his—and he couldn't possibly take those with him. He considered asking the girl to look after them, but that was like asking a child molester to babysit. Better to let the shoots fend for themselves. He walked over to the window sill and tucked his Nixon mask into his pocket. He also scooped up the girl's cigarettes and her lighter—that seemed like the least he was entitled to as compensation. When he turned around, the girl was blocking his exit.

"You're not being fair," she said.

"Okay," agreed Arnold. "I'm not being fair."

He attempted to step around her. She impeded his retreat.

"You're forcing my hand," she said. "If you leave, you'll regret it."

Arnold stepped toward her. "What is that supposed to mean?"

"Nothing," said the girl. "I hope it doesn't come to that."

She was going to turn him in.

"I'm not stupid," said the girl. "I either get you or $500,000."

That's when Arnold snapped. All the tension of the past two weeks roared up inside him and he grabbed the girl by the neck. His hands wrapped around her throat, squeezing, while her fingers tried to pry them free. She kicked at him too, but the blows glanced off the sides of his leg. Her head twisted and bobbed. At some point her hair fell backwards, revealing an expression too surprised to be terrified. He was killing her, second by second. And then the dog barked. Just once. But enough to break his trance. He released his grip and she was breathing again, choking, sputtering blood.

She inched backwards, the fear rising in her face. He didn't know what to say.

"You've got to look after my tomatoes," he said.

Then he fled through the door and out into the twilight.

CHAPTER 10

Arnold waited in the darkened entryway of a scrap-metal dealership until the pedestrian traffic thinned on the avenue. Then he burrowed his head into his shirt and walked briskly down to the Brooklyn Bridge and across the East River into Manhattan. But he returned to his native borough as a homing pigeon might, utterly unequipped with further plans for survival. To make matters worse, a profound and acute loneliness overtook him. He hadn't realized how good he'd had it in Cassandra's company, but now that his social circle had contracted from one to zero, he longed for human companionship. Alas, there were only two people in the entire world he could trust—and one was holed up behind a police cordon, surrounded by Spitford's minions, while the other was probably being skinned alive by the Peruvian version of the Stasi. Arnold couldn't even befriend his fellow homeless. Even if he might surmount the class and education barriers, not to mention the initial distrust that kept apart strangers in the city, their bonds would melt quickly at the prospect of reward money. No, he was on his own. And so began the two long weeks of social isolation during which Arnold eked out his sustenance in Central Park. During the day, he concealed himself in dense brush and watched the parade of joggers who crowded the meandering paths, the joyful picnickers and shameless lovers who congregated in what they thought were secluded groves. It was like being surrounded by a carnival and yet locked in solitary confinement at the same time. He couldn't even maintain a permanent campsite—if you could call a clump of dried leaves a campsite—because the police conducted random patrols. Their goal seemed to be to prevent vagrants from building cardboard cities, as they'd done in the 1980s. As a result, they chased the homeless from location to location. Their efforts reminded him of his own futile efforts to smoke out a woodchuck from under his pumpkin patch.

One night, Arnold slept in a mound of mulch near the zoo. On another occasion, he came across a ragged mattress lying beside the service drive that looped around the Metropolitan Museum of Art. It smelled faintly of vomit—but that was a small price to pay for the soft feel of polyurethane under one's head. For food, the botanist initially relied on grasses and wildflowers, occasionally supplemented by a crust of cold pizza or an apple core he unearthed in a trash can. He knew no shame. He could afford no shame. His clothing quickly wore away at the knees and elbows, tattered gaps that soon forced the amputation of the sleeves and cuffs below. Showering also proved impossible, as the park service had installed mesh security gates around all of its ponds. He slept further away from the trails, afraid his stench might give him away. Even Arnold's small successes rapidly degenerated into failure.

When he was fortunate enough to acquire a torn sleeping bag, apparently abandoned by a fellow park-dweller, he'd hardly dozed off before a pair of pre-teen thugs stumbled across his hideaway. He awoke to the patter of urine on his exposed feet and the back of his head. In hindsight, he was thankful that the boys hadn't set him on fire. Later that week, Arnold broke into a Goodwill dumpster and pilfered a new set of clothes. Unfortunately, the dungarees he selected were infested with fleas that raised burning welts on his ankles and around his groin. He scoured the curb side trash along 110th Street for protective pet collars to wrap around his ankles and penis. Again, Arnold tried to look on the bright side: At least the pants hadn't been infected with flesh eating bacteria. Or laced with biological toxins. But there were mornings when he wouldn't have minded a chaser of smallpox or anthrax to wash down his dandelion sandwiches.

Keeping abreast of the news also proved more difficult without access to Cassandra's radio and internet connection. Arnold found his best source of information were the old newspapers that the park police used to insulate the stable attached to their uptown headquarters. He didn't dare steal the newspapers from underneath the horses, of course, but every few days a groundskeeper stacked the old pages at the curb side for recycling. They smelled pungently equine. Often they came with a fresh supply of straw and horse droppings. But they did supply the news. And all of it, during those long weeks of summer, was bad. First, the old transvestites "broke under pressure" and confessed that they sold fake IDs in addition to costumes: passports, drivers licenses, liquor purchasing cards. But to college kids, they insisted. Not suicide bombers. The authorities didn't buy the distinction. In fact, they suggested that would-be terrorists like Arnold might even be using unsuspecting college students as middlemen. "Don't be surprised if a 'corrupting the welfare of a minor' charge is added to the indictment," one unidentified source told the *Daily News*. "We haven't found a minor yet. But we're looking." Prominent gay leaders were quick to condemn Gladys and Anabelle as "not representative of our community." A right-wing talk-show host branded them "The Women of a Thousand Faces" and the moniker stuck. Two days later, the police arrested Lucinda, Arnold's bookkeeper, on suspicion of harbouring a fugitive. It turned out that her brother, a security guard at a local department store, shared the name of a wanted Al Qaida operative. The newspapers ran the story of the pair's capture on page one. When the police finally figured out that the sixty-one year old diabetic guard wasn't the bomb-maker in their dossier, the same papers ran small corrections in their Metro section. None of this did much for Arnold's reputation. Eventually, Arnold stopped reading the news scraps entirely. Better to be uninformed than regularly demoralized. Besides, if anything truly important happened—if the messiah showed up, for example, or if the world ended—he was bound to find out eventually.

The only genuine pleasure of living in the park—as compared to life in Cassandra's apartment—was that Arnold was able to add wild mushrooms to his diet. He hadn't trusted the girl to distinguish the mouth-watering Coccora, *Amanita calytroderma*, from the one-hundred percent lethal Death Cap, *Amanita phalloides*. (Arnold could tell the species apart quite easily, but only from contextual clues of microhabitat; once they were harvested, the two species proved virtually identical.) To Arnold, his new outdoor home offered a seemingly inexhaustible variety of flavours. He lurked around the Great Lawn in the hours before dawn, gorging himself on morels and toadstools. He discovered a stand of black locusts near the southeast gate that proved a veritable smorgasbord for shelf fungi. A row of young cherry trees bordering the Sheep Meadow offered up a bounty of white polypores. For breakfast, Arnold supplemented his dandelion sandwiches with a raw paste concocted from clinker fungus, black knots and puffballs. He hadn't thought much about mushrooms in recent years, consumed as he was with petal-based meals, but he found that the know-how returned to him as quickly as a foreign language or the ability to ride a bicycle. Fungi soon displaced plant-life as the backbone of his diet and gathering these morsels consumed the greater portion of his time. The energy he expended distinguishing mycotic delicacies from closely-related toxins was effort not squandered in thinking about his former life. It was only when Arnold took a break from his foraging, maybe to examine the summer night sky, that he found himself thinking of Judith, and Gilbert Card, and what that crazy girl had done to his beloved garden. So he tried to think as little as possible. Scouring the high grass on his knees was a far better way to retain what remained of his sanity.

Arnold was hunkered over a grove of white-capped boletes one sultry evening, trying to recollect whether this particular species was poisonous, when he felt a cool, sharp sensation on the back of his neck. At first, he took it for a bead of water—but as he reached around to brush away the droplet, its pressure increased abruptly. He was feeling a weapon, he realized. His suspicions were confirmed when a deep male voice ordered him to place his hands over his head. "Slowly, man," said his assailant. "Okay, now stand up and turn around." The botanist did as he was instructed. He expected to confront a police officer wielding a handgun—or possibly an entire SWAT team ready to brutalize him at the slightest provocation. Instead, he found himself face to face with a naked man wielding a saber.

"Jesus Christ!" exclaimed Arnold. "You're the Bare-Ass Bandit."

"So I've been told," said the lunatic. He wore only sneakers and a long scabbard attached to a braided leather belt. "But I'm glad you recognized me. That means you know what to do next."

"This is unbelievable," answered Arnold. "My goddam life falls apart and on top of that I get attacked by a headcase."

He knew he ought to have felt frightened, but he didn't. He was too worn out to be frightened. Or maybe Cassandra's pseudo-student Calvinism had rubbed off on him. In any case, he was overcome with a powerful calm. Whatever was going to happen was going to happen. Being frightened wouldn't change a thing.

"It's time for you to remove your clothing," said the Bandit, matter-of-factly. He waved the sword only inches from Arnold's throat. "Then we'll see what other adventures might be in store for you."

Arnold kept his hands over his head. He smiled indifferently.

"I said, take off your clothes," ordered the Bandit. "Trust me, man. You don't want to end up human shish-kabob."

Arnold didn't move. He sensed he was grinning like an idiot.

"Dammit, I'm warning you," said the Bandit. "Are you going to do this the easy way or the hard way."

Arnold turned his palms upward in a quasi-shrug. "I'm not going to do it at all," he said. "If it's that important to you, stab me. See if I give a damn."

"Are you crazy, man? Your life is on the line here."

"I've already lost my wife, my business and my garden....So if this is how it's meant to end, I'm not going to fight it."

"Don't be this way," insisted the Bandit. "I don't want to have to hurt you...."

"Then *don't* hurt me," answered Arnold. "But you're not getting my clothing without a fight. In either case, make up your mind. Because if you're not going to kill me, I want to finish harvesting these boletes before it gets too light."

The Bandit frowned and lowered his sword to Arnold's navel. "You're into mushrooms?" he asked suspiciously.

"I used to be," replied the botanist. "I'm just getting into the swing of it again."

Arnold's assailant stepped forward and for a moment Arnold expected to be impaled on the lunatic's sword. He braced himself for the pain. Instead, the Bandit used the weapon to poke at the heads of the boletes. He decapitated half the stand with one wide blow.

"You don't want to be eating those, man. Better off drinking Drano."

"Excuse me?" asked Arnold.

"They're poisonous, man. Trust me. I'm something of an expert." The Bandit pointed at the severed cap of the nearest bolete. "See those ridges on the underbelly. Well the rule is: 'Bottom yellow, very mellow; bottom red, very dead.' It's not always as easy as that, of course, because sometimes you get in-between shades. But here, I'd say that's more of an orange-red than an orange-yellow...."

"I was debating that...."

"Mushroom eating isn't for amateurs," warned the Bandit. Arnold prickled at being called an amateur. "At least buy yourself a field guide...."

Arnold considered explaining that he wrote field guides, but it wasn't worth it. "I'll do that," he said. "Unless you turn me into shish-kabob."

The Bandit raised his saber again. The blade was extraordinary thin, as though designed for filleting fish, but Arnold didn't doubt it could disembowel him with ease. "I saved your life, man," said the lunatic. "Why not give me your clothes and call it even?"

"No," answered Arnold. "I can't do that." He thought over the demand for another moment and added: "Why don't you give me your sword?"

"What the hell?"

"You heard me," said Arnold. "Give me your sword. Then I'll let you go."

"Don't fuck with me, man," warned the Bandit.

Arnold lowered his arms.

"Hands up!" shouted the Bandit.

"Calm down. I'm just going to have a cigarette." Arnold reached into his jacket pocket for the girl's lighter and her pack of Camels. "You want one?"

"You really do have a screw loose, man," said the Bandit. "I could have killed you ten times by now."

Arnold took a deep drag on his cigarette. "You don't recognize me, do you?"

"Should I?" demanded the Bandit.

"I can't say whether you *should* or you *shouldn't*. But these days I'm known as the Tongue Terrorist."

Arnold's assailant examined the botanist closely. The lunatic actually circled him as though examining a sculpture. Then he sheathed his sword and whistled. "Wow, man," said the Bandit. "I'm totally speechless. All I can say is Wow."

"So you have heard of me?"

"Heard of you? I'm practically your number one fan. I own all of your books. Where do you think I learned so much about poisonous mushrooms?" The Bandit rubbed his eyes as though unsure that they were functioning properly. "Say, you must think I'm a total asshole for calling you an amateur."

"No big deal," said Arnold.

"You really are Arnold Brinkman, Ph.D., aren't you?"

"Unfortunately," answered Arnold. "It's not exactly something I brag about these days."

The Bandit braced his leg against a nearby log and rested his elbow on his bare knee. "What are you doing in the park at one o'clock in the morning?"

"Picking poisonous mushrooms," Arnold answered.

He wasn't sure how far to trust the lunatic—but they were both fugitives. It wasn't as though the lunatic could walk over to the nearest police station and turn him in. They were bound by the same sort of self-interested secrecy that protected the patrons of gay bars and methadone clinics. On the other hand, the lunatic *was* a lunatic. "I'm actually *living* in the park these days," he added. "Until I get back on my feet."

"Where abouts?"

"No place in particular....Wherever I can find a comfortable spot that the police won't find. I'm a fugitive too, you know."

"You can't let that get in your way," objected the Bandit. "Say, why don't you come over to my place for breakfast? I'll rustle you up some tucker and you can crash on my sofa for a few hours....Maybe you'll autograph a few of my cookbooks."

The prospect of sleeping on anything other than leaves was too good to pass up—even if it did mean placing his trust in a lunatic. He was also curious to see where the Bandit actually lived.

"Okay," agreed Arnold. "You've got yourself a deal."

"Awesome," exclaimed the lunatic.

"Lead on," said the botanist. "Let's get out of here before the sun comes up."

He started walking toward the path, but the Bandit

drew his saber quickly. "Hold on, man," he called.

"What's wrong?"

The Bandit blocked Arnold's path. "Take off your shirt," he ordered.

"This again? I told you I'm not giving you my clothes."

"It's not for me," explained the Bandit. "It's for a blindfold. You don't expect me to lead you straight to my hideout…."

"But I couldn't turn you in," objected Arnold. "Then they'd catch me too."

"It's for your own protection too," added the Bandit. "This way if they torture you—even if they pull out your fingernails or cut your testicles off and make you swallow them—you still won't be able to give me away."

"I guess not," conceded Arnold.

"There's no honour among thieves," observed the Bandit. "Even honourable ones."

Arnold reluctantly removed his shirt and allowed his companion to tie it around his skull. The Bandit appeared to have some expertise in the field of blindfolds, and the end-product was not the sort of eye guard one might peer around. It was doubled over so he couldn't even recognize patterns of light. The botanist sensed the night air drying the sweat from his bare chest.

"I can't see a thing," said Arnold. "Are we ready to roll?"

"Almost," answered the Bandit. "I've got to ask you to do one more thing."

"What's that?"

"Take off your pants."

"Not in a million years," snapped Arnold. "Enough is enough."

"It's not what you think, man," explained the Bandit. "It's so I can lead you across the park. You don't want to go for a stroll holding hands with a naked man, do you? People might get the wrong idea…."

"But they'll get the right idea if they see you leading me by the pants?"

"Be reasonable, man. I'm letting you crash at my place."

The botanist's eyes were already heavy. He was wondering if the Bandit would let him use a shower as well. "Fine, fine," he grumbled. "But the pants are the last of it."

"Sure thing," agreed the Bandit.

"I mean, I'm not taking off my underwear under any condition."

"Of course not. What do you think I am? Some kind of pervert?"

The lunatic sounded thoroughly indignant—so much so that Arnold felt genuinely guilty for questioning his intentions.

CHAPTER 11

They each took hold of one end of the dungarees and the naked man led Arnold across increasingly rougher terrain, presumably farther into the park, warning him at intervals to step over a root or to brace for a culvert. Soon the drone of automobiles gave way to the rhythmic cries of whippoorwills and the low-pitched groaning of night toads, though the men never fully escaped the periodic honking of distant yellow cabs. At one point, a barred owl swept across their path—or at least its shriek sounded like that of a barred owl—and the botanist fell belly-first to the trail. He landed himself with a mouthful of woodchips and windfall leaves. Birches, he thought, by the flavour. It crossed his mind that the Bandit might be toying with him, leading him to a secluded spot before subjecting him to some sort of creative and perverse depravity. Wasn't this the same man who'd once stolen the scrubs from an operating room full of surgeons and insisted they proceed with the appendectomy in their underwear? And hadn't he forced a Chasidic rabbi and the imam of a storefront mosque to exchange garb in an act of "religious reconciliation"? Arnold couldn't help second-guessing his decision to trust an outlaw with such a track record. But what was the worst that could happen? The man might steal his clothing. Humiliate him. Make him wade naked into the fountains outside the Metropolitan Museum of Art, singing *By the Sea*, as he'd done to the Lithuanian consul. But all of this was nothing compared to having lost his wife, his home, his garden. Besides, he *was* the Tongue Terrorist. He imagined *that* ought to win him some respect, even from a character as depraved as the Bandit.

They marched until Arnold's ankles throbbed. The botanist sensed they'd circled back over their path several times, and after two hours, he wasn't sure whether they'd covered a great distance or had returned to where they'd started. His guide, it seemed, was taking no chances. "Stop right here, man," said the Bandit. "Give me a second." Then Arnold heard the sound of stone grating against stone, as though the naked man were sliding aside a large boulder. "Come forward and take hold of the guide-rope. It's nineteen stairs down. When you get to the bottom, you can uncover your eyes." Arnold considered for a moment that this might be another of the Bandit's antics, even that the lunatic might be planning to bury him alive. But then the man gave him a gentle push between the shoulder blades and Arnold started off toward the stairs he could not see. He tested the first step with his toe before placing his weight upon it. The air temperature dropped precipitously as he descended. Several of the steps sloped downward, as though chiseled out of the rock-face. When he reached the bottom, he pulled the blindfold from his eyes, expecting to find himself entombed in darkness. Instead, he looked out upon a tidy, well-lit efficiency apartment with limestone walls. The Bandit had secured a boulder over the entryway and was now climbing down the stairs. "Pretty impressive, don't you think?" asked the lunatic. "I built it myself."

"Where are we?"

"Under the park," answered the Bandit. "If I told you any more than that, I'd have to give you the old run-through with my saber."

The naked man patted the hilt of his sword; he was smiling, but he didn't sound as though he were speaking in jest.

Arnold surveyed the chamber. One half of the apartment was furnished with a folding cot, a pair of threadbare easy chairs, and a bridge table upon which lay a half-played game of solitaire. A porcelain washbasin and flush toilet stood exposed in a far corner. The opposite side of the room contained row upon row of clothing racks—enough to fill a small department store. Even at first glance, the range of apparel was noteworthy: everything from dark business attire to vintage lingerie to what appeared to be a Native American headdress. The Bandit's wardrobe vastly exceeded the selection at Gladys and Anabelle's.

"I bet you have masks in my size," observed Arnold.

"What are you in the market for?" asked the Bandit. "Would you like the disguise that Ronnie Biggs wore during the Great Train Robbery or one of George Washington's death masks?"

"You've got to be joking."

"Help yourself to whatever you'd like," answered the naked man. "If you'll excuse me one moment, I'm going to put on some clothing."

The Bandit disappeared into the thicket of garments. Arnold heard the rustle of fabric as the lunatic rummaged through his trove.

"I don't need anything, thanks. Not anymore," called Arnold. He took advantage of the Bandit's absence to reclothe himself. "But when I first escaped, I was stuck wearing a dreadfully suffocating Nixon mask."

"Do you still have it with you?"

Arnold fished into his pants pocket. "Sure. You want it?"

"If you don't," answered the lunatic, emerging from the maze of astronaut suits and ballroom gowns. He was wearing a long beige trench coat and flip-flops; the point of his scabbard protruded beside his bare, hairless calves. "You never know when an extra costume will come in handy."

The Bandit took the mask from Arnold and tried it on. "Can I offer you a drink?" he asked. "Maybe a cup of cappuccino?"

"No, I shouldn't," replied Arnold.

"Really, I insist," said the Bandit. "I just acquired a new espresso maker."

The use of the verb 'acquired' struck Arnold as somewhat sinister.

"You're wondering about the electricity," observed the Bandit. "It comes from tapped lines. But I only borrow a little from a large number of customers, so nobody ever notices. Same with the water." The lunatic removed the rubberized mask and stashed it in his coat pocket. Then he set two coffee cups atop a stone countertop and switched on his new appliance. The machine let forth a low-pitched whir. "And as for food, that's where you come in...." For a moment, Arnold feared the Bandit might be hinting at cannibalism. He felt genuine relief when his companion added, "Your books on foraging are totally priceless, man."

"Thanks," said Arnold.

"Really, man. I mean it. I'd have starved down here if not for you," the lunatic added. "You know I went on one of your walking tours once. Years ago. Before I found my calling. It was a winter expedition out in the Jamaica Bay Wildlife Refuge, as I remember. You taught us how to chew the roots of bulrushes for nutrients."

"I'm glad I could be of help."

"I make a mean fern and scallion manicotti," boasted the Bandit.

"I'm sure you do."

The lunatic carried the two cups of cappuccino over to the bridge table. He set them down on a pair of round cork coasters and cleared away the playing cards.

Arnold opened up a wooden folding chair and sat down opposite him.

"You don't mind if I ask you something personal, do you?" asked the Bandit.

"Why not? Everybody else seems to."

"I'm sure you've been asked this before, too. But why'd you stick out your tongue? I mean, you had such an awesome job. Why give it all up like that?"

"You're right. I *have* been asked that before." Arnold remained on guard, watching the Bandit carefully. He was struck by how young and innocent the Bandit appeared close-up, far nearer to Cassandra's age than to his own. "It's hard to explain. That's like asking you why you steal people's clothes."

"Do you really want to know?"

"Sure," admitted Arnold. "It has roused my curiosity."

"Okay, I'll tell you," agreed the Bandit. "But drink up. Before it gets cold."

Arnold eyed the cappuccino nervously. Who knew what toxic herb his companion might have added to the beverage? It was even possible the Bandit had learned his poisoning techniques from the botanist's own book. Arnold had devoted an entire chapter of *The Flower Power Diet* to "plants to avoid" with warnings that even one azalea leaf or castor bean seed might prove fatal. Never had he considered that his writings could prove a trove for would-be assassins, that arrowroot might easily replace arsenic as the nation's poison-of-choice. He looked into the foamy cup and then downed the now lukewarm drink in one shot. It was hard to discern whether it tasted like foxglove and laburnum, or just like bad coffee.

"Believe it or not," explained the Bandit. "I used to be a lawyer. That's after they threw me out of the army on account of my being psychologically unfit—whatever that means. Basically, they said I frightened my commanding officer. So I went to law school and I specialized in intellectual property of the non-technological sort. Copyrights, trademarks. My expertise was in defending corporations with allegedly offensive names or logos. I spent an entire year of my life insisting that the term Redskins, when applied to football, had nothing to do with Native Americans, and another six months arguing that the Hooters restaurant chain took its name from the mating call of owls. Day after day of nonstop, futile document searches....It was hard to imagine that I'd spent six years in Special Forces and three more in graduate school to end up pushing papers in circles....And then 9-11 happened and it changed everything, man."

"Were you downtown that day?"

"No, I didn't even live in New York at the time," continued the Bandit. "But that doesn't mean the plane attacks didn't have a profound effect on my life—though my reaction was apparently different from most other people's. I guess I actually found the attacks exciting—a break from the daily grind. Like an action movie, but genuinely unpredictable. Maybe that makes me sociopathic. I kept thinking what a great job the terrorists had. Not the idiots who flew the planes, but the guys behind the hijacking. The guys in Afghanistan and Yemen who got to sit around campfires hatching new plots. It sure sounded a lot more challenging than filing endless briefs on behalf of a San Francisco Dairy Queen being sued by a group of homos."

The Bandit sipped his cappuccino while he spoke. He seemed perfectly calm, but Arnold found his placidity unsettling. If the lunatic had toyed neurotically with a carving knife, or rolled steel ball-bearings between his fingers—anything to confirm his status as a lunatic—it would have brought the botanist a great deal of reassurance. As it was, Arnold felt slightly loony himself in doubting the sanity of his host. He understood exactly why the Bandit's commanding officer had been terrified.

"After September 11th, I had a hard time concentrating on my work," said the Bandit. "I'd sit at my desk all morning and I'd think up countless ways of becoming a terrorist. One day, I'd map out plans to leave explosives in women's purses on the seats at half a dozen Broadway theatres, and the next night, I'd wake up with a scheme to put cyanide in the municipal swimming pools. One of my best ideas involved smuggling explosives into Disneyworld via carefully-weighted helium balloons and blowing up several rides simultaneously. At worst, that could kill fifty kids and cripple another hundred or so—not to mention the economic damage it would cause the tourism industry. I don't want to sound cocky, but I think some of my plans were well ahead of anything Osama bin Laden could come up with."

The Bandit looked at Arnold for approval.

"Children are a weak spot for a lot of people," said the botanist.

"That's the way I see it, at least," agreed the Bandit. "But there were a couple of problems with my plan. I didn't exactly have any of the advantages Osama had—a band of loyal followers...an attractive and coherent ideology...cash... a hiding place in Pakistani mountains. Your book proved really helpful to me on the poisons, and I learned a lot about explosives from the Internet, but none of it made a difference. The bottom line was that I just wasn't a violent person at heart. I learned that in the service. It's not that I'm against violence. I mean: Who cares if a bunch of strangers get blown up? I don't even know them. But violence doesn't have any *particular*... allure for me. And I'm not the sort of person to butcher a large number of innocent people if I'm not even going to enjoy it."

"What would be the point?" asked Arnold.

"Exactly. But then I read about how our interrogators in Iraq and at Guantánamo Bay would torture their prisoners by making them stand naked for long periods of time and by forcing them to wear women's undergarments—and I thought, 'Hey, that's something I could do.' Besides, what's the use of wearing clothes anyway? I mean, at least in the summer. It doesn't make much sense. So I resigned from my firm, and sold my stuff, and transformed myself into the Bare-Ass Bandit. It's not the name I would have chosen—I'd have much preferred Naked Osama or the Mad Clothesnapper or something a bit more ominous—but that's just how the media is. I may file for trademark protection anyway. And I came back to New York for all the obvious reasons. You know. If you can make it here, you can make it anywhere."

"And I guess you've made it.," Arnold offered.

The Bandit shrugged. "What exactly is making it, man? Maybe that's easy to say if you're a doctor or a jazz musician, but the benchmarks for bandits are much murkier. How can you compare yourself with John Dillinger or Jesse James? You see what I'm saying."

"You've got a point," agreed Arnold—though he wasn't sure what it was.

"So now your turn. Why the tongue?"

"I don't know. I guess I'm also sociopathic."

"The great ones always are," said the Bandit. He grinned and removed a large plastic clock from his pocket—the sort one might use to teach analogue time to a child. This apparently served the lunatic as a pocket watch. "Anyway, I'd better get going," he said. "It's getting late and I've still got at least one more job to take care of tonight."

"You're going to leave me here?" demanded Arnold.

"Unless you want to come with me," answered the Bandit. "You're more than welcome to tag along, man. I could use a partner."

Maybe because he'd been a fugitive himself for over a month, the offer didn't sound so unreasonable to Arnold. Although the Bandit made him nervous, he found that after days of social isolation, he actually enjoyed the man's company.

"What are your plans?" asked Arnold.

"No plans."

"You don't choose your victims in advance?"

"Not usually. I just wander around until something comes to me," said the Bandit. "Say, man, you don't have any enemies, do you?"

"It seems like all I have are enemies."

"I mean real enemies. Anyone you want to screw over."

Arnold sensed where the conversation was headed—and he liked it.

"You ever heard of the Reverend Spotty Spitford?"

"They guy with the sunglasses?" asked the Bandit. "The one who's got the thing against nudists."

"That would be him. He's not too big on terrorists either."

"I'd love to toy with Spitford, man," said the Bandit.

"Add one of his Brooks Brothers suits to my collection... But we're not going to."

The lunatic's words surprised and disappointed Arnold.

"Why not?" demanded the botanist. "He's an asshole."

"No argument from me," said the Bandit. "But he's a famous asshole. A very famous one, especially now that he's leading the crusade against the Tongue Terrorist. I've got a rule against going near big-name celebrities...You can screw with ordinary people all you want to, even prominent upper-middle class folks, and the authorities come after you with one arm tied behind their backs, but the minute you mess with some hotshot athlete or movie star or politician, it's kiss your ass goodbye. Sorry, man, but I'm not getting sent down to settle your score with Spitford."

"I knew it was too much to hope for," said Arnold.

"Anybody else on your hit list?"

Lots of people, thought Arnold. Dozens. Hundreds. Not to mention a few individuals he felt genuinely conflicted about—like Cassandra and Gilbert Card. "I have this neighbour of mine," he said. "Ex-neighbour, I guess. Ira Taylor. A real prick."

"You want to dish out a little payback?" asked the Bandit.

"Sure," said Arnold. "Why not?"

Of course there were a thousand reasons why not.

Because it was illegal, for starters. And because he'd be working side-by-side with a madman. But all of that seemed small potatoes when compared with the prospect of humiliating the bond trader.

"I like the sound of that," said the Bandit. "Maybe you are sociopathic."

He clearly meant this as a compliment. "Thank you," said Arnold.

The Bandit rummaged through one of the garment racks. "Let's get you some clothes."

"What's wrong with what I'm wearing?"

"Nothing, if you're a fugitive botanist," said the Bandit. "But any successful racket has to have a distinctive M.O." He stepped from behind a pile of angora sweaters, holding a long grey mackintosh. "Here, try this on."

Arnold put on the coat.

"Not like that, man," said the Bandit. "Take your clothes off and *then* put it on."

Arnold had little choice but to comply. He hadn't undressed in the company of another man in many years—possibly since junior high school—and he found the process of removing his clothing in front of the Bandit utterly mortifying, particularly because the man made no effort to look away. In fact, he watched closely as the botanist undressed. Arnold was beginning to sense what the lunatic's victims must have experienced. Wearing only the long coat, he felt like a flasher. If he could somehow get hold of a horn, at least he might pass as Harpo Marx.

"There you go," said the Bandit, pleased. "How does that feel?"

"Airy."

"You'll get used to it. Now all we need is to find you a weapon."

"What if I don't want a weapon?"

"Trust me, you'll want a weapon," said the Bandit. "Besides, it reduces the chance of violence....How are you with swordplay?"

"What do you mean?"

"Any experience fencing? Or in martial arts? Maybe kendo...?"

"What's kendo?

"Okay, let's skip the sword...."

"I like the sound of that," said Arnold.

"If you don't know what you're doing. You're much better off with a gun."

"A gun—?!"

The Bandit didn't answer directly. Instead, he dragged a large steamer trunk out from beneath one of his clothes racks. It contained an extensive assortment of pistols, rifles, shotguns and even a crossbow. "How about a .38 Smith & Wesson?" he offered, handing Arnold a jet black revolver. The lunatic might just as well have suggested a water pistol or an AK-47—Arnold wouldn't have known the difference. "Watch the recoil on that," warned the Bandit.

"The what?"

"Jesus," muttered the lunatic. "It jolts backwards when you fire."

"I don't intend to fire it," answered Arnold.

He tucked the revolver into the holster that the Bandit provided. The weapon had Philadelphia Police Department engraved in the barrel.

"I've got to blindfold you again," added the Bandit. "Nothing personal."

He quickly secured a cloth rag around Arnold's eyes.

"Ready to roll?" asked the Bandit.

"I guess," answered Arnold. "But Ira Taylor lives all the way down in the West Village. Aren't we going to look pretty damn conspicuous dressed like this."

"Don't worry," responded his companion. "There's a police station very close by here.

"That's supposed to reassure me?"

"We'll go by squad car, man. I do it all the time," explained the Bandit. "You know how cops are. They leave their cars in front of the stationhouse day and night—with the engines running. They figure: Who the hell is going to be stupid enough to steal a police cruiser from in front of a stationhouse? Arrogant bastards. Besides, if you turn on the sirens, you can make damn good time...."

"You're totally nuts."

"Maybe. But it works."

It sounded too easy to Arnold. "Don't they have tracking devices in police cars these days?"

"You must think I'm a total moron, man. Of course they do. But the tech is newer than the cars themselves are, so it's not built in. There are special boxes attached under the hoods," explained the Bandit. "That makes it real simple. Before you borrow a car, you exchange the tracking box with the tracker on another cruiser. That confuses the hell out of them. By the time they figure out what you've done, you could have driven cross country."

"You really have thought of everything," said Arnold.

"More or less," said the Bandit. "The best part is listening to the police on the radio in the cruiser. There's nothing more fun than a bunch of confused cops searching for their own vehicle."

They turned on the sirens and arrived downtown in record time. While they darted their way through late-night traffic, the police radio did broadcast a heated argument between two cops over whether their car had been stolen or merely misplaced. When the Bandit tired of this debate, he flipped off the radio and quizzed Arnold about the botanist's animosity toward the bond trader. "I try to custom design my projects," explained the Bandit. "In the army they called this a God-complex. But I don't have the foggiest idea why. Does it seem to you like God custom designs his projects?"

"I guess not," said Arnold.

He was struck by the ease with which the Bandit relied on a personal vocabulary of euphemisms: not just 'acquire' and 'projects' and 'calling,' but also 'beneficiary' for victim and 'comfortable' for naked. If he were ever to give another media interview, Arnold decided, he intended to refer to the baseball game incident as his 'project' and the Yankees fans as 'beneficiaries.'

"I'm the opposite of God," said the Bandit. "God is careless."

"I never thought of it that way."

"Most people don't. They assume that God has some sort of grand design. But He doesn't, as far as I can tell," said the lunatic. "That's why I have to help Him out sometimes in the meting-out-justice department."

The Bandit cruised down Ninth Avenue and then cut west on Seventh Street. As they approached Arnold's own home, the familiar sites of the neighbourhood—the leafy branches of the linden trees, the brickwork advertising Goldstein's Packaged Meats—sent a shiver down his back. "We'll sneak up on him from behind," explained the lunatic. "That way we'll avoid the chaos outside your place." But when they reached the block behind Arnold's townhouse, that street was also lined with police and a handful of determined demonstrators. The protesters had brought along aluminium lawn chairs and pup tents.

The authorities must have discovered Arnold's ladder trick—maybe Cassandra had given him away—and they were taking precautions to prevent him from sneaking back inside.

"What now?" demanded Arnold.

"Easy," answered the Bandit. "We'll have to go in through the opposite building."

"Dressed like this?" asked the botanist.

"Just watch."

The Bandit parked the car and opened the wrought-iron gate of the renaissance brownstone immediately behind Taylor's. An unambitious row of pansies lined the short slate path leading up to the house. Garbage cans and recycling bins stood beside the bright-yellow Dutch doors; the brass knocker was shaped like an elephant. Arnold's companion rang the bell and waited patiently.

They heard footsteps approaching. A studious-looking, sallow-skinned man in a cashmere pullover opened the door and examined the two of them suspiciously. "Yes?" he demanded. Arnold noticed that he wore a flesh-coloured hearing aide.

The Bandit reached into his jacket and produced a badge. "NYPD," he barked. "We need access to your back yard."

"Well, all right..." stammered the sallow-skinned man.

"We're undercover," explained the Bandit. "Backup

is on its way."

"Is there a problem....?"

"You're fine," said the Bandit. "It's your neighbour we're after."

"Oh, the tongue fellow—"

"No, not Brinkman. We're after a man named Ira Taylor. You know him...?"

"Taylor....Taylor....I know the one. His son used to throw rubbish on my lawn. Until a couple of years ago. Then I paid the kid $100 and he stopped. Carrot always works better than the stick, as they say."

The Bandit stepped past the home owner, and they crossed through a study into a kitchen. The air smelled of mildew and the appliances might easily have come from the set of a 1950s sitcom. Arnold followed the lunatic down the back stairs, through a garden of Bell peppers and patty-pan squash, and over a low retaining wall into the bond trader's yard. It was immaculately tended and without so much as a gum-wrapper or cigarette butt. All grass, no clover. A large variety of tea roses blossomed beside the stockade fence. Arnold was still admiring the greenery, which included a series of topiary hedges cut to resemble human breasts, when the Bandit pounded on the back door of Taylor's townhouse.

Taylor came to the door in his weekend casuals: a cambric shirt, beige khakis, penny loafers. "What the hell—?" He hadn't unhooked the latch, but the Bandit barrelled into the door and snapped the chair off the moulding. That sent the bond trader stumbling backwards, where he landed on his behind. The lunatic kept him pinned to the ground by levelling the saber at the man's abdomen. Arnold followed the Bandit through the shattered door.

"You!" shouted Taylor when he spotted Arnold. "Mother-fucker!"

"Watch your language," ordered the Bandit. "Is there anybody else home?"

"No...." spluttered Taylor. "They're out on the Island already. I'll be joining them in the morning."

"I highly doubt that," observed the Bandit. "But first things first. My friend Arnold here will need your clothing."

"It's in the bedroom. First door on the—"

The Bandit jabbed Taylor lightly. "What you're wearing," he clarified. "Stand up slowly and remove your clothes."

"You have to be out of your mind if you think—"

Arnold's companion jabbed him harder with the sword. He drew blood.

"Okay, okay," said the bond trader. "Just let me up."

He stripped out of the shirt and slacks. The Bandit slammed his sword against a seascape in the foyer, slashing the canvas in two, and Taylor quickly handed over his boxer shorts as well. "That's an original Winslow Homer," he said in alarm.

"Was an original Winslow Homer," countered the lunatic. "Now it's confetti." He slashed the canvas several more times. "What do you say, Arnold? Shall we tar and feather him?"

"You're the boss."

"That's right, I am," agreed the Bandit. "Why don't you put those clothes on, man, and then we'll get the hell out of here."

Arnold tossed the bond trader's shirt over his shoulders. He was disappointed that the Bandit didn't intend more damage. Taylor must have had the same thought, because he appeared somewhat relieved.

"You got a car?" asked the Bandit.

The naked bond trader stood with his arms folded across his muscular chest. His limbs were blanketed in curly auburn hair.

"I asked you a question," shouted the Bandit. He held his saber above his right shoulder with both hands as though wielding a sledge hammer.

"In the garage. The Mercedes….Amelia took the Hummer to the Island."

"Then let's go for a drive," said the Bandit.

"You want me to come with you?" Taylor asked incredulously. "Like this?"

"It's an invitation I wouldn't turn down if I were you." The lunatic then walked around the ground floor of the apartment overturning furniture and slashing paintings. A cabinet of figurines toppled onto the piano with a cacophonous reverberation. "Just so you don't forget us, Ira," the Bandit explained.

The victim—the beneficiary—endured the destruction stoically. He was either searching for an escape route or calculating his insurance payouts. Arnold continued changing into Taylor's outfit. The clothes fit loosely.

"You ready?" the lunatic asked Arnold.

"Lead the way."

"Let's have our special guest lead the way," countered the Bandit. He prodded the naked bond trader with his sword and they followed him down the basement steps into the two-car garage. Arnold's companion ordered Taylor into the driver's seat of the Mercedes and instructed Arnold to sit up front as well. "If he makes any sudden moves," urged the lunatic. "Pop him one." The Bandit settled in behind Taylor with his saber resting on the driver's scalp. He instructed his victim to pull onto the street.

"Drive north up Broadway," ordered the Bandit. "Keep driving until I tell you to stop."

"Where are we going?" asked Arnold.

"Staten Island," said the Bandit.

"Staten Island?"

"You said our friend here has a thing for garbage. Well I figured he wouldn't mind a trip out to see the municipal landfill."

Ira Taylor didn't dare turn his head, but his eyes darted nervously from the gun to the rear-view mirror. "You won't get away with this," he warned. "I'll sue the pants off you, Brinkman. I'll take you for every last dime."

"What was that about pants?" asked the Bandit.

The bond trader's cheeks and ears turned a fiery pink.

"I wouldn't say you're in a great position to be levelling threats, Ira," observed the Bandit. "Besides, aren't you the one who's always telling people to lump it? What happened to all that community spirit? Taking one for the team? You're not the sort of stickler who'd sue over a minor kidnapping, are you?"

"Fuck you," snapped Taylor.

The Bandit tapped the man's skull with the saber blade. Taylor winced.

"I think it's time for a silent contest," said the Bandit. "Just like when we were kids. Let's see how long our friend Ira can stay quiet for. Do you know what the winning prize is, Arnold?"

"What's the winning prize?"

"If he stays quiet long enough, I won't scalp him."

The Bandit's threat betrayed absolutely no emotion—he could as easily have been speaking of filleting a fish. They continued driving up Broadway. It was already late in the evening, so traffic was light.

"Isn't Staten Island south of here?" asked Arnold.

"It was last time I checked," said the Bandit. "But we can't risk crossing the Hudson in the city. Too many cops guarding the bridges and tunnels. What we'll do is drive up to the Catskills on local roads and cross there, then we'll come back down on the New Jersey side."

"The Catskills!" shouted Taylor. "That could take hours."

"You just earned yourself a scalping," said the Bandit. "I'm afraid that will have to wait until we get there. But one more word and I'll cut your testicles off on the spot."

That silenced the naked man for the remainder of the four hour drive.

They crossed into the countryside, cutting through secondary growth forests of hickory and basswood. Orion's bow grew visible in the night sky. Deer grazed on the grassy mounds at the roadside. While they drove, the Bandit spoke at great length on the potential benefits of castration and the historical contributions of castrati. He told of Cai Lun, the Chinese eunuch who'd invented writing paper, and the Byzantine general, Narses, who'd reconquered Italy for the Emperor Justinian. He also shared with them his expansive knowledge of the self-castrating *skoptzy* of nineteenth century Russia. Listening to the lunatic's eloquent soliloquy was almost enough to convince his audience that only a true fool would want to hold onto his testicles. But just when the Bandit's words were actually starting to make sense—far too much sense—the lunatic broke off his lesson and started singing Frank Sinatra's "My Way" at the top of his voice. Then he stopped as suddenly as he'd begun and gave Ira Taylor orders to turn down a narrow gravel road. By now they were already on Staten Island, near the municipal landfill, and a series of increasingly hostile signs warned them against trespassing.

The Mercedes pulled up in front of a gatehouse. It was a small, wooden structure with a mansard roof; moss covered one of the exterior walls. A bright orange control bar blocked their farther advance. Beyond the access point rose mounds of household garbage, some five stories high, surrounded by a high chain-link fence. Coils of barbed wire rimmed the upper edge of the gates. A pair bulldozers and a backhoe stood lifeless on the opposite side. At the window of the gatehouse, a pot-bellied, grey-haired guard sat listening to a transistor radio. When they stopped, the guard looked up indifferently.

"You guys are lost, aren't you?" he asked.

"Do you mean that in a physical sense or a moral sense?" retorted the Bandit.

That's when the guard must have noticed that Taylor wasn't wearing any clothing, because he reached for his phone, but by then it was too late. The Bandit was already outside the vehicle with his saber point resting against the guard's flabby throat. Arnold kept his revolver trained on the bond trader.

"I'll have to ask you to step outside and remove your clothes," said the Bandit.

The guard looked as though he might weep. "Please, please don't do anything to me," he begged. "I have money. In my wallet…."

"We don't need your money," answered the Bandit. "We need your clothes."

"Oh my God," blubbered the guard. "Perverts. Like... *Deliverance.*"

The Bandit opened the gatehouse door and pushed the guard out onto the pavement. "*We're* not perverts," he said. "But the man driving that car is a very dangerous sexual predator. Aren't you, Ira?"

The bond trader said nothing.

"Okay, pop him one, Arnold," order the Bandit.

"—No!" cried Taylor. "I mean yes! I'm a famous sexual predator. A dangerous one too."

The bond trader bared his teeth in an effort to look threatening.

"That's the spirit, Ira," said the Bandit. "Now if you don't start removing your clothing by the time I count to three," he warned the guard, "I'm going to hand you over to our naked friend. He prefers to work with children, you understand, particularly little boys, but he'll take what he can get."

"One," counted the Bandit.

The guard's entire body was shaking.

"Two."

Now the guard reached for his shirt buttons and began undressing. He fumbled with them one at a time.

"Good job," said the Bandit. "I thought you'd see it our way."

The man continued blubbering while he undressed, but the Bandit ignored him. He took off his own trench coat and put on the guard's overshirt.

"Wait a second," said the guard. "That guy in the car. He's the asshole from the baseball game."

"That is *Mr.* Brinkman," said the Bandit.

"You never think it will happen to you..." muttered the guard.

"Underwear too," the Bandit demanded. "And socks."

"Please," pleaded the guard—but he didn't stop undressing. "Okay, I'm naked," he finally said. "Now will you let me go?"

"You don't look naked to me," observed the Bandit. "Say, Arnold, does he look naked to you?"

The guard did appear decidedly naked to Arnold. His hairy barrel of a belly hung forward over his flaccid, uncircumcised penis; a blotchy rash covered much of his chest. Even a lunatic should have been able to tell that the man had run out of clothing. "I can't see from here," said Arnold.

"Well, I *can* see from here," answered the Bandit.

"What's that?"

He poked at the guard's throat with his saber.

"That's my Saint Christopher's medal. It brings me good luck."

"Obviously, man," answered the Bandit. "You're clearly a very lucky guy."

The guard gulped. Arnold watched his Adam's apple moving.

"Next time, you're better off with Saint Jude. He's for desperate causes, right?"

The guard's face had gone white; he looked as though he might vomit.

"I asked you a question," barked the Bandit.

"St. Jude," stammered the guard. "Desperate causes, yes. I think so."

"You think? Or you know?"

"I know. Yes, I know. I know."

"Aha!" declared the lunatic, lowering his sword. "You're a religious man. Why didn't you say so?"

"Oh, please," begged the guard. "I'm very religious."

"That changes everything. I'd never decapitate a religious Christian."

The guard exhaled audibly. "You wouldn't?"

"It's much more fitting to crucify one," said the Bandit.

Arnold hadn't been prepared for this. But he'd exposed himself to the mercies of a lunatic, so now he had to follow through. He waved the gun as a reminder to Taylor.

"Hand over the medal," commanded the Bandit.

The guard unclasped the chain and gave it to him.

The Bandit handed the medal to Arnold. "Here's a souvenir for you. St. Christopher's the patron saint of gardeners."

Arnold wrapped his fingers around the chain.

"Now up against that fence," insisted the Bandit. "Arms above your head. Legs spread." Then he ordered the bond trader out of the Mercedes and had him tie the naked guard to the fence in a giant X formation. "They should find you in the morning, man," observed the Bandit. "This is a good lesson for you. Always wear sun block… even if you're not headed out to the beach." He tested the guard's bonds. "But no screaming until then. Or we'll have to come back and use nails."

"I won't scream," promised the guard. "I swear I won't scream."

"That's the spirit," said the Bandit. "And now that leaves only you, Ira."

The bond trader stood helpless on the macadam. It was a chilly night and he'd started to shiver.

"I think it's into the garbage with you," mused the Bandit. "How does that sound to you, Arnold?"

"Sounds good to me."

"You heard him," said the lunatic. "Into the

garbage. Now!"

Taylor looked from the saber to the gun and walked toward the nearest mound of household waste. The light from the guard house illuminated the millions of soiled packages, left-over wrappers, and undigested meals. It let off a truly noxious stench.

"Now!" shouted the Bandit. "Garbage or death!"

To emphasize this point, Arnold discharged the revolver. It actually bounced off the waste pile far closer to the bond trader than he'd intended, but that sent Taylor scurrying into the mounds of human refuse.

Arnold fired again and again and again. He was careful to keep his weapon pointed far from the bond trader, but he kept firing until the man disappeared into the dunes of rubbish. Then he started laughing. Terrorizing his enemies was far more enjoyable than he'd ever imagined.

CHAPTER 12

The humiliation of Ira Taylor marked the beginning of the two weeks of widespread mayhem that would earn Arnold and the Bandit their places beside Butch Cassidy and the Sundance Kid in the annals of outlawdom. They targeted a number of the botanist's adversaries. One night, they broke into the home of the father of nine who'd made a name for himself describing Arnold's conduct at the baseball game, and they forced the man to call a local radio station and to confess on the air to harbouring sexual feelings for poultry. The following afternoon they showed up at the posh suburban residence of Arnold's sister-in-law and surprised Walter the Republican Chiropractor on the toilet. They had read that Celeste's husband, in an effort to distance himself from his unpopular relative, had put up his own reward for Arnold's capture. The naked duo accompanied the man to a drive-thru automated teller machine at knifepoint, where they ordered him to empty out his bank account and to eat the bills one at a time. Celeste's husband consumed nearly three hundred dollars in twenties before he threw up on his seersucker lapels. Even Arnold's medal, draped around his neck, became the subject of media speculation. The *New York Times* reported, from an unnamed source, that its secret compartment held enough plutonium to build a dirty bomb.

When the *Daily Vanguard* ran Cassandra's interview with Arnold—a highly-doctored transcript alongside an editorial that branded him a "bourgeois infiltrator intent upon discrediting the Left"—the naked pair corralled the editor at a branch library in Queens and had him perform five hundred jumping jacks in his birthday suit for the benefit of the other patrons. But the Bandit and Arnold also continued their practice of targeting total strangers. They crashed a Prospect Park wedding and carried off the bride's gown. They hit a midtown bank, leaving all of the cash but making away with the tellers' undergarments and stockings. In an act of unprecedented audacity, they bought tickets to the Metropolitan Opera, wore false beards to Puccini's *Madame Butterfly*, and charged onto the stage in the middle of the spectacle to demand Cio-cio-san's kimono. Within days, all gossip in the metropolitan area focused on the union of the Tongue Terrorist and the Bare-Ass Bandit. The city council speaker and the mayor squabbled over the merits of imposing a community-wide curfew. Street vendors began merchandizing clothing with kryptonite locks. The naked duo also spawned a host of copycat bandits, including the Bare-Breasted Burglar and the Loinclothed Gang, who swung down upon unsuspecting visitors at zoos and aquariums, but these amateurs were all apprehended rapidly.

Arnold was amazed at how easily he adjusted to his newfound life of delinquency. He had always thought of himself as a highly moral person, despite Bonnie Card's accusations, but now he relished a chance to thumb his nose at the law. He suspected there were limits to his newfound vice—he couldn't imagine physically harming anybody, or inflicting abuse on children or the elderly—but embarrassing strangers and disrupting the workings of society didn't trouble his conscience. After all, hadn't they started this? He'd have been content to live out his days gardening and selling plant books, but they'd been all so quick to fall in line behind rabble-rousers like Spitford in calling for his head. The masses had taken an innocent man and insisted that he was a terrorist. So now he *was* a terrorist. And yet there were weekday afternoons when he lurked around the edges of the park, watching a coal-skinned Senegalese man in a beret instructing a half dozen middle-aged women in painting, their easels angled around the edges of the reservoir, their brushes immortalizing a great blue heron, when he felt a deep longing for Judith welling up inside him. He'd heard nothing of his wife since his flight from Cassandra's. The morning papers, which catalogued the naked duo's exploits, reported only that she remained under home detention and unavailable for comment. But he could easily conjure up the silky feel of her hair and the faint scent of turpentine that she carried on her fingers. It was enough to leave his eyes watering.

Late one night, after invading a gentleman's club and forcing the patrons to strip and the nude dancers to dress, the pair sat in their underground apartment playing cards. The Bandit continued to blindfold Arnold during his entrances and exits, but made less effort to conceal the general location of the hideaway. He dropped hints that they were north of the reservoir, south of the uptown woods. This may have been the lunatic's way of expressing his trust in his new companion. But it was a confidence that had its limits. "You have every right to take your blindfold off," explained the lunatic. "But that's where Isaac Newton's laws come into play. No action is without its consequences. If you do take your blindfold off, that will force me to poke your eyes out." From experience, Arnold understood that the bandit *wasn't* joking. He never joked. Or laughed. That was out of his M.O. Yet despite these occasional threats, Arnold found his companion to be an overall decent guy. He was also an astoundingly lucky card player. Arnold managed to lose two hundred straight games of gin rummy.

"Gin!" announced the Bandit.

"Can I ask you something?" asked Arnold.

"You think I'm cheating?" demanded the Bandit defensively.

"Oh, no. What would be the point?"

"Because I don't cheat," insisted the Bandit. "I just play the odds."

Arnold slid his exposed cards to the centre of the table. "Do you ever miss your old life?" he asked.

The lunatic shook his head. "Nope, not really. What's there to miss about getting up at six in the morning and working in a suit and tie all day?"

"You don't miss *anything*?"

"Not family, if that's what you're driving at, man. My father died in the state asylum. And my mother was a first-class bitch. Still is, I imagine. She's a professional hypochondriac. For real. She makes a living suing doctors for imaginary injuries and settling with their insurers. We had a major blow-up when I refused to keep doing her legal work." The Bandit shuffled the cards nimbly in his hands. "So, no. I don't miss my old life. I'm glad to be done with all that."

"What about other stuff?" asked Arnold. "Do you ever miss the ordinary routine of things? Being able to walk into a store and buy a bag of dog food or a tube of toothpaste or a cheese sandwich?"

"I can have all the toothpaste I want, man," answered the Bandit. "All I have to do is rob a dentist. And as for dog food…I don't own a dog."

The Bandit said nothing about the cheese sandwich—but after two weeks of the lunatic's cooking, which for Arnold verged on the toxic, the botanist found himself thinking often of ready-made and processed foods. He didn't share these feelings with his host, who believed himself a first-rate chef.

"So you really don't miss being able to live among

other people?" Arnold asked.

"Life is about trade-offs," said the lunatic. "You can have a steady paycheck or a job that doesn't require clothing. You can stand for a song or you can stand for your principles. The difference between happy people and unhappy people is that happy people accept the trade-offs and unhappy people complain about them. Personally, I prefer to be happy."

The Bandit turned over the deck of cards and spread it out. He'd managed to sort the cards by rank and suit without looking at their faces.

"Say, you're not going soft on me, man?" asked the Bandit.

"No. I'm just thinking....You really do live by a philosophy, don't you?"

"Not bad for a sociopath, is it?" quipped Arnold's companion.

Not bad for anyone, thought Arnold. He felt actively jealous.

"Do you remember how you said you make a point to stay clear of celebrities?" asked Arnold. "Back when we were talking about Spitford...."

"It can't be helped. Wait a few years. When he returns to obscurity—and they always do—then we'll nail him."

"What if I don't have a few years?" persisted Arnold. "How would you feel if I...decided to hit Spitford on my own?"

The Bandit frowned. "Without me?"

"I'd only be putting myself on the line."

"You know how I feel."

"Are you ordering me not to?" asked Arnold.

"I can't order you to do anything. You're a grown adult. You've got to do what you've got to do." The Bandit stood up and pocketed his cards. "I was just offering a few words of friendly advice. Trust me, Arnold. If you take on a fish as big as Spitford, the last laugh will be on you."

Arnold recognized the wisdom of the Bandit's warning about attacking celebrities. The prisons were full of small-time felons who'd chosen the wrong targets: If Charles Manson and Sirhan Sirhan had bumped off Mexican day labourers, they'd likely have drawn sentences numbered in years rather than decades. But that just made the thought of getting even with Spitford all the more tempting. It was like an itch he might easily reach but had been warned not to scratch. Arnold had always wondered why the victims of violent crimes lobbied so strongly for the execution of their assailants, why life imprisonment wasn't good enough for them. Now he understood. The knowledge that the minister was out there in the world—that the man might walk into a convenience store and purchase a sack of dog food—kept Arnold awake at night. Not that he intended to kill Spitford. At least, not physically. But the prospect of breaking the minister psychologically, even for a few minutes, was enough to get Arnold through the day. The need for revenge overtook him with the same fervour as his love for Cassandra once had. It was almost as though one had replaced the other. By the end of his fourth week with the Bandit, Arnold was pacing the apartment and chain-smoking. He puffed the unfiltered cigarettes through a long meerschaum holder that his companion had stolen for him from a Greta Garbo impersonator, but the ferocity of Arnold's habit concerned even his host.

"Are you okay, man?" asked the lunatic. "You seem jittery."

"Too much cappuccino," answered Arnold. "And I miss my wife."

That was a lie, of sorts. He did miss Judith, but she'd been far from his thoughts at the moment. With this remark, he realized, he'd crossed into uncharted territory: If it was objectionable to lie *to* one's spouse, wasn't it also a mistake to lie *about her*—to use her like that for one's own convenience.

"You could pay her a surprise visit," offered the Bandit. "I have a couple of girlfriends I pop in on now and then—to break up the pace of things, you know."

Arnold recognized that visiting Judith wouldn't help. "Your girlfriends aren't under house arrest and surrounded by a mob of protesters," he observed. "They don't have

Spotty Spitford camped on their front porches."

"Maybe you can sneak in through a window or something," suggested the Bandit. "It's worth a shot, man. Better than coming down with an acute case of lung cancer."

"I can't spend all day here choking myself to death, can I?" muttered Arnold.

"You can. It's a free country. But it isn't how I'd want to live."

"Okay, you've inspired me," Arnold said. "Take me to the surface."

He continued smoking while the lunatic blindfolded him—and it crossed his mind that he must have looked like a Hollywood prisoner facing a firing squad, although he'd seen very few film convicts enjoy their last smoke through a telescopic meerschaum tube. The Bandit led him up the stairs into the warm night and paraded him around the park for twenty minutes. They came to rest under a lightning-scarred hickory. This was their rendezvous point if they split-up during getaways. Arnold tucked the blindfold into his shirt pocket and lit a cigarette.

"You love your wife a lot, don't you?" asked the Bandit.

"Is it that obvious?"

The Bandit picked up a long, jagged stick and poked at several knots in the hickory. "I've been thinking over what you were saying, man," he said. "About missing the ordinary life."

Something in the lunatic's tone made Arnold feel genuinely sorry for him. "I wish I hadn't brought it up. It's different when you're married. If not for Judith, I think I could get used to life on the lam."

"No, man. I'm glad you brought it up," persisted the Bandit. "Because I've been thinking about what you said. About being able to walk into a store and buy a cheese sandwich or a tube of toothpaste or a bag of dog food. When I was a kid, what I wanted more than anything else in the world was a puppy…." Here the lunatic's eyes took on a distant gloss, as though he were gazing through time as well as space. "But my bitch of a mother was afraid she might develop an allergy. Not that she actually had one, mind you. She didn't let me have any pets because she could only see the downside. Veterinary bills, torn upholstery. Never once did it cross her mind that a dog might do us good."

"You could have a dog here in the park," suggested Arnold.

"It's too late," explained the Bandit. "The truth is I'm not fit to take care of anybody or anything, at this point. I'm hardly capable of looking after myself. But if I could do it again, do you know what I'd want?"

"A puppy?"

"Kids. Lots of them. Dozens. Hundreds. You know how you talked about walking into a store and buying a cheese sandwich. Well I'd like to be able to walk into an adoption agency and take my pick of the litter. Because I'd raise them the right way. All for one and one for all. Like the five hundred musketeers. If anybody did me wrong, I'd have a ready-made army of followers to revenge me. That's what children were all about hundreds of years ago, before this twenty-first century bullshit about teaching children to pursue their own dreams." The Bandit looked up suddenly and snapped the stick over his knee. "All pipedreams, man," he said. "It's too late for that now. They don't give babies to terrorists."

Arnold had never had an interest in adopting children himself—that was Judith's craze—but the suggestion that he too might be excluded actually stung him deep down. It seemed an injustice, a violation of his fundamental human rights. "Maybe if you apologized—"

"Don't be a fool, man. Some things are unforgivable," said the Bandit. "Now back to business. How long do you need?"

"I don't know." Arnold glanced at his wrist instinctively, although he'd stopped wearing a watch. "How does four hours sound?"

"Depends what you have in mind," answered the Bandit. He slapped Arnold on the back. "Good luck, man. And don't get caught, dammit. I don't want to have to go back to playing solitaire."

Arnold sensed that the Bandit was trying to be

affectionate, so he hugged the lunatic to his chest. The man's body remained stiff and uncomfortable.

"Four hours," said Arnold.

"I'll be waiting," agreed the Bandit.

Arnold started walking south, keeping to the edge of the path. The botanist ducked onto the grass whenever he passed a streetlamp. He looked over his shoulder several times, and the Bandit gave him a thumbs up. But then he passed through a dense thicket of maple saplings and climbed over a steep rise, taking him out of the lunatic's line of sight. That's when he changed direction—first hiking several hundred yards to the east, then retracing his steps northward toward Upper Manhattan.

The return journey to Spitford's residence was complicated by Arnold's status as a fugitive. Although it was already past midnight, the streets of Harlem were teeming with late-night club-goers and revellers. Teenage boys lounged on the stoops, listening to cacophonous music. A pair of street preachers chanted Hallelujah on opposing corners. Every few blocks, a multigenerational conclave was locked in a fierce bout of dominos. Arnold walked rapidly, holding his hands over his face and faking a severe cough. People gave him a wide berth. Only one time was he recognized—by a homeless guy selling paperback novels on the sidewalk—and then the fugitive ran down a series of alleyways until he'd lost both his pursuers and himself. When Arnold finally reached the wrought-iron gates that protected Spitford's block, his feet were two large blisters and his underpants had chafed his sweaty thighs raw. He sensed liquid squishing between his toes, but he wasn't sure whether it was puddle water, sweat or blood. A closer examination under a streetlamp revealed it to be a combination of all three.

Spitford's Church of the Crusader still bore battle scars from Arnold's previous visit. Plywood boards stood in the window sockets, giving the structure a burnt-out appearance. A banner dangling above the main entryway solicited donations for a HEAVENLY REBUILDING FUND. He rounded the corner of the hulking structure and stripped naked. He stashed his clothing beneath the "God Hates Sin" sign, retaining only his sneakers and the handgun. Then he crept along the slate path that ran between the minister's home and his church, under a row of leafy beeches, to where a solitary security guard had dozed off on the job. The man was one of the same dark-suited bodyguards who'd accompanied Spitford on his protests outside Arnold's brownstone. He was sitting on the concrete porch, a flashlight and a radio at his feet, a large black nightstick resting on his lap. That made Arnold's next step all the easier. The botanist slid the cudgel out from between the man's lax hands and, as the guard stirred, bashed him over the head. He was surprised how easy it was. Just one hard blow. That was all it took to knock another man out cold. The victim let forth a deep groan and disappeared into unconsciousness. Arnold checked the guard's pulse—to be certain he hadn't done any permanent damage—and then he set about removing the man's garments. He even pried the man's dentures from his gums and tossed them into the undergrowth. In another ten minutes, he'd lugged the naked body down to the church and bound it quite snugly to the altar. Morning services, he suspected, would never be quite the same.

Arnold hadn't come all that way, of course, to humiliate a nameless security agent. His real target remained the fascist minister himself. But he dared not ring the front bell, as he'd done on the previous visit, trusting himself to Spitford's hospitality. Instead, he circled the building in search of an alternate entrance, and coming across a set of glass sliding doors, shattered them with the club. Then he tiptoed up the carpeted stairs and along the low-ceilinged corridors into the minister's bedroom. He knew it was the minister's, because it faced the front of the house—the same location where, on his previous visit, he'd seen the glow of a reading lamp. Sure enough, he he found himself in a large bedchamber heavily furnished with nautical décor. A free-standing globe and a ship's wheel stood sentry under the windows. Several large trophy fish—mackerels, barracuda—were mounted above the bureaus. Over the king-size bedstead itself loomed the antlered head of a bull moose. There was also a highboy whose drawers stood open and empty, and a wardrobe of vacant hangers, as though one of the two Mrs. Spitfords had recently departed in haste. Who could blame her? What could be worse than infidelity except infidelity and a passion for animal heads? The room smelled pungently of damp wood. A box air-conditioner provided its only sound. From the window coursed an effervescent stream of moonlight.

Arnold noticed a rotary telephone on the end table and yanked the cord out of the jack. Then he rattled the fleshy lump under the sheets. "Wakey, wakey," he cooed.

The minister grumbled and shifted onto his opposite side.

"Rise and shine," said Arnold, louder. "It's time for naked roll call."

Spitford must have recognized something amiss, because he froze suddenly. All but his right hand remained under the covers.

"You heard me," Arnold said sharply. "Stand up and get your hands over your head or you'll be taking a lead sandwich in the stomach."

"Sweet Lord Jesus," muttered the minister. He poked his face over the sheets and raised his hands toward the headboard. "As I live and breathe," he said.

"You won't be living and breathing for long if you don't do exactly what I tell you," retorted the botanist. "Now stand up slowly."

"Let's talk this over," offered the minister. "I'm more

than willing to negotiate…."

"The only negotiating you'll be doing is negotiating yourself out of those clothes," ordered Arnold. "You have exactly fifteen seconds."

The minister was wearing striped cotton pyjamas, but not a stocking cap. That had apparently been an accoutrement added solely for the media's benefit. The man stumbled out of bed and stood in the centre of the carpet, enormous and helpless as a beached sea mammal.

"I'm sure we can work things out, " pleaded Spitford. "I'm a man of the cloth. A man of God."

"Well let's see how God made you," answered Arnold. "Time to show that trim body of yours…."

Spitford sneered at the jibe about his weight. "Think what you're doing, Mr. Brinkman. It's never too late to step back and reconsider. Many of our greatest martyrs began life as profligates. St. Augustine—"

"Knock off the sermon and start stripping. Now!"

The clergyman slowly undid the buttons of his top. It fell open to reveal his enormous paunch—a torso crisscrossed with keloid scars from various medical interventions. Arnold caught Spitford's narrow eyes darting toward the corridor, so he waved the gun. "Don't tempt me," he warned him. "I'm already facing God-knows-how-long a prison sentence. One more dead fascist isn't going to make or break me one-way-or-the-other….Now off with those pants."

Spitford reluctantly slid out of his last article of clothing. Manoeuvring his flabby legs through the pyjama bottoms required considerable effort. It was several minutes before the oversized Black minister was standing stark naked in front of Arnold. He'd allowed the pyjamas to fall to the bearskin rug. Arnold let him stand like that in silence. The Bandit had taught him the "humiliation power" of waiting.

"Now what?" Spitford finally asked.

"Did I tell you that you could speak?" demanded Arnold.

The minister gulped. He tried to cover his groin with his hands.

"I thought you might be willing to show some decency," said Spitford. "Now that you're done humiliating me—"

"—Done humiliating you?" cried Arnold. "*Done?* I haven't even begun."

The minister nodded. He looked more perturbed than actually frightened.

"It's time to sing," announced Arnold. "Are you ready to sing?"

"If that's what you want," answered the minister. "You have the gun."

"Hands over your head," barked Arnold. "And I want

to hear *We Shall Overcome* at the top of your lungs."

The minister raised his arms again, but he didn't sing. "My mother is sleeping, Mr. Brinkman. If you'll kindly—"

"Sing goddammit! Either you sing or *she* sings."

Spitford winced. He began singing, barely audibly. "*We shall overcome...*"

"Louder!" ordered Arnold.

"*We shall overcome... We shall overcome someday....*"

Spitford paused for breath. His voice was painfully monotonal. Arnold stepped forward and levelled the barrel of the gun at his prisoner's forehead. Now the minister appeared genuinely frightened. He squeezed his eyes shut, but continued singing: *"Deep in my heart, I do believe.... We shall overcome someday."* Then he stopped.

"Keep singing," demanded Arnold.

"I don't..." stammered Spitford. "I don't know the words...."

This admission made Arnold even angrier.

"The next verse is, We'll walk hand in hand," said Arnold.

"We'll walk hand in hand...," sang Spitford. *"We'll walk hand in hand....."*

"Now up on that chair," commanded Arnold. "Keep singing...."

He kept the Black minister standing on the armchair through *We shall all be free...* and *We are not afraid....* Then he grew bored and had Spitford croon *Puff the Magic Dragon* and *Deutschland über Alles.* By the end, the clergyman was sobbing while he sang.

"I guess I'm done now," said Arnold.

The minister sighed, but didn't lower his arms.

"Oh, wait," said Arnold. "I forgot the part about me being a racist. I guess I can't let you go until I give full flight to my prejudices, can I? So what do you know in the way of minstrel music…."

"Enough Brinkman," his hostage begged. "Enough already…."

"No, *not* enough. Not nearly enough. We're just warming up….How about a chorus of *Old Man River*?"

But then they heard a noise in the corridor. A tiny, prune-like creature wearing a hairnet appeared at the door. She had hideous growths under her jowls, and her skin, if it could be classified as any colour, was a brutal mix of bronze and purple. The old woman's presence made Arnold feel acutely self-conscious.

"I heard music," said the clergyman's mother.

Spitford immediately took control of the situation. "Don't worry, Mother. It's just an old friend visiting," he said. "Please go back to bed."

Mrs. Spitford nodded. "It was such dreadful music. Like the devil himself singing," she said. "I'm Loretta Spitford," she added, extending her bony arm out to Arnold. He reached out to take it—and then realized he was holding the revolver. He quickly shifted the weapon to his opposite hand and let the old woman squeeze his fingers. Arnold introduced himself as Spitford's new choral director. "Delighted to meet you," she said.

"Please go back to bed, Mother," urged the minister "We'll talk in the morning."

"Why yes, of course," agreed the old woman. "But you should put some clothing on, Spotsylvania. You're liable to catch a chill."

"Yes, mother," agreed Spitford. "I was just about to get dressed."

"Be sure to put on your long underwear," said Mrs. Spitford. "Especially if you're going to stand up on a chair like that. You're liable to get caught in a draft."

"I promise, Mother. Long underwear. I'll get dressed this minute."

"You do that," said his mother.

Then the old woman grunted several times and vanished into the corridor.

"She's not what she used to be," said the minister. "Please don't bother her."

The appearance of Spitford's mother reminded Arnold of his own parents. How little he'd understood them when they'd been alive, but how much he had missed them after they'd gone. It took only a touch of reflection to divert him from his torment of the Black clergyman—and once he'd been diverted, it was impossible to regain his enthusiasm. He had Spitford sing a few Stephen Foster tunes, as a matter of form, but then he bound the man to an armchair and departed in haste.

The Bandit was waiting for him under the hickory tree.

"Four hours exactly," said the lunatic. "Did you make the most of them?"

"I did the best I could," said Arnold. He didn't like lying to the Bandit.

"I'm sure your wife was glad to see you."

"I'm feeling much more relaxed now," answered the botanist.

"Good. Feel relaxed, man. That's what's most important."

The Bandit offered Arnold the blindfold and tied it tight.

That night Arnold slept more soundly than he had in months. It wasn't that he'd taken any great pleasure out of humiliating the minister, but more like a great burden had been lifted off his shoulders. He hadn't tormented the man because he'd wanted to. He'd done it because it needed to be done. As though the entire balance of the planet had been out of whack and punishing Spitford had helped knock it back on course. So Arnold slept the sleep of a man without responsibilities. It was the same deep rest he enjoyed during the first days after completing a manuscript, or discovering a new recipe, in those short lulls before the urge to tackle another project overtook him. For nearly two months, he'd despised Spitford. He'd relished the thought of making the man suffer in indescribably horrific ways; he'd dreamed up methods of torture sure to make the most hardened Spanish inquisitors blush. Now Arnold found himself entirely without hate. He still didn't like Spitford, of course—in fact, he disliked him intensely. But now his attitude was entirely cerebral. He held the Black minister in contempt for what he'd done and for everything he stood for. At the same time, Arnold no longer felt what had been an overwhelming need to do the man any personal harm. The score between them was settled. It was time to move on. And there was nothing quite like a long sound sleep to tamp out the fires of revenge. Already, Arnold sensed that the coming days would open up a whole new world of promise and opportunity.

When Arnold awoke the following morning, his head was sweltering and his body was shaking with chills. He reached his hands up to his face and ran his fingers over what felt like a rubberized mask. The Nixon mask! Arnold jolted upright with a start and, as his surroundings came into focus, he realized that he was sitting stark naked in high grass. Someone had moved his body while he was asleep, carried him to the edge of the Great Lawn in Central Park. It was still early morning, he sensed, as the sun hadn't yet risen over the luxury buildings lining the avenues. Their roofs, some red tile, some grey slate, glistened in the pristine light. The grass itched on the back of the botanist's legs. He also felt a cool, mud-like sensation on his chest. All around him the air smelled of pollen and honeysuckle and what must have been a nearby mound of dog shit. That's when Arnold looked down at his own body and saw the lettering: TRAITOR. Printed vertically from his collar bone to his navel. He didn't need any reflection to recognize that the medium was human faeces and the perpetrator was the Bare-Ass Bandit.

CHAPTER 13

Arnold's initial panic at being abandoned, at having had his body desecrated, soon gave way to that most primal of all human yearnings—the desire to clean himself. The botanist raised his frame up on his elbows, and a horde of black flies, which had settled on his body as though it were carrion, scattered in surprise. He swatted at the empty air in their wake, as though revenging himself on these pests might in some way undo his debasement. Then he rubbed his skin along the grass like a snake until he'd managed to remove as much of the faeces as was possible without water. This dry bath proved highly imperfect and gobbets of excrement remained entangled in his chest hairs. Not that it mattered. It wasn't long before the botanist's efforts gave way to an overwhelming sense of futility. Arnold felt disoriented, possibly feverish. Like a rat that had been spun by its tail for several hours and then left to die. Tears of frustration and self-pity and sheer exhaustion overcame him and soon he was sobbing and shaking. He was *so* unnerved that he lost control of his own bladder, and the stench of his urine mixed with that of the lunatic's shit. It was a pungent odour, and he fought the urge to vomit. But even throwing up required a certain reserve of energy—and Arnold's was entirely depleted.

He wasn't without his faults, he knew. Nobody was.

Had he really caused enough harm to deserve this fate? That's when he recalled the terror in Ira Taylor's eyes as the bond trader struggled to free his naked body from the chain-link fence. Then he remembered Spotty Spitford's voice quavering as the minister strained to reach the lower registers of *We Shall Overcome.* But it was the indelible memory of his own hands around Cassandra's throat that finally drove him to a horrid realization. Good God! Maybe he *had* caused enough harm to deserve his fate.

Human voices, not too distant, shook Arnold. He understood that this wasn't an opportune time for reflection or self-assessment. The sun had already risen over the nearby trees, and with each passing moment, a steady stream of early morning dog-walkers and bird-watchers were converging on his escape routes. He knew he needed to get off the Great Lawn and into the woods as rapidly as possible. But how? And where was he to go from there? What he really wanted was a piece of clothing, anything to reduce his feeling of exposure, of helplessness, but now even something as basic as underwear seemed far beyond his grasp. Only hours earlier, he'd have had no qualms about forcibly unburdening passers-by of their jogging shorts, but that entire mind-set suddenly seemed like a distant shadow. What sort of human being attacked strangers for their wardrobes—even under exigent circumstances? Maybe excuses could be made for a true sociopath, like the Bandit. But Arnold recognized that he *wasn't* a sociopath.

He could offer his own rationalizations, of course—that he'd gotten carried away in the moment, that the world served up many injustices far greater than any he'd created. That was Bonnie Card's sort of thinking. She'd find a way to justify his behaviour with her ethicist's abracadabra.

Arnold realized now that he wanted no part of that. Never again. He thought back on all that had happened to him, all that he'd done: the humiliation of Spotty Spitford, the torture of Ira Taylor, his kiss with Cassandra. It all seemed like a bizarre nightmare. Only his own nudity confirmed for him that he'd ever really lived through these events. Somewhere, somehow, he sensed that he had crossed over a barrier—and he wanted more than anything wade his way back over the Rubicon.

Luckily, the Bandit had laid him to rest on a patch of turf along the outskirts of the Great Lawn, a shady nook which hadn't recently been mowed. The crabgrass was just tall enough for Arnold to slither forward without exposing himself. He kept his belly flat to the ground, his elbows and knees bent outward—like a World War I soldier trying to surprise an enemy trench. He tried to keep his mind blank. He sensed that if he thought too much—about either the horrors that had been done to him or those that he'd perpetrated—he might come entirely unhinged. That was what became of real terrorists, he'd heard. Some, of course, remained intransigent to the end. But others, when confined alone with their own thoughts for a long enough period of time, degenerated to madness under the weight of their shame. So best not to think. Just crawl. Inch by inch. One knee in front of the other. So simple—like a child. But it was only a matter of time before unwelcome ideas crept into the recesses of Arnold's head. The sounds of pedestrians on the nearby trails propelled his unhealthy thinking. He heard the voice of young woman reasoning with her poodle, as though it were a human being, and he was instantly seized with a memory of Cassandra snuggling against the nape of her beloved Son of a President. And now he would never see the crazy girl or the oddly-named beast again. Because he'd been unable to compromise, unable to forgive. Arnold's dilemma was that, in his gut, he wasn't so sure that Cassandra deserved to be forgiven for what she'd done—but, at another level, he missed her intensely. Then he hated himself for missing her, because she wasn't Judith. And he longed for Judith so deeply that, when he thought about it, that his feelings for the girl seemed entirely trivial. The more Arnold tried to decipher his own emotions, *or what they should be,* the less they made sense. All internal debate, at some level, was like reasoning with a dog.

Arnold was certain of only one thing: He was running short on options. Having been cast out both by society and by its rejects, each time as a result of his own pigheaded intransigence, he no longer had any safe harbour to claim as his own. It was true that he didn't love America. The idea of loving a country still seemed ludicrous to him. But he *did* love the idea of having a place to go—a place to call home—and if that meant allying himself with a country, in a pact of mutual convenience, it was a step he was more than willing to take. Better than living as a refugee, alone and hunted. Or trusting himself to the enemies of his country. That was one lesson he'd learned from the Bandit: The enemy of his enemy was *not* his friend. As he crawled across the tall grass, trying to conjure up his next move, he realized how wrong he'd been to envy the poor lunatic. Arnold's stupefaction gave way to a sense of revulsion—not so much horror at what the Bandit had done, as awful as it was, but horror at the unfortunate creature's existence. Even prison seemed more appealing, all of a sudden, than that sort of isolation.

Arnold arrived at the edge of the grass, opposite a poorly maintained footpath. A homeless couple was arguing under a disease-ridden spruce, threatening each other with all sorts of hyperbolic physical injuries, but they were too engrossed in their own altercation to notice the naked man as he darted into a nearby hedge of privet. Arnold collapsed in the thicket, catching his breath while he listened to them shout. It was impossible to pick up the origins of their row—or even its purpose—but it left Arnold feeling even more empty than before. He'd been a fool to fight with Judith. Ever. It wasn't as though apologizing or adopting a few children was the end of the world. What

Arnold wanted now, more than anything, was his old life back: His playful arguments with Willie Zambrano and his bitter ones with Ira Taylor; his back-breaking morning weeding sessions; even Judith's unforgiving lectures when he tracked up the carpets in his gardening shoes. Ordinary life was what he longed for more than anything. That, and his wife. To wake up in the morning to find she'd stolen all of his blankets and pillows—"appropriated," she called it—and to love her all the more. To sit at the kitchen table while she mocked the results of his stab at the Monday morning crossword puzzle. To have someone to whom he didn't have to explain anything—because she knew what he was thinking before he thought it, and what he was going to do before he did it. There was nothing better in life than sharing it with someone who loved you no matter how much of an ass you made of yourself—who would forgive you even if you didn't deserve to be forgiven. Judith was certainly that person. But Judith was one hundred blocks away in a townhouse surrounded by police barricades and self-proclaimed patriots with far too much time on their hands. Even if he could find a way home—and you couldn't just crawl across Manhattan stark naked—he had no way of getting inside.

Soon the homeless couple reconciled and wandered off hand-in-hand. Arnold used the privet leaves as makeshift tissues to scrub more of the excrement from his chest hairs. Then he continued north toward the reservoir.

His first thought had been that he might wait until dark and then dunk himself into the water for a quick rinse. It wouldn't exactly be a bubble bath—the pond was covered with a thick layer of scum—but baptism by stagnant water was preferable to the stink of human waste. Unfortunately, when Arnold arrived at the southern shore, he discovered that a high mesh fence had been erected around the entire man-made lake to accommodate a drainage project. The one advantage of this renovation—was that a small section of the park had been cordoned off from pedestrians as a workstation. It appeared unoccupied. Arnold darted around a parapet of sandbags and hid alongside the rear wall of the boathouse. It crossed his mind that he could empty the sand out of the sacks and fashion the canvas into a makeshift wardrobe. Like a scarecrow's outfit. But he had nothing with which to cut into the heavy, tightly-woven cloth. The work crew had taken their tools with them, leaving behind only wrappers and duct tape. Arnold was still attempting to tear open one of the bags when two Parks Department maintenance employees rounded the corner of the shuttered snack bar in a golf cart. The botanist abandoned his refuge and dashed into a raspberry hedge. He was sure the men had spotted him—that they'd chase him into the brush. But the cart drove on, its occupants rehashing the previous night's Yankees game.

Arnold's failure with the sandbags enforced his desire for clothing. He crept through the raspberry bushes to the opposite side of the boathouse, where several large metal dumpsters stood brimming over with trash, and he set about combing the refuse for discarded garments. All he managed to do was to slash his palm on a broken bottle. A few minutes later, he was still perched atop the garbage bin when he heard a trio of joggers debating whether they might ignore the construction barriers. Their approach forced him to plunge again into the undergrowth—this time head-first into a thicket of briars. The branches tore at his bare flesh. His bare arms and chest stung. It was impossible to tell where the blood stopped and the faeces began. He picked the thorns out of his flesh one-by-one. In a moment of weakness, Arnold even considered throwing himself on the mercies of the passing joggers.

All that separated Arnold from surrender was inertia. And possibly his nudity—because the thought of exposing himself to total strangers seemed suddenly and inexplicably humiliating. But he had no home, no prospect of security, no hope of seeing his wife again. He didn't even have any cigarettes—the Bandit had stolen them along with his pants. If he'd still had the revolver, he'd have shot himself. Unfortunately, the lunatic had taken that too. And Arnold's sneakers. His feet, already torn up from his hike to Spitford's, stung with every step.

Arnold took a deep breath and stepped out into the open—determined to beg the next passer-by for assistance. But the joggers had already disappeared over a rise and the footpath remained momentarily quiet. The one time he *wanted* to be caught, he managed to find himself all alone. If there were a God and that God were going to show him mercy, Arnold pleaded, it was now or never. That was when he spotted an abandoned pair of men's undershorts lying on the concrete beside the boathouse bathrooms. The briefs were crumpled into a ball beneath a dripping spigot, sopping in a pool of icy water. On closer inspection, they also proved to be smaller than Arnold had hoped. But they were better than nothing. He stretched the fabric several times, as best he could, and then inched the frigid cotton up his legs and over his groin.

For a moment, finding the wet underpants seemed like a great victory to Arnold. But that was merely a reflection of the abject state to which he had been reduced. When the euphoria wore off and he saw things more clearly, he realized how hopeless his situation was. Even surrendering seemed pointless. All he wanted now was to see Judith one more time—to apologize for what he'd put her through—and then he'd be willing to accept whatever additional tortures that fate chose to throw his way. But with the police cordon and Spitford's army of demonstrators, even that brief solace appeared denied to him. He found himself missing the Bandit—wishing he might ask the lunatic for advice. Because the poor lunatic's existence might be unfortunate, but he *was* resourceful. That was another thing Arnold had learned about himself:

He *wasn't* resourceful. On his own, he wasn't much good for anything.

Then the kernel of an idea congealed in his mind. It was implausible, maybe a one-in-a-million. Within minutes, his mood raced from dejected to joyous. With a sudden burst of determination, he navigated through the park—from hedge to hedge—until he arrived at the security headquarters, a long rectangular building with faux gas lanterns hanging from the eaves and a roof shaped like a pagoda's. Sure enough, there were a pair of recreation department police cars idling at the curb side. Arnold darted out from the brush and exchanged the transponders. Then he pulled onto the gravel road and steered his way toward Fifth Avenue. Soon he was heading south, toward home. They'd catch up with him, he knew, but he at least might have an hour or so of cushion while they figured out what he'd done. Maybe longer. He doubted the police stashed their most astute investigators on parks' patrol.

Arnold abandoned the cruiser in front of the sex toy museum and scaled the chain-link fence designed to keep vagrants out of the adjacent lot. His back and hands were still bleeding, and he left a trail of blood along the dust. It took him half an hour to uncover the entrance to the Weatherman's tunnel, now overgrown with clover, and another spell of hard labour to dislodge the storm grating. Then he crept into the underground passageway and lugged out the cinderblocks one by one like a miner.

Each brick felt as though he were carrying an entire city on his bare, bloody back.

All of the muscles in Arnold's body ached, and several had stopped functioning, when he finally crawled out the other end of the tunnel into the remnants of what had once been his garden. Since his departure—it had been nearly two months—the pachysandra and crabgrass had suffocated what remained of the flowers. Poison ivy vines curled their tentacles around the linden and poison sumac blocked the entrance to the tool shed. Deep black-rot lesions scarred the trunk of the apple tree. An infestation of aphids had left the tea roses with desiccated leaves. Woodchuck burrows pocketed the lawn. Even the bird feeders had collapsed under the weight of rainwater. The gardens of Pompeii and Herculaneum could not have appeared as desolate. But to add insult to injury, Ira Taylor's kid had transformed the entire northern border of the yard into a makeshift trash dumpster. Where the azalea hedge had once run along the stockade fence, empty beers kegs now bloomed. Also Styrofoam cups, and rotting steak bones, and an impressive collection of used condoms. A small stretch of the fence was charred black as though a discarded cigarette had been left to burn out of its own accord. They were all lucky that the entire neighbourhood hadn't ignited. Then he caught sight of the open door to the back hallway and all thought of anything other than Judith melted from his mind.

Arnold saw the back of his wife's head at the bay windows in the living room, her long sandy tresses cascading over her shoulders. He charged across the lawn and up the rear steps, like a soldier returning home from the battlefield, but at the last moment he recoiled at the sound of laughter. Male laughter. There was no mistaking the resounding baritone of Gilbert Card's mirth.

"You really *are* the man of my dreams," he heard Judith say. "You drive me up a wall ninety-nine percent of the time, but the other one percent makes up for it."

A long silence followed. In the foyer, the grandfather clock tolled off the seconds.

"It's so strange how life works out," drawled Gilbert. "You search and you search and you search—and then suddenly you find someone. And they're either right or they're wrong....but it has so little to do with whether you actually get along. Sometimes I think you fall in love with someone *because* they drive you crazy."

Every word pierced Arnold like a saber. He'd known it all the time, of course—but he'd chosen to interpret every clue in Judith's favour.

Arnold was on the verge on striding into the living room—of revenging himself on his treacherous friend—when he heard additional footsteps coming from the kitchen. He ducked behind the china cabinet. To his amazement, the next voice he heard was Bonnie Card's. "What no good are you two up to behind my back?"

"I was just telling Judith how you drive me up the wall ninety-nine percent of the time," said Gilbert. "Give or take."

"I guess I'm losing my touch," answered Bonnie. "You wouldn't accept only 99% from an airplane or a pacemaker, would you?"

Arnold heard the sounds of chairs moving. "You didn't have any popcorn in the cabinets," said Bonnie. "All I could find was a bag of frozen leaves."

"Oh, those are forget-me-not sprouts," said Judith. "They taste sort of like guacamole....only not."

"I say we order in Chinese food," suggested Gilbert.

"It's not going to happen," answered Judith. "The delivery guys won't pass through the protesters. They view it like crossing a picket line."

Arnold crept closer and placed his ear against the French doors. That's when he heard the sound of his own voice. "Food's ready," he shouted. "Jimsonweed burgers and daffodil hotdogs! Just like at Nathan's."

He remembered that barbecue. It was three summers ago, when he'd first installed the gas grill behind his wife's studio. So they were watching home movies. That was all. Judith had been speaking *on tape.* About *him.* She must have purchased a TV and a VCR in his absence.

"I'm so glad you found these tapes," Judith said as though on cue. "You're entirely forgiven for poking that video camera of yours in our faces all these years....No matter how much you miss someone, it's so easy to forget the details. The shape of his voice and the particular motions of his body and all that. Eventually, it becomes like describing a dead person to someone who's never met him…I'd nearly forgotten how Arnold used to loosen his belt a notch before eating."

"I've got to hand it to him," he heard Bonnie say. "I thought Arnold would have given up weeks ago. Wherever he is, he really is a man of principle."

"Some good that does *me*," said Judith. "I'd trade all the principle in the world if he'd just slide down the chimney or something…."

"It's not good to think like that," answered Gilbert. "The best thing to do is to pretend that he's gone forever… Even if he does come back, he may not be the same Arnold anymore….You've read about what he's been doing…How he tried to rape and strangle that girl…Sometimes a shock can change people permanently…"

"You can't believe that bullshit," snapped Judith. "She's just a hussy out to turn a profit at our expense."

"I don't know what to believe anymore," answered Gilbert. "A man steals clothes from strangers…It's hard to make sense of that…To be honest, it's possible he's gone truly insane."

"Say what you like," Judith said sharply. "But I know Arnold better than anybody, and I'm telling you he's going to come back as sane as he ever was—even if it's only to drive me over the edge."

Arnold stepped through the doors. His audience drew back in alarm—and he realized that, for the first instant, they hadn't recognized him. He was smeared in grime and faeces, after all, bearded and unshorn for months. And he was wearing only a damp pair of underpants.

"Arnold?" gasped Judith.

"Don't believe everything you read in the papers, Gil," said Arnold. "That same girl is the head case who tore up my garden."

"Is it really you?" demanded Judith.

"What's left of me," answered Arnold. "But I don't think I'm as changed as some people seem to think. Rumours of my insanity have been greatly exaggerated."

Arnold's wife stood up and moved toward him. "Good God! Are you alright?"

"I'm trying to make a fashion statement," said Arnold. "What do you think?"

Judith reached out to touch his cheek. He wrapped his soiled arms around her and kissed her face. Her eyes. The end of her nose. It was so good to feel her warmth, her skin against his—but then she started sobbing.

"It's okay, honey," he soothed. "I'm back now."

Judith drew away from his embrace. Arnold noticed the crow's feet around her eyes, the silvery strands in her hair. They'd always spoken of growing old together as though it was like visiting some far-off kingdom, only that kingdom seemed suddenly less distant. Judith held her hands over her mouth and examined him closely—her face inscrutable, but possibly displeased.

"What's wrong?" he asked.

Arnold's wife took a deep breath. "I want to know the truth about that girl," she said. "Whatever it is, as bad as it is, I *need* to know. After all these years, goddammit, I have a right to know…"

Judith stared down at the carpet, her hands clasped together as though in prayer. Gilbert Card inched his way toward the door. "I think we'll head out now—"

Arnold held up his hand. "There's no need for that," he said. "We're all friends here. I'm not going to keep any secrets…" He glared at Bonnie, who'd made no effort to leave, then reached forward and took Judith's hands in his own. "The truth is that there's nothing to tell….Absolutely nothing…."

He hated lying to Judith. The old Arnold would have told her the truth—told her in order to be forgiven—but he'd have been a selfish ass to have done so. Judith's peace of mind depended upon his lying and, if that was what it took to make her happy, he could live with that. Sometimes you had to compromise your values to get through the day, to protect your home and your loved ones. Beyond that, the more Arnold spoke about Cassandra, the less his words sounded like lies. His romantic feelings for the girl had faded as rapidly as they'd arisen—so much so that they too now seemed inexplicable. Maybe it was a case of circumstance, of war making strange bedfellows. All that remained in his heart was a paternal benevolence, tempered by the residue of his anger at what she'd done to his flowers. But she was, when you got down to it, just a child—and you couldn't stay upset with a child too long. In a few months, a few years, he'd have a new garden. Then the girl would fade pleasantly into memory, a lost friend who ebbed deeper and deeper into his past. But Judith would remain at his side forever. That's why there wasn't any need to confess. "You're the only one for me, darling," he said. "Really. I swear. Nobody else would be stubborn enough to put up with me."

"I knew it," sobbed Judith. "I knew it was all lies."

They embraced again. This time, when Judith drew away, she kept her fingers locked around his hand. "What are we going to do now?" she asked in renewed despair.

"I love you," said Arnold "*That's* what matters."

"I love you too, my dear," said Judith. "But where does that leave us? I don't know if I have it in me to run off to Fiji or God knows where…."

"Who said anything about running off?"

"In case you've forgotten, you're the most wanted man in America right now," his wife answered. "You can't exactly walk to work tomorrow morning as though nothing has happened. They're going to put you in jail."

"She has a point," interjected Bonnie Card.

"I'll tell you what we're going to do," said Arnold. "We're going to adopt children. Lots of them. Black ones. White ones. Boys, girls, in-betweens. A whole goddam army of kids. Fifty musketeers...."

Bonnie held her index finger at her temple and wiggled it. "He's gone off the deep end," she said. "All that time on his own must have addled his brain."

"Nobody's brain is addled," said Arnold. "Or at least mine isn't. Yours with its half-baked ideas is another matter." He stood up "Adopting dozens of children might be the first good idea I've had in ages."

"Dozens?" gasped Judith.

"Or hundreds. If they'll let us...."

The Bandit had been right about children, he realized. Children could just as easily be ammunition in his effort to improve the planet, a secret plan B to launch when his own stamina failed. Like a ready-made army. He'd raise his kids to keep up the struggle against the Ira Taylors and Spotty Sptifords of the world. They would be his legion of crusaders against hypocrisy and knee-jerk patriotism. His dozens would do more good than the harm caused by other people's one or two or nine.

"Since when do you want kids?" asked Judith. "Not that I'm complaining...."

"It's complicated," said Arnold. "But I know I want them. I even know a guy I want to send the adoption announcements to."

That would also repay the Bandit.

Arnold poured himself a glass of wine and downed it quickly. Then he walked toward the entryway.

"Where are you going?" demanded Judith.

"Outside. To apologize."

"Oh God, honey. It's too late for that. You don't understand...."

"Of course, I understand. That's one of the great things about America. It's never too late to apologize."

"You can't just walk out there like that," pleaded Judith. "You'll be lucky if the police snipers don't shoot you...."

"This is where having a good lawyer comes in handy," interjected Gilbert Card. "Why don't I phone the police and negotiate a surrender. I'll tell them you want an opportunity to issue and apology before they take you into custody...."

"You really think an apology will do any good at this point?" asked Judith.

"It's worth a shot," agreed Gilbert Card. "It worked for Spitford. He's twenty points ahead in the mayoral polls."

"And for all those televangelists," added Bonnie. "And a whole host of politicians."

"But this is different," objected Judith. "You can't just apologize your way out of robbery and vandalism and Lord knows what else."

Arnold patted her shoulder. "Of course, you can," he said. "The worst thing they can do is jail you....and then, when you get out, you're doubly forgiven. People genuinely feel guilty that you went to jail after apologizing."

"But be sure you actually apologize," warned Gilbert. "I don't think you can afford another tongue-sticking incident."

"No worries," agreed Arnold. "I'll be as contrite as the dust."

Bonnie Card smiled at him—her "I told you so" smile. He didn't give a damn. If she wanted to live her life at odds with the world, that was her privilege. Arnold had more important rows to hoe.

He waited with the wives while Gilbert phoned the police. The lawyer returned from the kitchen with a thumbs-up. "Once you're outside, they'll give you ten minutes," he said. "But keep your hands up while you speak."

"I can handle that," agreed Arnold. "I'll reach for the heavens."

He wrapped his arms around Judith and kissed her on the lips. Then he braced himself for the masses.

"Wait!" shouted Judith.

"It's too late," he said. "I'm going through with it."

"Okay, darling. But at least let's make you look presentable." She dabbed some water on a cloth napkin and washed the grime from under his eyes. "Why don't you take a shower, put on some clothes...."

It was another half an hour before his makeover was complete. He wore a light grey shirt and a conservative blue tie. His hair was trimmed and parted on the right. He could have campaigned for governor. For a final touch, Gilbert pinned a tiny American flag to the botanist's lapel.

"You want some moral support?"

"Thanks, but no thanks," Arnold answered. He thought of the army of crusading children he intended to raise with Judith. "I got myself into this mess. I suppose it's my responsibility to get myself out of it."

Then he opened the front door and stepped out onto the porch.

ABOUT THE AUTHOR

Jacob M. Appel is a physician, attorney and bioethicist in New York City. He is the author of more than two hundred stories that have been published in major American literary journals including *Missouri Review*, *Southwest Review* and *Virginia Quarterly Review*. His fiction has been short-listed for the O. Henry Award, Best American Short Stories, and Pushcart Prize anthology on numerous occasions. His collection, *Scouting for the Reaper*, won the 2012 Hudson Prize and is forthcoming in 2013. Dr. Appel also writes about the nexus of law and medicine, contributing to The New York Times, Chicago Tribune, San Francisco Chronicle and many other leading periodicals. He is a graduate of Brown University, Harvard Law School, Columbia University's College of Physicians and Surgeons, and the MFA Program in Creative Writing at New York University. This is his first novel and the winner of the 2012 Dundee International Book Prize.